LIV

VOL III

A BLESSED LIFE

ELEANOR *C-PASS* JONES

KNOWLEDGE POWER BOOKS

Copyright 2020 by Eleanor H. Jones

All rights reserved. In accordance with the U.S. Copyright Act of 1976, the scanning, uploading, and electronic sharing of any part of this book without the permission of the publisher is unlawful piracy ad theft of the author's intellectual property. If you would like to use material from this book (other than for review purposes), prior written permission must be obtained by contacting the publisher at info@knowledgepowerinc.com

Thank you for your support of the author's rights.

ISBN: 978-1-950936-25-0 (Paperback)
ISBN: 978-1-950936-26-7 (Ebook)
Library of Congress Control Number: 2016953386

Cover Art Direction: Eleanor "C-PASS" Jones
Cover Design: Juan Roberts, Creative Lunacy, Inc.
Literary Director: Sandra L. Slayton

KP Publishing Company
Publisher of Fiction, Nonfiction & Children's Books
Valencia, CA 91355
www.kp-pub.com

Printed in the United States of America

DEDICATION

Volume III in the LIV series is dedicated to my siblings—Yvonne J., Barbara A., Alvin Jr. (deceased), Lavetta Kaye, Gwendolyn M. (deceased), Howard W., Athene D., and Elton K.—my best friends.

Acknowledgements and Kudos

As was true in the prior volumes, I continue to acknowledge and thank God through my Lord and Savior, Jesus Christ, for His presence in my life and for all the good gifts given to me that can only come from above.

I am very grateful to Willa Robinson, who continues to be encouraging, inspirational, and supportive. My kudos to Juan Roberts, who is a fantastic graphic artist and is insightful and crafts his work to fit the spirit of the story.

I want to acknowledge all those who have helped me and encouraged me through this journey. Included in this group of fantastic people are my friends in my aqua aerobics class, my walking partners at the track, my Tai Chi classmates, and my friends in the L.A. Leggers marathon training group.

A Heads Up for New LIV Series Readers

As a point of reference for those who have not read LIV Vols. I and II, following is an excerpt from Vol. II, Chapter 27—"The Wedding Night." This portion is shortly after they have consummated their union. This information is key to understanding the significance of a recurring theme in Vol. III.

Morgan took that opportunity to test and see where Liv's head was regarding their physical intimacy by casually asking a few innocuous questions. "Liv, are you familiar with the King James version of the Song of Solomon Scriptures, particularly with respect to his love affair with the Shulamite woman?"

Liv thought it to be a strange question to be asked out of the blue at that particular moment, and she wondered what the motivation could be. She rolled over to raise herself up to look at him, but with his arms still around her, he rotated so that they were facing each other on their sides. "Yes, I am familiar with it, but why are you asking me about that *now*?"

"I just wanted to get an idea of how much explaining I would have to do before I can make my next statement or ask my next question." That response certainly did nothing to shed light on the subject for Liv. She was more curious than ever.

"Just what are you trying to say, Morgan?"

"I want you to know that I am your King Solomon, and you are my Shulamite woman!"

Liv blushed so profusely that Morgan was hesitant to ask her the more important question. He waited for her response.

"That's. . . . That's. . . . Gee whiz, Morgan! You've got me stammering! You have made me blush! Again! But I like the idea of being your Shulamite woman, O King!" she said, looking seductively at him.

Greatly encouraged by her response, Morgan hopefully asked a follow-up question, "Do you believe what the Bible says about the marriage bed being sacred, undefiled?"

Liv thought a moment and responded, "I have a long answer and a short answer. Which do you want first?"

Not wanting his hopes to be dashed abruptly, he replied, "Long version first, please!"

"The long answer is that I love you, all of you. I love your body, I love your spirit, I love your mind, I love the way you look at me, I love the way you make me feel, I really love the feel of your hands caressing my butt. I love being your wife, I love everything about you, but especially I love the incredible way you have made me feel tonight! If there is anything more to love and feel, I can't imagine it!

"The short answer is 'yes,' and I want more!"

"No holds barred?"

"No holds barred!"

"As I recently cautioned some friends of mine, be careful of what you ask for! Therefore, I propose one caveat—excluding S & M, no holds barred as long as we both agree and are comfortable with it?"

"Agreed! Excluding S & M, no holds barred as long as we both agree and are comfortable with it!"

Morgan was as happy as a hungry rabbit given free rein in a carrot patch! "Oh, lovely wife of mine, my own Shulamite woman, we are going to have a bed-rockin' good time! A rockin' good life!"

Liv resumed her former position and replaced Morgan's hands on her buttocks. The activity and the anticipation of possibilities were such a turn-on for both of them that the COW *[Hormonal Committee of the Whole]* voluntarily cut short its rest period by eight minutes! Long story short, their first-night celebration continued nonstop until morning, with teasing, testing, exploring, caressing, manipulating, experimenting, touching, kissing, and mutual pleasuring until they finally drifted off into blissful sleep!

(Author's Note: Any references throughout the book to "King Solomon," "King," "My King," or "Shulamite Woman" are an indication to the reader of the couple's sexual activity with purposely no graphic detail.)

PROLOGUE

LIV Vol. I—Once Upon A Time and LIV Vol. II—Happily Ever After (?) tell the story of Olivia Louise Washington and Morgan Avery Calais. Their story can be described as one of the greatest love stories ever. Their union was destined as they embarked upon the fulfillment of their shared dream and was the impetus for setting in motion the "Master Plan" which created a paradigm shift in the status quo, involving a vast network of individuals committed to positive, perpetuated changes in virtually every America institution, especially education and politics.

The victim of severe sexual and other abuses during her first 16 years of life, Olivia used the tools available to her to survive. Despite her horrific home life, Liv found solace in her music and in her new-found, child-kike understanding and belief in God, a result of what became her life-long friendship with Elizabeth and an invitation to her family's church. It was her violation by that church's youth pastor during a week-long youth camp that not only shattered Liv's fragile faith, but also gave her the strength and determination to take control of her life and to resolve to never be the victim again.

The most frightening thing she had to do was to confront her father before she was ready. As a result, she was forced to flee from home immediately, under threat of death. On the run, she met Theodore McCoy Henry, a wise and insightful 88-year-old widower who befriended her and offered her a job as his live-in housekeeper and caregiver. Accepting the job, Liv began her new path to becoming the whole person she was meant to be. From Theo she received and returned unconditional love and gradually began to trust again. Nevertheless, she had to overcome a myriad of deep-seated, complicated issues.

Liv's life was impacted by Walter La Salle, who watched over and guided her, initially at Theo's request. He became first a trusted friend, a surrogate father, and, eventually, her step-father.

It wasn't love at first sight for Liv, but she fell in love with Morgan Calais, whom she first knew as "The Mysterious Stranger." They became acquainted; and after a visit to Morgan's part-Cherokee grandmother, Birdie, the two knew for certain they would become husband and wife. While Morgan was away on a trip, Liv was reunited with her best friend, Elizabeth, and another friend from the church they attended, Holly, who had been searching for Olivia as a possible second victim of the youth pastor, Holly's being the first. The reunion of the three young ladies led to their bonding as life-long friends and future partners in the CCECA.

Morgan returned from his trip to a "different" Liv. Their engagement was announced on New Year's Eve at a celebration at her supper club, and Morgan was able to be with and support Liv and her friends when the youth pastor was arrested in the middle of a presentation in the church's Sanctuary—described as a "Public Defrocksion," by Elizabeth, a tern she coined.

Morgan and Liv adopted Alex, a three-and-one-half-year-old girl they both loved, and the three had a unique, fabulous, storybook wedding. For a wedding present, Morgan surprised Liv by presenting not only her mother, Lydia, whom she had not seen since leaving her home, but also the grandparents she had never known. Liv surprised Morgan by interrupting their honeymoon to take him to see the facility of his dream to house the school and community center they would found.

A significant event was the subsequent marriage of Lydia to Walter after she was assaulted by an obsessed, rejected fan who mistook her for her look-alike daughter. He was put down by Liv, who was also attacked when she came to her mother's aid. Instinctively, her self-defense training kicked in, and she retaliated, permanently disfiguring him. Morgan arrived to finish the job by completely disabling the culprit, Tyrone Adams, who earned their nickname for him, "Casanova Adams," because of his womanizing. Tyrone is one of the many characters from Vols. I & II reprised in Vol. III.

Other returning characters include Elizabeth and Holly; Kyle and Travis, Morgan's best Friends since elementary and middle school; Frank Bynum, the PI who found Liv's mother and grandparents; Birdie, Morgan's deceased grandmother, referenced because of her prophetic predictions; and Liv's grandparents, Dionne and Arlan.

Although not mandatory in order to thoroughly appreciate Volume III and all it has to offer, having read Vols. I & II first would greatly enhance the reader's enjoyment.

CHAPTER 1

CELEBRATING TEN YEARS

(2/16/2023) For this, their 10th wedding anniversary, Morgan and Liv chose Hawaii to spend the week. They had already spent an anniversary in Canada, Brazil, Cancun, the Virgin Islands, Paris, Italy, Tokyo, Argentina, and Jamaica. They had decided on Hawaii after visiting there with their children following a traumatic family ordeal in an attempt to regroup and return their family to normalcy.

They had arrived at their suite very late in the evening of February 15, only minutes before the midnight hour on the eve of their exact anniversary date. Because of an urgent situation that had occurred regarding their schools, they were forced to change their plane reservations to a much later flight. Exhausted, they showered and fell asleep immediately.

"Happy Anniversary, my Shulamite woman!" Morgan said, awakening Liv the next morning with a kiss.

"Good morning, and happy anniversary to *you*, my King Solomon!" Liv replied sleepily and returned his kiss. "It really has been 10 years! It seems as though it were only yesterday that we were on our *honeymoon*, Morgan."

"That's because it was only yesterday, Love. With *you* I have been on a perpetual honeymoon that has lasted for 10 years! And you are still as fresh, and new, and wonderful to me as you were the first time we 'knew each other in the Biblical sense!' You haven't changed a bit—still just as hot, sexy, and beautiful as ever!"

"Oh, I *hope* I have changed, at least for the *better*! But I can say the same for you. Ten whole years of . . . phenomenal! What shall we do first?"

"First, I want you, my Shulamite woman!"

"Your wish is my command, O King!"

The pair spent their first day in their suite mimicking the first extraordinary days of their honeymoon, and it was just as exciting and wonderful for them. As they had done on the evening of every anniversary, on the 16th of every February before retiring for the night, they danced to Liv's recording of her original song that Athene had sung at their wedding ceremony, *"This Is Love."*

As they danced, entranced in the moment, lost in their sensual embrace, it was as if they had been transported back 10 years to the original place and time. The music had stopped, but the music in their hearts played on. With his wife's body melted into his, Morgan kissed her ear and whispered, "Liv, My Love, My Life, My Joy, My Shulamite woman," punctuating each phrase with a kiss, "I made a promise to you 10 years ago that we would relive that night over and over again, that it would never get old. It hasn't. It won't."

Morgan kissed her passionately in a lingering kiss and easily swept her off her feet and carried her to the bed.

"My King!" Liv smiled.

After breakfast the next morning, they went for a leisurely walk on the beach.

"Morgan, this is such a beautiful place—so tranquil!"

"Yes, it is," Morgan agreed. "It is easy to put aside any worries or concerns when you can just admire the beauty of these surroundings."

"Let's not think about or even *mention* worries or concerns. Lord knows we have had our share!" Liv stated.

"That is true, Sweetheart, but the challenges we have experienced in these 10 years are a mere pittance compared to what many couples have had to endure. We can be thankful for all of the good things and events in our lives that have *far* outweighed any negatives. Besides, any negatives that we have encountered have only served to make us and our love stronger."

The stage was set for the pair to reflect over the past 10 years of their lives together. This they did throughout the week as they relaxed between and during their many activities, especially on long walks along the shore, or just sitting quietly enjoying the breathtaking scenery. There was little talking in their suite. They ruminated on the various events, not necessarily in chronological order, but as they were triggered in their conversations and reflections.

The first few years of their marriage had been ideal and full of successes, prosperity, and happiness, with a few major exception. The first of three major events that took place during their 10-year journey was the Casanova incident that occurred on Liv's father's birthday. One of Liv's obsessed fans attacked her mother, mistaking her for her look-alike daughter, and then Liv herself.

They experienced *many* joyous occasions during that time. Among the significant personal events that occurred, besides the birth of their two sons, were the marriages of close friends and family members.

The first marriage to take place was that of Liv's mother, Lydia, to Walter, her surrogate father. Immediately after the Casanova attack, Walter told Lydia he was not giving her the option of waiting to be sure marriage to him was the right move for her and for the right reasons. He was sure enough for both of them. The quickie wedding took place within a week in the garden at the Big House, the major residence of Liv and Morgan. The only ones in attendance were Lydia's parents, Arlan and Dionne; her son, Kevin; Liv and Morgan as Matron of Honor and Best Man; and last, but not least, her granddaughter, Alex.

Lydia didn't mind not having a fabulous wedding as her daughter's had been. She was happier than she had ever been and knew Walter cherished her. He promised her he would make it up to her in the future, and he did in a classic way!

Three months later, Liv's brother, Kevin, was married to Eleanor, a relative of Theo by marriage. They took up residence in the home given to them by Liv and Morgan as a wedding present.

The next marriage was that of Holly Albright to William Lacey. Theirs was a relatively small wedding with only 300 guests, but it was fabulous, nonetheless, and lots of fun. Liv was the Matron of Honor, and Morgan was a groomsman.

Elizabeth, Liv's best friend, chose a different route when she and Allan Reynolds were married. The only ones in attendance at their Las Vegas wedding were their parents, her brother Roger and sister-in-law Barbara, and her two best friends and their spouses—Liv and Morgan, and Holly and William.

When Elizabeth approached her friends with her plans for a Las Vegas wedding and invited them to come, they were happy for her. Both were surprised that she, of all people, would not be saying her vows in a church; but Holly was the one to question her about it.

"Elizabeth, it is a puzzle to me that you are not going to be married in a church locally where all of your *friends* and *family* can attend. Is there any particular *reason* why you made that choice?" she asked. "I can remember as a little girl dreaming of the wedding I would have some day. Although that dream was stymied for several years because of, you know, I *did* end up having the wedding of my dreams."

"Yes, your wedding, and yours, too, Olivia, were both *dream* weddings. I suppose at one point in my life I looked forward to a storybook wedding. It's no reflection on *either* of *your* weddings, Ladies, but I believe that it's not about how big a wedding you have, or how much *money* you spend on it, or how many *celebrities* are in attendance, *none* of that.

"Look at your *mother's* wedding, Olivia. I'm sure she could have had a wedding that would have made yours, as fabulous as *it* was, *pale* in comparison. They were married in your beautiful garden with just the immediate family as witnesses. Are they *not* the *cutest*, happiest couple you know? It's all about the love, Olivia!

"*My* parents had been contemplating *my* marriage for longer than they ever thought they would and were about to give up hope. It was hard for my mom, especially, to accept our plans, but she came around. I told her they could splurge to their hearts' content on our wedding reception, which will be held locally."

"I understand, Elizabeth," Liv interjected, "but was there a *specific* reason you changed your mind about the wedding of your dreams?"

"Olivia, *you've* known me long since before we had *training* bras. You know my outgoing personally, my take-charge attitude . . ."

"Your bossiness?" Holly interrupted to clarify.

"Yes, my *'bossiness,'* as you put it, Holly. Big Brother Roger tells me I order and lead Allan around like a little puppy dog. I made all of the major decisions in our relationship, and Allan *allowed* me to. I sort of thought that was what he wanted me to do, he was so compliant and never complained."

Elizabeth continued, wanting her friends to understand her reasons. "I have been forced to take a good, hard look at myself. I have prayed about it because I want the Lord to bless our union. I really, really *love* Allan, and I *know* he really loves *me*. Why else would he put up with me? I was led to the Scriptures that talk about marriage and the relationships between husbands and wives and God. I don't want to be the boss of William. He believes in God. He is *saved*.

"I confessed to him how I was feeling and what I was thinking. He told me he loves me just the way I am and that I didn't have to change anything for him. He said he cared more about *my* happiness than his *own*. That's when it really *hit* me. He was willing to sacrifice *his* happiness for *mine*. I realized that what *I* wanted more than *my* happiness was *our* happiness.

"I think all my life I have felt the need to be *perfect*. That included being *surrounded* by perfection. That to me meant controlling my environment and people *in* it. I came to understand as I grew and matured in my faith that what I envisioned was impossible. In the first place, there is none perfect but *God*! I gradually came to understand that, since perfection is impossible for me, it was more important for me to be the *best* that I can be. I learned to accept the imperfections in life, in myself, and in others. As I am still a work in progress, I have to correct myself and say that I am *learning* to accept imperfections, knowing that there is always room for improvement.

"I fall short sometimes, *often*, and I accept that fact in myself as well. I couldn't do a full 180° instantaneously! But what I *strive* for now is *excellence*, instead of *perfection*. Since I *know* there is room for improvement, I don't beat myself up when I fall short.

"I find that I am freer *and happier*. I wasn't *meant* to be the epoxy of the world. After our long, heart-to-heart talk, Allan and I are now pretty much on the same page. I can see the difference in *him* since I have changed my ways, as it were. He let me know that he was uncomfortable and didn't want a huge, fancy wedding. Our compromise is that we are having a small, intimate wedding in Las Vegas with our immediate families and our very close friends, you guys. We will have a sizeable reception when we return from our honeymoon. Our families are happy with that situation, and more importantly, we are *both* happy with it.

"I hope that answers your question, Holly."

"I heard you loud and clear, Girlfriend!"

It was relatively much later that Morgan's two main buddies, Travis, and then Kyle, took the plunge into marriage. For Travis, it was more a case of his not being ready to settle down, that is, until he found his soulmate, Kyonne, who made him *want* to settle down.

Several months after their wedding, Morgan's Best Man Kyle began to travel quite a bit to parts unknown for lengthy periods of time. Although he always kept in touch with Morgan, his best friend since elementary school, Morgan never really knew what was up with his travels. Besides, Morgan was always very busy in his own life with his growing family, their schools, and his career as a public speaker and writer.

Kyle ultimately settled down and married Aly Wesson in 2022. Morgan and Liv were participants in or in attendance at the weddings of all of their friends and their family. They gave fabulous, thoughtful gifts to all of them and continued to enjoy the close relationships that grew with time as their families also grew.

A regular event was the hosting of a lavish get-together at the Calais estate, hosted, of course, by Morgan and Liv for their close friends and family.

A spectacular highlight was the renewing of the vows of Lydia and Walter La Salle on the second anniversary of their quickie, backyard wedding. Walter chartered a high-end cruise liner whose passengers were all invitees of the couple to witness the reaffirmation of their vows. The seven-day Mexican Riviera cruise for the 3,000 guests was phenomenal and netted an astronomical amount in donations to the Calais Education and Community Centers of America (CECCA) in lieu of gifts.

The CECCA spawned from the Calais Education and Community Center of Los Angeles (CECCLA) which opened its doors on April 1, 2013. It had continued to thrive and grow yearly. Because of its unparalleled results, the successful replication of its model nationwide permanently changed the face of education in the nation.

As President of CECCA, Morgan was able to begin a prolific writing career and became a best-selling author and sought-after motivational speaker. He was a frequent guest on talk shows, radio and television. Liv continued to write music and perform in her club. She had her share of public appearances as a guest on various shows as well. In their second year, she opened a second supper club in the South Bay with Ms. C-PASS as the resident performer. She continued to showcase promising students of the Music Program at CECCLA, who were given opportunities to obtain paid bookings on off nights and weekend afternoons at both clubs.

With the encouragement of Morgan and their friends, who were all familiar with her propensity to orchestrate plots and scenarios, Liv began writing short stories, graduating to writing one-act plays, and ultimately to writing full-scale screen plays. Her first one-woman show, an immediate hit, catapulted her into a career as an actor on stage and in film.

Liv began recording her original compositions and occasionally covered other songs with much success, first in the school's recording studio, and later in their state-of-the-art home studio Morgan had constructed for her. Having performed successfully for years in her well-known supper club, Liv had already been established as an artist, and her career was in high gear. In their third year, Liv received the first of many nominations and awards for her original music, scripts, songwriting, and acting.

CHAPTER 2

SHARING THE GOOD NEWS / WELCOMING RANDY

Sharing the Good News

Liv found herself in her Mother's neighborhood after her presentation at a Chamber of Commerce breakfast meeting. She had not seen her mother, or Walter, since the previous Sunday dinner. She had not had a chance to talk with her privately and was taking this opportunity to do so in person. Liv was anxious to share her news.

"Hi, Sweetheart," Lydia greeted Liv with a kiss. "Come on in. I was just about to fold some laundry."

"Oh, let me help you, Mom. We can talk at the same time. Remember, I told you Sunday that I had something to tell you?"

"Yes, I remember. I also remember how *mysterious* you were about it!"

"You know me, Mom, the *dramatic* one in the family."

"How well I know! What character will you be this time?" Lydia asked.

"No character, Mom, just me," Liv replied, smiling, suggesting something tantalizing. "The good news is that you and Daddy are going to have another grandchild to spoil!"

"Oh, Olivia! That's *great* news! I was wondering when Alex and Little Morgan's brother would come on the scene. They will have such fun growing up together with not too big a gap in their ages. Does the rest of the family know?"

"Mother, we wouldn't tell anybody before we told you and Daddy! Alex is the only one who knows. I suppose we will tell Little Morgan soon and start preparing him."

"Well, how pregnant *are* you?"

"About as pregnant as one can get. If you mean how *far along* I am, I am about a month behind Eleanor. Oops!" Liv covered her mouth with her hand. "I'm sorry, that was a slip! I had lunch with Eleanor last week, and she told me she and Kevin are pregnant. I should not have spilled *her* beans if you didn't know. She didn't say it was a secret, but . . ."

"Don't worry, you're not breaking any confidences. I *knew* it even before she *told* me. I remembered when they told us about the soon coming of your niece, Lydia, how she was so all-aglow! She would *never* be able to hide a pregnancy from *me*. On the other hand, *you* are a mystery. You have so *many* faces, and you were *always* so adept at masking your true feelings. The only thing I can see in *you* readily is your love for Morgan and your family!

"Speaking of Morgan, I know how much you love each other. *Anyone* can see that. What puzzles me, though, what I have often wondered, is why you never call him, or address him as anything other than 'Morgan.' He uses all of those endearing terms and pet names for *you*. It's either 'Sweetheart,' 'Honey,' 'Babe,' 'Baby,' 'Love,' or something else. You use pet names for Alex and Little Morgan and

Lydia, and for many of the children at school, but never for Morgan. Why is that, if you don't mind my asking?"

Liv didn't have to try to think of an explanation. She answered gladly, "Mom, Morgan is *all* of those pet, endearing names to me. When I call him '*Morgan*,' it encompasses *everything*! He *knows* that. He told me long ago that the sound of his name was like music to his ears when it was *my* voice speaking his name. He says it turns him on!" Unabashed, she added, "And, Mom," I *love* turning him on!"

Liv fondly recalled that evening he had told her how he was turned on by hearing her call his name. "Really?" she had asked. "Morgan, oh Morgan, Morgan," she sang his name over and over until he had to respond with the outcome she wanted. Enough said!

Hearing those words coming from her daughter caused Lydia to blush. "Relax, Mom, we're *both* adults. For your information, I *do* have another way of addressing him which you may never *hear*."

"Oh? What is it?"

"'King' as in 'King Solomon,'" Liv responded without hesitation or explanation.

"King Solomon?" Lydia repeated. "I suppose that's an appropriate name for him. He is very wise, I have found."

To spare her mother any further embarrassment, Liv just smiled and sagaciously let it go at that. "On that note, if you have no more laundry to fold, I'm going to be on my way, Mom. I will see you Sunday, if not before."

"Okay, Honey." Lydia walked her to the door and said 'goodbye' with a hug and kiss.

Alex had taken the news of another baby in the family with excitement. She was no longer curious about *where* they come from.

She was highly gifted and had been placed in the independent learning program at school designed for those gifted students who were able to learn and excel at their own pace without being restricted by grade-level assignments and curricula. In turn, each of her brothers was also included in the program. Even so, the students in the program had plenty of opportunity to interact socially with their peers in age.

Her best friend, Christiaan, also in the program, excelled in math, science, and scientific research. Alex had a healthy dose of science with a specialty in medicine. By the age of eight, she was performing at grade level 12. Morgan and Liv did not try to hold her back academically, but they wanted to ensure that her social development was age appropriate. The fact that Christiaan was close in age and equal in scholastic development made it easier.

Alex had done research on her own in pediatrics, her choice for specialization. After the birth of her cousin, Lydia, she decided she wanted to be a "baby doctor." She wanted to start with the *development* of her future patients and had begun her quest for knowledge from the very beginning, conception.

Having been planted much earlier, the seed was in full bloom after Alex witnessed the birth of her first brother, Morgan, II, aka Little Morgan, aka Morgy. She was amazed and became more curious than ever. Thus began her quest for even more knowledge. By the time she learned her *new* brother was on the way, she had no need for an explanation from *anyone*. She had excellent reading, retention, and comprehension skills and read prolifically on many subjects, but mostly on the development of babies and children, from conception on.

Liv and Morgan were thrown for a loop when they told Alex about the expected arrival. "Alex, do you have any questions about babies you want to ask us?" Morgan had inquired, remembering her curiosity when Little Lydia's birth was announced.

"I don't think so, Dad. I remember what you told me about my cousin, Lydia."

After seeing her cousin shortly after birth and witnessing Little Morgan's birth, she had delved into her quest for knowledge with a passion.

"I have since found out what I need to know," she continued, "and I know just about *everything* there is to *know* about it!"

"What do you mean, Sweetheart? What is '*everything*?'" Liv queried. They knew they had a little genius on their hands, but still they weren't prepared for her matter-of-fact discourse.

"If you want me to *explain* it to you, I *will*. But let me just tell you that I *know* how babies are made—conceived. I know the part *you* play, and I know the part *Daddy* plays. I know the *body parts* and the *mechanics* involved . . ." Noticing their discomfort, she asked, "Must I continue?"

"No!" they immediately chorused. Needless to say, they had a new respect for their knowledgeable daughter!

Easily falling back into her age-appropriate role, Alex's excitement at the prospect of a new "pupil" was evident. She was ecstatic about it. She loved being the big sister and big cousin to Little Morgan and Cousin Lydia, and she was looking forward to adding her new cousin- and brother-to-be pupils to her class.

She enjoyed reading to and teaching her willing pupils. She read several of their favorite books so many times, she often recited them verbatim. Her pupils were so attentive, they were soon mimicking reading while reciting from memory as well while turning the pages at the appropriate times. It was not long before they were actually reading, learning to write, and memorizing math facts to impressive degrees.

Morgan set up a make-shift classroom for Alex in the enclosed portion of the patio with desks and chairs and a blackboard, because she liked writing on the board. In the latter years of her phenomenal career, in addition to her medical practice, Alex taught part-time and lectured in medical schools across the country and internationally.

The routine in the Calais household didn't change much due to Liv's pregnancy. Just as before, she continued with duties at CECCLA; performing at her club; writing; dates with Morgan, Alex, and Little Morgan; their family outings; and her personal and family exercise routines. Everything was business as usual.

Both felt Little Morgan was too young to really pay attention to what was happening with his mother as the pregnancy progressed, or to even be curious as Alex had been about Cousin Lydia. As the time grew closer, they learned Alex had added the subject of childbirth to her curriculum.

Liv had referred her sister-in-law to the doula who had delivered Little Morgan. When questioned, Liv assured her that the doula was certified and could legally attend to births. Eleanor gave birth to their son, Kevin, Jr., six weeks before Randy was born to Liv and Morgan. Both births were family affairs occurring at home, and both were uncomplicated, joyous occasions. Mothers and babies did very well and were normal and healthy in every respect.

When Cousin Kevin Jr. was born, the women in the family were present for the event, including Grandmother Lydia, Great-Grandmother Dionne, and Auntie Liv in addition to Daddy Kevin and, of course, Cousin Dr. Alex. Watching as Kevin assisted in cutting the cord, Alex was completely fascinated.

"Mommy," she said, turning her attention briefly to Liv, "when my new brother Randy is born, can I be the one to cut the cord?"

Liv remembered the birth of Morgan, II and the look of awe and pride on Morgan's face when he cut the cord. She didn't want to promise away his opportunity to do the same for Randy. At the same time, she didn't want to discourage Alex's enthusiasm.

"Alex, Honey, that is usually the daddy's job, but why don't we discuss it with your dad? We'll see. Maybe you can help *him*."

"Okay, Mom!" she said, quickly returning her attention to the birth at hand.

Welcoming Randy

On the morning of Randy's birth, Liv was awaken very early with the strong feeling that today would be the day Randy would arrive. Mild labor pains had begun the evening before, and Liv recognized the feeling from her previous experience. Her water had not broken, but it had not broken on its own with Little Morgan, either. She decided to let Morgan sleep another hour or two before awakening him.

Liv felt like an old hand at giving birth. Morgan, II had been an easy, joyful experience. She saw her doctor regularly and had continued to take very good care of herself, gaining little weight. Overnight, it seemed, her body returned to normal, none the worse for the wear. Likewise, again, she had gained under fifteen pounds and maintained her nutritious diet and healthy exercise routine. She expected the same result this time around.

Lying there beside Morgan, Liv reflected, as she often did, on her life with him from the time he came on the scene. Even after all the years they had been married, she still felt more and more blessed every day. She was surrounded by love that she felt and knew was real—a stark contrast to her life as a child.

She was inundated with love from her husband, her children, her parents, her family, her friends and her fans. She was completely happy in every respect. Liv thought fleetingly about the admonition they had received from Morgan's grandmother Birdie, not to become complacent and to take nothing for granted. Liv couldn't see at that point anything on the horizon to cause concern. They both believed together they could weather any storm, face any foe.

"Morgan, wake up," she sang to him and kissed him gently on the lips.

"Hey, good morning, My Babies' Mama!" he said, pulling her to him and kissing her passionately. Aware of the nontraditional wake-up call, he asked, "What's up, Sweetheart?"

"Morgan, I'm pretty sure today is the day Little Randy will make his debut!"

"You're *sure*, Honey?" he asked, suddenly alert.

"Pretty sure, Morgan. Do you remember what to do?"

"Oh yeah! I'll make the necessary calls. You stay in bed and relax. I'll get the kids together and get their breakfast. What do *you* want?"

"Nothing right now. Maybe a glass of orange juice in about an hour."

"You got it, Babe." Morgan patted her bump, leaning down to talk to Randy, "Hey, Little Man, take it easy on your mommy, you hear?"

By 4:30 that afternoon, everyone was in place to greet Randy when he made his entry into the Calais family. Morgan was calmly holding Liv's hand while Alex was shadowing the doula, watching her every move. The atmosphere was reminiscent of a hen party plus one rooster and one chick. Lydia and Eleanor were exchanging war stories about their birthing experiences while Liv and Dionne listened politely. Alex was busy making mental notes, especially when the doula broke Liv's water bag. Morgan devoted all of his attention to his wife, making sure she was relaxed and comfortable, constantly kissing her hand and telling her how much he loved her.

Little Morgan was keeping his Uncle Kevin, his grandfather, and his PawPaw entertained in the den. Kevin and Eleanor's newest edition was sleeping in his carrier, and Lydia had fallen asleep in her father's arms as they waited for the new arrival.

Little Randy wasted no time in making his entrance about 20 minutes after the water bag was broken. He was plump and pink all over, except his hair, which was plentiful, thick, and *very* red!

"His hair is red!" Alex exclaimed in surprise. "*No* one has red hair in *our* family that *I* know of. *He* must be *special*!"

"Yes, he *is* special, Alex," Morgan confirmed, "but so are *you*, and *Little Morgan*, and *all* of the children. In fact, we are *all* special."

As time passed, the babies grew and thrived normally. When Randy was six months old, Liv and Eleanor taught him and his cousin to swim the same way Little Morgan and Lydia had been taught at that age. All of the children had taken to the water readily with no fear whatsoever. Eventually, frolicking and swimming became a favorite pastime for the cousins whenever the opportunity arose.

The cousins were very close and thoroughly indoctrinated into the Calais Culture at home and at school. They were all exceptionally bright and excelled even before entering school, under the tutelage of big sister/cousin Alex.

CHAPTER 3

ANOTHER MAJOR CHALLENGE / THE PHOTOGRAPH / THE NOTE

Another Major Challenge

Morgan and Liv found, in deed, Birdie's pronouncement was right, that there would be challenges ahead. The first major challenge, the attack on Lydia, Liv's mother, and subsequently, Liv herself, came much sooner than either of them could have predicted.

Although they chose not to always be looking for and expecting challenges at every turn, the pair was confident that together they could rise to any situation. They were also aware that a challenge could have any face, could be overt as well as covert, and could seem innocuous on the surface. Each of them was extremely attractive to the opposite sex. Because of their strong commitment to their family and each other, they were quite secure in their abilities to resist temptations and to thwart concentrated attempts or temptations.

Morgan, as president of their well-known and respected corporation as well as an active public speaker, received many requests to meet with individuals and groups and to make presentations. In one of those many engagements, he happened to attract the attention of a certain young woman by the name of Camille Cavanaugh, a socialite who had been spoiled rotten by her father.

This social butterfly was beautiful, and she knew it, too. Her "beauty" was relegated to what could be brought, constructed or reconstructed, and visualized on the surface. She was extremely successful in getting any and everything she wanted or pursued. She saw Morgan, liked what she saw, and wanted him for herself, for as long as she chose.

Morgan's calendar had him scheduled to meet with a community group at its regular monthly meeting on Saturday, June 15. He learned the group included mostly parents who were interested in receiving a presentation geared to the implementation of the Calais Culture in a private middle school in the area. The rotating meeting location that month was in a very affluent, exclusive neighborhood, which happened to be in the home of Ms. Camille Cavanaugh.

.Morgan arrived about 15 minutes early to get more information about the group and to organize his handouts. He rang the doorbell, hoping that he would be first on the agenda as he had requested. After an inordinate amount of time, Ms. Cavanaugh opened the door, soaking wet, clad only in a skimpy bikini with a diaphanous, damp cover-up that was clinging to her body. She might as well have been wearing nothing.

"Oh, Mr. Calais! I'm *so sorry*!" she opened the door fully and acted surprised. She pretended to cover herself, knowing she couldn't. "I wasn't expecting you until *next* week! There must be some mistake!"

"Yes, there *must* be a mistake, and *I* didn't make it," Morgan replied, managing to mask his displeasure. Irked, he kept his eyes focused pointedly on her eyes, his expression blank. "I would never have accepted an engagement for next week as I have a family commitment," Morgan continued. "You may call my office to reschedule if you wish," he said as he was turning to leave.

"Oh, *please*, Mr. Calais," she pleaded, "Just give me a moment to put something on. Can you at least leave some materials that I can give to our members? The parents will be so disappointed."

Morgan was not fooled for a moment. He did have brochures and other materials that he had planned to distribute, and the thought of having to come back there prompted him to acquiesce.

"Since I *am* here, Ms. Cavanaugh, I will leave some materials. If you will go and cover yourself, I will prepare the materials."

"Thank you, Mr. Calais. There is a table over there you can use. Please let me take your coat. I think you will be more comfortable, or I can turn on the air."

Morgan reluctantly handed her his coat and sat at the table to concentrate on his materials while she left with his coat. She returned several minutes later clad in a pair of short-shorts and a tank top. Ignoring her, Morgan finished with the materials.

"Here you are, Ms. Cavanaugh. I think these should be sufficient for your group. Anyone who wishes more information can obtain it from our website. All the information one might desire is contained there."

"Thank you, Mr. Calais. Please call me Camille. May I call you Morgan?"

"No, thank you. I prefer to keep my professional business professional, Ms. Cavanaugh. 'Mr. Calais' is quite appropriate. If you will give me my coat, I will be on my way."

"Mr. Calais, I know my group will have questions, and I think based on our previous meetings I know what they would ask you that is probably *not* included in your package. If you don't mind, will you please take just a few more minutes to answer a few questions? I can take thorough notes and will be able to relate the information to the group."

Morgan saw this as a chance for her to perpetuate her purposes, but he also saw an opportunity to prevent a return trip should her group want to reschedule. He removed a notepad from his case and a pen and handed it to her, effectively removing a reason for her to get up and walk away with the hope that he would be watching the visual she no doubt planned to show as she sauntered away.

"So, what are their concerns?" Morgan asked. She proceeded to pose questions to him, all of which were addressed in the brochures and pamphlets, which he indicated to her would be sufficient.

Realizing she was getting nowhere, she changed her tactic. "Mr. Calais, can I be honest with you?"

"That would be novel, Ms. Cavanaugh."

"I know you are a married man with a family."

"Yes, I have a wife and three children, to be exact. I happen to be a devoted, committed husband and father," he added, unsuccessfully attempting to ward off further comments.

"Mr. Calais, you *must* know that women, *including* me, find you attractive. But, after all, you *are* a man, *quite* a man, I must add. I have found that men are mostly all alike. Don't *you* find me attractive, Mr. Calais?" she shamelessly teased.

Morgan, his poker face never wavering, answered, "I can see how *some* men *might* find you attractive."

"But what about you?" she continued, licking her lips as she looked him up and down.

"I *am* attracted to *inner* beauty," Morgan said in a not-so-subtle put down. "I am fortunate enough to be married to a woman who possesses inner *and* outer beauty and more, to whom I am *completely* and *irrevocably* committed."

"Surely, you *can't* say you're not *tempted*!"

"Surely I *can*, and I *do* say I am *not* tempted in the least. I love my *wife*, the mother of my children. I would *never* do anything to dishonor her *or* myself, just as I know *she* would never do anything to dishonor *herself* or *me*. Now, if you are quite through being *honest*, I will take me coat. I am leaving."

Ms. Cavanaugh was happy to learn Morgan had three children. She felt it gave her an advantage. She reasoned a body that had borne three babies would show tell-tell signs—extra weight gain, belly fat, stretch marks, and perhaps even sagging breasts.

"You are here alone, without her, so you are obviously not joined at the hip. Are you *afraid* to stay lest your male hormones take control?" she asked, again blatantly trying to seduce him.

The COW yawned in boredom. "Ms. Cavanaugh, it is *not* my nature to be rude to *anyone*, but you are seriously crossing the line. You're right, though. We are *not* joined at the hip. Even better, we are joined at the *heart*! Now, will you *please* be so kind as to get my coat!"

"I must say you are stronger than most, but I am not accustomed to *not* getting what I want, by hook or by crook. I bet if your wifey were to *cheat* on you, you would be singing a different tune, and you just *might* want to seek *me* out. Just so you'll know, the door will always be open to you. One never knows what can happen. I'll get your coat."

She shimmied away to get his coat, and Morgan just looked up at the ceiling, shaking his head. He took his coat when she returned, picked up his attaché case, and made a beeline for the door to let himself out.

Morgan was appalled at the brazenness of Ms. Cavanaugh and was musing over what Liv would say when he told her about it. There was no question that he would tell her. They made a habit of sharing the events of their day. For sure, this was *not* to be an event they would discuss over family dinner.

"Hi, Sweetheart, I'm home!" Morgan announced as Liv came to greet him with a kiss. "You won't *believe* the morning I have had!"

Liv's bloodhound nose immediately picked up the scent of perfume that was not hers. "I'm *sure* it will be interesting, judging by the non-*Liv's Scent* reeking from your *coat*." Liv was curious, but not jealous.

"Has the cleaning been picked up yet?"

"No, it should be soon, though."

"Good." Morgan removed his coat and handed it to Liv. "Please add this jacket to the pile. I certainly don't want any scent but *Liv's Scent* on *my* clothes. Be sure to check the pockets first, Hon. Thanks."

Liv took the coat from him and noticed the lipstick spear on the lining that was definitely not *her* shade. "I can't *wait* to hear your anecdote, especially about how this *lipstick* smear found its way *inside* your coat!" Liv said, mimicking jealousy.

"What?" Morgan asked, taking the coat and examining the smear. "Well I'll be!" he exclaimed. "She didn't!"

He was shaking his head in disbelief as he handed the coat back to Liv, who made a search of the pockets. She found the inside and the right pockets to be empty, but from the left pocket she pulled out a skimpy, silky thong! Holding it between her index finger and her thumb, she held it up with her arm stretched out and said, "Just how did *this* nasty, cootie booty floss find its way into your *pocket*?" before letting it drop to the floor.

Morgan looked at the thong in surprise. "Oh, that is just *too* much! When that coat gets back from the cleaners, I want you to donate it!"

"But that's one of your favorite suit coats, Morgan. You really want to get rid of it? It *can* be cleaned."

"It will *never* be clean enough for *me* to wear it again!" Emptying his pants pockets, he removed his pants and handed them to Liv. "No point in separating the suit. Take these, too. Some lucky guy will get an expensive suit dirt cheap."

"What do you want me to do with *this* thing?" Liv asked, picking up the thong with a tissue.

"Put it in the trash where it belongs. After I get into some more pants, come and let me tell you about my 'presentation' today."

Morgan proceeded to tell Liv all about the events of that morning, leaving out nothing.

"What are you going to do about it, Morgan?"

"I'm not going to do *anything*! I don't want to give her the satisfaction of even knowing that it, or she, was given a second thought.

"Where are the kids?"

"They're with Grandma and Grandpa until after church tomorrow."

"Do you mean we have the rest of the day to ourselves until we go to the Club?"

"We have all day and *night* to ourselves. Athene gave such a great show last night, I gave her tonight as well. So we have all day. We can have dinner at the Club and catch her first set, and have the *rest* of the night to ourselves."

"That's great! I feel like a king. Are you game?"

"You have to ask?" Liv coquettishly replied.

(The following Tuesday) Camille Cavanaugh was leisurely relaxing with a fashion catalog when a courier arrived at her door with a package. Inside the courier's packaging was a clasp envelope with no return address. She opened it first and found the thong she had slipped into Morgan's coat pocket before she gave it to him and a terse, typewritten note in bold, capitalized 36-point font that merely said, **"IT DIDN'T WORK!"**

Although she knew what it meant, she did not know who had sent it—Morgan or his wife. Mildly speaking, she was not a happy camper. Her ego was sorely bruised, and her pride was crushed. It was a defeat, a slap in the face she was not going to accept quietly.

She had called the corporate office the previous day expecting to be able to talk to Morgan and was peeved to learn that he was not available. She left a message for him to return her call. Since she had not received a return call as of the time she received the package, she made plans to present herself in person the next day. She was planning to demand a meeting with Morgan!

The Photograph

(A few weeks later) Morgan's meeting with the Mayor's representative was much shorter that he had anticipated. His presentation was so thorough it left little need for questions or detailed explanations. He wanted to surprise Liv with his presence earlier than she was expecting him. He decided to check his mail first and went to his office.

"Good morning, Morgan," Elizabeth said as they passed. "Is your meeting over so soon?"

"Yes, they are getting easier and easier as more and more people are becoming aware of our protocol and the successes of our programs."

"We *are* the best, aren't we! Tell Liv I will get back to her by Monday on the scheduling changes and the breakfast and lunch menus we discussed."

"Sure thing."

Morgan entered his office and eyed the pile of mail on his desk. The mail clerk habitually stacked his mail according to size when his secretary was away. Usually the secretary opened and sorted the mail and put on his desk just the correspondence only he could handle.

Morgan quickly skimmed the pieces noting the sources to determine if he needed to open anything. If not, he would deposit it on his secretary's desk. He didn't need to handle anything until he reached the last piece of mail, a 10"x12" clasp envelope stamped in bold red letters on both sides, "PERSONAL AND CONFIDENTIAL."

Morgan used a letter opener to open the flap which was securely taped closed. Nothing could have prepared him for what he found when he removed the content! He became furious, immediately blinded with rage, the likes of which he would never have thought himself capable. His emotional response when his wife and mother were physically attacked, and when he was infuriated by the insensitive questioning and innuendo of the detective who questioned Liv about the incident could not even come close to the anger he was experiencing at that moment! He struggled valiantly to contain his emotions and to regain his composure. He put the photograph back into the envelope and sat back in his chair with his eyes closed, his fists clenching and unclenching, trying to slow down his breathing to normal and to calm his rage.

After 45 minutes, he thought he was calm enough to call Liv. Hearing his assigned ringtone, Liv answered cheerfully, "Hi, Morgan!"

"Olivia, we need to talk. I'll be home in 45 minutes."

"Will we be going *out* for lunch, or do you want me to fix something?"

"I'm not hungry. I'm leaving now." Morgan abruptly ended on that note.

Liv was perplexed by the call. She perceived that Morgan was upset, but she had no idea why. He had called her "Olivia," something he *never* did. Absent was his customary greeting, "Hi, Sweetheart!" He ended the call without even saying "goodbye," or "love you."

She knew that whatever was on his mind, she would eventually find out. In the meantime, she was going to try not to worry about it. She decided to fix a light lunch anyway. She went to the garden and picked some spinach and tomatoes to put on the tuna sandwiches she would make. She made enough for snacks for the kids in case they were hungry when they got home.

After calling Liv, Morgan realized he had not given himself enough time to overcome his anger. He was remorseful and mortified not only that he had lost control and was unable to control his rage, but that he had allowed it to spill over onto Liv, something he never wanted or intended to do.

He realized he had been harsh with her and that he had called her "Olivia." He decided to take more time and try to desensitize himself so that he could contain his anger until it could be dispelled or channeled appropriately. Removing the photograph again, Morgan studied it carefully. There was nothing written on the back, nothing else in the envelope to indicate *why* it was sent or to what end. He just knew he had to find out everything there was to know.

The photograph causing such strong emotion in cool, calm, patient Morgan was of his beloved wife apparently nude in the arms of another man. Her cheek was on his chest as was her hand with her wedding rings that had been his mother's plainly visible. She appeared to be asleep, while the man was propped up on pillows with a lit cigarette in his hand and smoke rings being blown from his mouth. He had the unmistakable look of extreme satisfaction on his face.

There was nothing in the picture that could be identified other than Liv and the man. The sheets, the pillowcases, everything was white. The headboard was draped in white sheets, and a white sheet was covering the wall behind the bed. There were no pictures, nothing else visible that could be described.

Looking at the photo again rekindled Morgan's rage, and he wisely decided he would give himself much more time before he would discuss it with Liv. Knowing his wife, Morgan knew that he would have to be extra gentle with her, but he also knew that only she could provide him with the answers he needed. He would wait.

He thought—hoped—that if he waited, there might be some kind of follow-up that would shed light on a possible motive. He considered perhaps blackmail. He tried to put the matter out of his mind for the time being and concentrated on Liv.

Before leaving, Morgan made arrangements to have Alex, Little Morgan, and the baby transported home on the second bus run at 4:30 to have that extra time alone with Liv. He stopped at a specialty store on the way home and purchased a "Please Forgive Me" teddy bear. He chose a 12-inch black bear with a sparkly red ribbon around its neck.

Liv was reticent, not knowing what to expect when Morgan arrived home. She stood quietly, waiting for him to make the first move. Looking into her eyes, Morgan could see the questioning, confusion, and the tinge of hurt that was evident; and it made him regret his behavior even more.

He reached into the bag, removed the teddy bear, and handed it to Liv. "Liv, Baby, Sweetheart, I am so sorry. I just love you *so* much." He kissed her gently and held her tightly, kissing and then resting his chin on the top of her head while holding her in his arms. Liv took the teddy bear and gladly melted into his arms, holding onto him as tightly as she could, still holding the bear.

When he released her, Liv searched his eyes and saw his regret and his pain. "Morgan, what is the matter? *Whatever* it is that we need to discuss, it *can't* be *that* bad, *can* it?" When she saw his eyes soften even more, she relaxed.

Morgan did not want Liv to see that picture of herself any time soon because he knew just how disturbing it would be for her. Besides, *he* didn't want to see it again soon either.

"Honey, I sort of jumped the gun. Don't worry about it. Everything's fine for now. I was angry and should not have called you when I did. It's okay. Have you had lunch? Do you want to go out?"

Liv was relieved, although not totally convinced that everything was fine and dandy. After all, she knew her husband almost as well as he knew *her*. She chose to let it go. Whatever it was that angered him, she knew that in time he would share it with her.

"No, we don't have to go out for lunch unless you just *want* to. I made some tuna salad sandwiches the way you like them with fresh spinach and tomatoes. Is that all right?"

"Oh, sure, Baby. I *am* hungry after all, and we can have lunch and relax. Why don't you bring a tray up to our suite, and I will bring some iced tea. We can eat on the balcony and watch the view."

"That sounds good. I have been in the house all day working on my script. I do need a break and can use some fresh air and sunshine!"

During the time they were having lunch on the balcony, Morgan found he was still thinking about the photo and was having a hard time keeping his feelings, his anger, under control. He knew he had to replace those feelings with feelings and emotions that always brought him joy.

When they had finished their lunch and were taking time to relax and enjoy the scenery, Morgan was paying more attention to his wife than to the view. The Hormonal Committee of the Whole (COW), usually Johnny on the spot, had been subdued by the uncustomary negative emotions of that morning. It was now getting the usual signals and was beginning preparations.

Morgan stood and took Liv's hands, compelling her to stand as well. He looked at her in that special way he had that made her blush and said, "My Shulamite woman, thy king hath need to show thee his contrite heart. I beseech thee to accompany thy king to the bed chamber."

Liv happily responded, "Thy Shulamite woman doth gladly comply with grateful heart for the gift thou hath given to thy handmaid, O King."

When Liv raised her head from Morgan's chest and glanced at the clock, she was alarmed that it was almost 3:00. Starting to rise, she alerted, "Morgan, wake up! We will be late picking up the kids!"

Morgan replied, "Don't worry, it's okay," as he pulled her back down and clamped his arms around her. "I made arrangements before I left for them to be transported home on the second run. Holly said she would take care of it. We have a good hour plus before they will be home."

"Oh? Okay then!" she said, nestling again in Morgan's arms. "We'll have to make sure we're up and dressed in time. We don't want them to find us like *this*!"

"Don't worry, I'll get up about 4:00 and start dinner, and you can just relax if you want."

"I like that idea. I made extra sandwiches to tide the kids over until dinner is ready in case they are hungry."

The Note

More than a month had passed, and there had been nothing further concerning the photograph—no more photos, no demands for money, no notes, nothing. One Friday, following a lengthy, late luncheon meeting of the corporate officers and key members of the Advisory Committee, the officers returned to their offices in the North Wing of the Administration Building of the Calais Education and Community Center of Los Angeles.

Liv and Morgan's offices encompassed both corners of the wing with Holly and Elizabeth's offices on the east and west sides. A conference room, which was accessible only through either of their offices, separated Liv and Morgan's offices. The two shared a private bathroom at the rear of the conference room that included a shower and likewise could only be accessed through either of their offices.

In the center of the large wing was a reception area and office space for the officers' support staff. As they each entered their respective offices, Morgan's secretary handed him an envelope saying, "Mr. Calais, I found this small envelope for you that slipped through the cracks. All the matters that couldn't be handled are on your desk. I didn't open this one because, although it is not marked as being personal, it looked to me like a personal greeting card or something. I hope you don't mind."

"No problem, Jennifer. Thank you." Morgan took the envelope and examined it. There was only a post office box return address, no name. Morgan did not take that as a good sign. He opened the undated card and read the hand-written note which said,

Morgan,
If you are ready, my offer is still
on the table! The door is wide
open, just like my legs!
Camille

Morgan was disgusted by the note. His first instinct was to crumple and toss it. For a split second, he was reminded of a thought that had occurred to him when he first received the photo of Liv, that it might be the work of Camille Cavanaugh. He had dismissed it then as not plausible, and he was still inclined to doubt she would be so determined to have her way that she would do something so exceedingly low, despite her outrageous behavior.

Nevertheless, he had already shared the experience with Liv and saw no reason to hide the follow-up note from her. He thought Liv might take pleasure in destroying it herself, so he took it to her office and handed it to her.

"What's this, Morgan?"

"I thought you might like to destroy this note yourself, Liv."

Liv read the note, frowning. "That wench doesn't know when to quit, does she! Are you going to just let her get *away* with this? Do you want *me* to intervene? I *will*, you know!"

"Now, Liv, I didn't show it to you for you to *do* anything about it. I just showed you because we don't have secrets, right?"

Liv avoided his eyes thinking about how she "disposed" of the thong a while back. "You're right. *Here. You* dispose of it," she said, handing the note back to him. "I can't blame the wench for *trying*, though. I might do the same thing if I were her.

"I don't understand. If I remember her from that article in the magazine, she is rather attractive. Though she couldn't do better than you, surely there must be other men out there who would *gladly* have her."

"She's attractive all right; she is as attractive as her father's money can make her with the face-lifts, the implants and enhancements, the liposuction, the peals, the injections, and who knows what else. Let *me* have it. *I'll* dispose of it *myself*. If I hear from her *again*, we *both* may have to pay her a visit. Or, I *just* might let *you* handle it in your own unique way," he added jokingly.

Liv gave him a devious look that made him add, "Liv, you know I'm *kidding* about that!"

"Yes, I know, Morgan. I'm tired. Let's get the kids and go home. Do you want to do dinner tonight, or should we order something?"

"We've both had a long day. Why don't you call Walter's caterer. She always does a good job, and she is good with last-minute orders. Besides, we *know* we will be getting healthy, home-cooked, organic food. We can spend the time with the kids and help Alex with her homework."

"That little smarty-pants *never* needs our help! She just likes it when we are with her while she does it."

Morgan laughed, "So you've figured that out, too? That little girl is something else!"

"Yes, I have figured that out. And don't let *her* hear you refer to her as 'little girl.' She hasn't considered herself a 'little girl' since her baby brother was born and she became a 'big sister'."

"Okay, I'll watch it; but she will always be my little girl, just like you will always be my baby," he said, kissing her. "Let's go."

CHAPTER 4

THE PHOTO IS UNVEILED / THE MYSTERY BECOMES CLEARER

The Photo is Unveiled

Receiving the note from Camille Cavanaugh the week before brought to the surface for Morgan the matter of the photograph. During the weeks that had passed since he first received it, Morgan had been trying *not* to concentrate on it; but doing nothing left him with the uncomfortable feeling of waiting for the storm to hit. He believed his rage had been assuaged to the point that he would be able to deal with the situation on a more rational and controlled level. He felt he could keep his emotions in check, especially for Liv's sake.

He also believed that Liv may be able to deal with it better, at least he hoped so. His being in control of himself would enable him to support her. He knew seeing the photo of herself in that position would be extremely traumatic for her. He hated that she had to see it, but he knew it was necessary if they were going to get to the bottom of it.

Alex and Little Morgan had been looking forward to spending Saturday with MiMi and PawPaw, Liv's grandparents, who lived on the property in the house on the other side of the garden. Randy was just always happy, no matter *where* he was or *who* he was with.

The children had spent Friday night with their great-grandparents and did not go to the Club, so Morgan and Liv slept in Saturday morning and had a leisurely, late breakfast. Morgan chose that time to approach Liv about the photograph.

When they had cleaned the kitchen, Morgan took her hand. "Liv, please come and sit with me." He led her to the couch in the den where they sat facing each other. He picked up the black teddy bear from its place on the couch among the pillows that had been its roost ever since he gave it to her.

"Sweetheart, do you remember the day I gave him to you?"

Liv took the bear, remembering the circumstances under which she had received it, and she felt a sense of foreboding. She remembered that he had been upset and apologized to her. She also remembered that whatever the issue was, it was not settled and would be raised again. She knew that this was the time.

"Yes, Morgan, I remember," she said tentatively. "There was something you said we needed to discuss, but that it could wait until another time. I suppose this is now the time," she said, her heart beginning to beat faster.

"Yes, Sweetheart. First, I want to apologize to you, *again*, for being so short and abrupt with you when I called that day. I was extremely upset and allowed my anger to affect my interaction with you. You didn't deserve that treatment from me, or *anybody*, for that matter, but *especially* from *me*. I thought I had given myself enough time to calm down, but obviously I hadn't. When you see what I have to show you, I think you may understand *why* I was so upset, but that's still no excuse for my taking it out on you."

"Morgan, we knew from the start that our lives would not always be smooth sailing. I've told you more than once that anything that comes up we will just have to deal with it. That means me, too. I'm a little skeptical, a little afraid, I have to admit; but we're supposed to be able to conquer *anything* as long as we do it together. So go ahead, Morgan, show me *whatever* it is."

"Before I show you this picture, Liv, I want to make sure you *know* that my anger was *never* directed at you. I *know* you, Liv, and I love and honor you. One look at that picture, and I *knew* there was *no* way you would *ever* knowingly or willingly be a party to what it suggests."

Despite her earlier assurance to Morgan, Liv's trepidation was steadily growing. She took a deep breath, closed her eyes, and waited. Morgan removed the photo and put it in her hand. Liv opened her eyes, and it was as if her worst nightmare had been multiplied a billion times!

"Oh, my God, Morgan, no! No! No!" she screamed, shaking her head vigorously. Leaping up, Liv dropped the photo and ran to the bathroom, where she promptly upchucked every cookie she had. Morgan was right behind her. He handed her a damp facecloth and tried to console her. She was shaking uncontrollably and screaming, "No, no! Oh, my God! No!" over and over again until she went limp, falling into Morgan's arms.

"Baby, Baby, it's okay, Sweetheart. Breathe." He picked her up and carried her back to the den and held her on his lap and rocked her the way she would rock Little Morgan or Randy when either came running to her and crying because of a booboo or mishap.

After about 45 minutes, Liv was considerably calmer and initiated conversation. She knew why Morgan was so enraged, and she knew why and how he knew of her complete innocence. What she *didn't* know was that one of his greatest concerns was that she may have been raped in the process. Liv *refused* to entertain the thought that it might have happened.

"Morgan, thank you for your tenderness with me. I know we have to talk about this. I just don't know what I can say," she said on the verge of tears again.

"Do you have any idea when, or where this could have happened?"

"Morgan, I just don't have a clue. This is worse than a nightmare. I don't know of *anyone* who would want to do this to me . . . to us. The only person I know who wanted to hurt me is in *prison*. It *couldn't* be *him*. Do *you* have any ideas, Morgan?"

"The thought did occur to me that that Cavanaugh woman could possible do something like this, but that was a long time ago. I had no further feedback from her, that is, until the note I received last week. I didn't give her any reason to . . ."

At the mention of the note from "the wench Cavanaugh," Liv's body noticeably tensed and caused Morgan to stop talking and look at her. Liv's eyes widened in remembrance, and she couldn't hide her thoughts from Morgan. "Liv, I *know* that *look*! What did you do that I don't know about?"

Liv averted her eyes, shying away from eye contact. She knew she would have to confess to her deed, but first she wanted to mitigate the impact, or at least delay having to face it.

"Liv?" Morgan repeated, stringing out her name and elevating the ending, expecting an answer. Liv peered up at him with penitent eyes, but remained silent.

"Liv, *talk* to me."

Liv shifted her body and took a slow, deep breath. "Morgan, remember when you told me, *several* times in fact, that *whatever* I did was *okay* with you?" she asked meekly.

"Yes, of *course* I remember that. I *also* remember *your* telling *me* that *you* didn't want to hold anything *back* from me! So, now, tell me what you *did*."

"Do you promise not to get angry with me and that you will still love me unconditionally?"

"You know I can't *promise* I won't get angry because I don't *know* yet what you've *done*. I *can* promise that I will continue to *love* you unconditionally, and that I *probably* won't get angry because, God knows, I have used up my quota of anger for at least a decade." He leaned over and kissed her to reassure her. "Now tell me, please, Sweetheart, what you did," he said softly.

"Okay, Morgan. Do you remember the thong that wench put in your pocket?"

"Yes, I do. I told you to toss it. Go on."

"I *know* she was trying to make me jealous. I wanted to get even with her, to *punish* her."

"Wait a minute, Liv! Are you about to tell me you *did* something to retaliate after *I* said I wasn't going to do *anything* about it?"

"But, Morgan, you didn't say *I* couldn't!"

"No, Liv, but you *know* that in that instance I meant '*we*.' That's why I said to put it in the *trash*!"

Remembering how in disguise Liv invaded his bachelor party,

how she punked Kyle at their rehearsal dinner, and her sting of Casanova Adams, the obsessed fan who retaliated by attacking her mother, believing it was Liv, Morgan was gearing up for some elaborate ploy. "Well, what did you do *this* time?"

"I just mailed her thong back to her," Liv answered innocently.

Disappointed, but very relieved that it was not worse, Morgan asked, "Is *that* all?"

"No, not quite, Morgan," Liv said haltingly.

"What *else*, Liv?" Morgan asked, eyeing her piercingly.

"I included a little note," she added cautiously.

"And just what did that *little note* say, pray tell?"

"Just three little words—in bold type: 'It didn't work!' I didn't *sign* it. As far as *she* knows, *you* could have sent it. But, yes, I know, you didn't. I'm sorry, Morgan. I couldn't *resist* doing it," she said, holding her head down and looking up sideways at Morgan.

Morgan breathed a sigh of relief. "If *that's* all there was to it, I don't see her having anything to do with something as sinister and vindictive as *this*. That *is* all, right?

"Yes, Morgan. That's *all*! *Really!*"

"Obviously, *somebody* did this, and we've got to find out *who* and *why*."

"Am I off the hook, Morgan?" Liv asked, still contrite, looking up at him with doleful eyes.

"Yes, Baby, you're off the hook," he said as he put his arms around her. "But in the future, will you please leave vengeance to Him to Whom it belongs!"

"Thank you, Morgan. I'll try."

"You'll *what*?" Morgan demanded with mock sternness.

"I mean, I *will*. Can I have a reassuring kiss?"

Morgan shook his head in resignation and kissed her. "We can probably cross your 'wench' off the list, but we still have to solve this."

The Mystery Becomes Clearer

Liv was still at a loss to try to even imagine, let alone explain how the situation depicted in the photo came to be. She was racking her brain to come up with a possible answer. They remained quiet for a while as Morgan held her. She retreated to her "go to" place for answers and inspiration, or just plain comfort—her private prayer closet, her haven.

Although she was loathe to do so, she reached for the photograph. "I need to look at this again. The answer is here, I just have to discover it, Morgan."

"Are you sure, Sweetheart? I don't want you to put yourself through that again. It's even hard for *me* to look at it."

"It was mostly seeing myself with my face and my hand on his hairy chest—and his hairy arm and hand on my body." She faltered somewhat at the thought, but continued, "I think the initial shock is passed enough for me to do what I must do, as much as I hate to."

Morgan was watching and supporting Liv with his arm around her as she pored over every detail of the photo, scrutinizing it thoroughly. After a few moments, Liv announced matter-of-factly, "Morgan, I know! I know *when* it was, I know *where* it was, and I *think* I know *who* did it, or at least had a *hand* in it! I just don't know *why*!"

"Really, Liv?" Morgan asked in surprise. "How do you *know* that? How can you be *sure*, Sweetheart?"

"I can be sure because of what I am *wearing*!"

Morgan was puzzled. "But you're not wearing *anything*, Sweetheart! You are completely *bare*!"

"Look *again*, Morgan! Look at my *ear*!"

Looking more closely, Morgan saw part of an earring that was not totally obscured by her hair. "I see a piece of your earring, but how does that help you? You can't *possibly* remember the earrings you wear on any given day, *can* you?"

"No, I can't. But I *can* in *this* instance. *This* was the *only* time I have worn those earrings when I wasn't on a mother-daughter date with Alex. Don't you recognize it, Morgan?"

Morgan concentrated on the visible portion and recognized the earring. "Why, that's that gaudy pair of earrings that *Alex* made for you!"

"Yes, Morgan, but don't ever let *Alex* hear you say that! She was so proud because she made them all by herself, just for *me*. She asked me why I never wore them to '*regular*' places, only when I was with *her*. I hadn't realized she noticed that. I should have known that little smarty pants would!

"I told her I didn't have anything appropriate to wear them with because of all the different, unusual colors. She insisted we go shopping so she could help me find a dress that would have the right colors, which I knew would have been impossible. We decided, I should say, she *agreed* to go with the dress *I* picked out. It was the white eyelet sundress that I wore to my appointment that Saturday. I made sure she saw me with them on, and she insisted on taking a picture of me wearing them. She was really happy!"

"Okay, Liv, this is a good start. What was the date, where did you go, and who did you see?"

"I went to this house in Gardena to audition a young lady who was trained at Juilliard and wanted to book a few nights at the Club. Her former music teacher called and left a message for me at the Club. When I called her back, she told me about her student and wanted to set up an audition.

"I was very excited for the opportunity to audition a bona fide Juilliard-trained artist. That's why I opted out of providing the luncheon entertainment at that special meeting of L. A. County School District Administrators where you were to be the key-note speaker, remember?"

"Yes, I do. That would have been a Saturday in June," Morgan noted.

"That was when the young lady was scheduled to be in Southern California. If the audition worked out, as I was hoping it would, it would have been great to present her to my audiences!"

"Where was the audition?"

"It was in the teacher's home in Gardena."

"Okay, Liv, back up a little bit. We can check the date. What was her name?"

"It's all recorded on the master calendar."

"Wait, I'll get it."

While Morgan went to retrieve the calendar, Liv was going over in her mind everything she could remember about that day. She knew it was in June on a Saturday, and she arrived early for the 11 a.m. appointment. She vaguely remembered the lady's name, but she could see her, a pleasant woman probably in her 60s, somewhat taller than she and weighing about 145 to 150lbs.

Morgan brought the calendar, flipped the pages back to June, and handed it to Liv. Liv looked for the sticker representing her doctor's appointment and pointed to the previous Saturday. "Here it is, Morgan! Your luncheon and my appointment—June 15! Her name is Thelma Olman. Since I was early, we chatted a minute. Mostly, she talked about her student, whose name she said was Traci."

"Did you get any strange vibes?" Morgan inquired."

"No, not at all. She was very pleasant, really friendly. Besides, I was excited and looking forward to meeting this young lady and hearing her sing.

Liv related everything she could recall without interruption until she mentioned drinking a glass of iced tea the woman offered her.

"Liv, we are always preaching to the kids about accepting food and drink from strangers. You actually *accepted* it?"

"Well, yes, Morgan. I had left my bottled water in the car. Even though, as you said, we don't accept food or drink from strangers, it *was* warm, so I did.

"When it turned out after some time the young lady wouldn't be able to come after all, I agreed to reschedule. I prepared to leave and found I had developed a rare headache. When I started to rise, I remember feeling woozy and sitting back down in the chair. She asked if I were okay and suggested I wait for the feeling to pass. I must have dozed off. The next thing I remember, Mrs. Olman was asking me if I felt okay, and I *did*. I was surprised that so much time had passed, but that was the *end* of it."

"You didn't tell me about that, Liv."

"No, Morgan. I really felt fine, and I didn't want to worry you. You've never known me to be sick. I'm as healthy as a horse! Besides, I knew I would be going to the doctor for my physical that Monday. As I expected, everything was fine, and I never gave the episode another thought.

"I *did* call you before I left, but when you didn't answer, I didn't leave a message. I remembered you were speaking that day. In hindsight, I wish I had never opted out of performing at that luncheon. I was just so excited about the audition."

"Liv, I wish you had told me about your experience anyway. Did the woman, Thelma, ever call back to reschedule?"

"No, but she *did* let me know that the young lady had auditioned for an Italian opera company and had been accepted. She had temporarily relocated to Italy and was touring with the opera company."

"That seems suspiciously too convenient to *me*, Liv. I believe she drugged you with that tea. I see *her* as the key to solving *all* of this."

Feeling very remorseful, Liv said, "If only I hadn't accepted that tea, this would not have happened. It's all my fault. I'm sorry, Morgan. I'm really sorry."

Knowing her pain, Morgan consoled her. "Honey, it's *not* your fault. *None* of it is. Don't blame yourself. Anyone who wanted to do this would have found another way to hurt you. It *could* have been worse. At least you are alive and well, and we *will* get over this!" he said, giving her a reassuring embrace.

Morgan took the photo and replaced it out of sight inside the envelope. They sat for a while in silence, each pondering the event and experiencing a resurgence of the thought, the possibility, that neither was anxious to address.

They were almost always in tune with each other's emotions, and often their thoughts. They had been thinking along the same line. Finally, Morgan faced her, his angst clearly visible. Not wanting to voice it, but compelled to do so, Morgan revealed to her his deep concern.

"Liv, seeing you in that picture, my first thought was of your father. I remember how you described him when we were on our honeymoon as a hairy monster. I *knew* what seeing the photo would *do* to you. I also knew without a doubt that you would *have* to have been drugged to be in that position. What I can't seem to get out of my head is the thought, the possibility, that he could have *raped* you, and you would not remember it."

Liv felt a sharp emotional pain in her heart. She could not bear knowing how painful that thought was to Morgan. Despite her own fear, Liv knew she had to ignore her own feelings to reassure him. The only way she could possibly reassure him would be to don a character who was strong, convincing, and assured of her truth. This had to be the most realistic, sincere, believable character she would ever have to portray.

After taking a moment to become the character she needed to be, Liv began to perform. "Morgan," she said, taking his face in her hands compelling him to really look into her eyes, "as you *know*, I have been raped before, many, many times—more times than I can or ever *want* to remember. I *know* when I have been *raped*! Please believe me when I tell you that I was not *raped*, or violated in any way more than what you can see in that awful photo. I was not raped!" she repeated emphatically.

Morgan searched deeply into her eyes looking, hopefully, for confirmation. "But how do you *know*? How can you be *sure,* Sweetheart, since you didn't remember anything about it?"

"I can't *explain* it to you, Morgan, how or why I know it's true. I just *know* with all my being; my *body* knows. So *please,* Morgan, *believe* me. *Trust* me! I was *not* raped!" she repeated simply.

She was so convincing, Liv was convinced in her own psyche. She smiled a smile of relief as she saw Morgan's relief and realized the easing of her own mind.

CHAPTER 5

IF THE TRUTH BE KNOWN

On June 15, 2019, Liv arrive at the home of Thelma Olman at 10:45 a.m. for her 11:00 o'clock appointment to audition a young lady for possible booking at Liv's Supper Club and Lounge. She was dressed comfortably in the white spaghetti-strapped eyelet sundress she had purchased specifically to be able to wear the multi-colored earrings Alex had made for her.

"Mrs. Calais, please come in," Mrs. Olman greeted her cheerfully. "It is a pleasure to meet you! Ms. Moran should be here any moment. In the meantime, please have a seats."

"Thank you. Please call me Liv," she said, following her into the living room.

"Okay, thank you, Liv. I'm Thelma. My, what unusual earrings you're wearing. I've never seen any quite like them!"

"Oh, you are so kind! My daughter made them for me.

"I am looking forward to hearing Ms. Moran sing."

"You won't be disappointed. She has a wonderful instrument, and I am proud to have had a hand in preparing her to be accepted at Juilliard," she said as her telephone rang.

"Hello," she answered . . . "Yes, she is here already. . . . Ten to fifteen minutes? Okay, it's still a little early. See you when you get here, Traci."

In answer to Liv's inquiring expression, Thelma said, "That was Ms. Moran, Traci. She will be a little late. She said the traffic on the 405 was beginning to slow, almost to a standstill. Why don't we go into the den and wait. We will be more comfortable there."

Liv followed her into the den and sat in the recliner suggested as being the most comfortable.

"I can open the patio door so that it will be cooler, and I won't have to turn on the air. Besides, that's where the piano is, and you won't have to move when Traci arrives.

"I do apologize for the temperature. I am a senior citizen on a fixed income, and I have to economize when and wherever I can. It's not that easy now since I have been widowed and no longer have the number of pupils I once had. My husband's life insurance was barely enough to pay for his burial. Oh, excuse me. I didn't mean to burden you with my problems," she said in a tear-jerking manner.

"That's quite all right, Thelma. I understand how it can be. I'm very sorry for your loss."

"Thank you, Liv. I made some raspberry ice tea. Can I bring you a glass? That's the *least* I can do."

"Yes, thank you. That would be nice."

Liv dialed Morgan and left the message that she may be gone a little longer than she originally anticipated. Thelma returned with the ice tea, and the two sat sipping the tea and chatting casually when the telephone rang again several minutes later. Thelma left to answer the phone and returned to the den. "Mrs. Calais, *Liv*, I am so sorry. That was Traci. Evidently, there has been a big rig jackknife that resulted in a 7-car pileup on the 405. The freeway is completely blocked." She continued in a dismayed tone, "According to the news report Traci said traffic is not expected to move for at least an hour or more.

"I can't ask you to wait for her, Liv. I told her that we would try to reschedule the audition at your convenience. Can we do that, please?"

Disappointed, Liv responded, "Oh, that's too bad. I was really looking forward to hearing her. But no problem. We can reschedule. Just give me a call."

Liv prepared to get up and found that she had a headache, and the room was beginning to spin. Feeling dizzy, she tried to rise, but fell back into the chair.

"What's the matter, Liv, are you all right?" Thelma asked.

"I don't know. I've suddenly developed a headache, and I'm feeling rather dizzy."

"Why don't you just lean back and relax a moment. Perhaps it will pass."

Thelma reclined Liv's chair. Liv leaned back, closed her eyes, and was almost immediately out like a light. "Mrs. Calais? Liv?" Thelma called her name several times without response.

Certain that Liv was completely under the influence o f t he drugged tea, Thelma called to her accomplice who had been waiting in the adjacent room and who had placed the calls.

"Okay, Stanley, she's out. Take her into the bedroom," Thelma ordered.

Stanley just stood looking admiringly at Liv. "She is *beautiful*!" he said as he reached down to fondle her.

"Don't you *dare* touch her! You're not getting paid big bucks to get your jollies. We have a job to do and not much time to do it! You don't touch her until I tell you, and only *where* I tell you, is that clear?"

"All right, all right!" Stanley grumbled. "You can't blame a guy for tryin'!"

"Now pick her up and take her into the bedroom and put her in the bed."

Following directions, Stanley picked up the sleeping beauty, carried her into the bedroom, and placed her in the bed on her back where the sheet had been turned back.

"Now lift her so I can undress her."

With Stanley holding her up, Thelma quickly unzipped Liv's dress and slipped the straps over her shoulders. She then pulled her dress down to just below her waist, baring her torso.

"Okay, Stanley," Thelma ordered, "strip and get in beside her."

Stanley reluctantly placed Liv down on her back and rose to take off his clothes. "Can I take off my briefs, too?"

"That won't be necessary," Thelma said as she placed the pillows on the bed so that he would not be lying flat but would be reclined on the pillows. "Now get in," she directed.

When he was in place, Thelma directed him to turn Liv over and pull her on top of him so that her right cheek was resting on his chest. With his left arm under her and her right arm raised so that it was over his shoulder, he easily pulled her limp torso on top of him into the desired position.

Thelma positioned the sheet so that the two were completely covered up to Liv's lower back so that they both appeared to be completely naked. She placed Liv's left arm with elbow bent so that her hand was on his chest close to her face, her wedding rings clearly visible. She directed Stanley to place his left arm and hand on Liv's back.

"Can I do what I want with my right hand as long as it can't be seen?" Stanley asked, hopefully.

"I'm not going to remind you again, Stanley. No monkey business! If we are caught, we'll be in enough trouble without adding rape or sexual battery to the mix. You can do that crap on your own time and your *own* dime!"

"How is anyone going to find out? I told you, with the drug I gave you to give her, she won't remember *anything*, I *guarantee* you. By my calculations, we have another ten to twenty minutes. She'll wake up and will be none the wiser. So, unless *you* tell, no one will possibly find out. That is, no one besides the one who is paying for all of this! By the way, how much are *you* getting paid?"

"Never mind what *I'm* getting as long as you get your $7½ Gs! That's more than you have probably made in the last five years as an actor. We're wasting time!"

She then disheveled Liv's hair, carefully displacing a few locks, being careful not to conceal her face. She lit a cigarette and handed it to Stanley. "Here. Let's see how good of an actor you are. Take a puff and show me your best after-sex expression of satisfaction."

Thelma got her camera and, after checking various angles, she made her choice and snapped the photo as Stanley was blowing smoke rings. When she was satisfied that the preview was perfect, she ordered Stanley to get dressed and help her to restore Liv to her former position in the recliner. When they had done so, Stanley left with his envelope full of cash.

Thelma was anxiously waiting for Liv to awaken from the effects of the drug. After about half an hour, she began to seriously worry as Liv showed no signs of arousal. She contemplated calling for paramedics as it had been almost an hour since she had administered the drug. She certainly didn't want to face a murder charge in addition.

She was in a quandary and didn't know what to do. Liv's system was so clean, the drug she ingested was much more effective, akin to giving an infant an adult dose of medication. While Thelma pondered her situation, Liv began to stir. Thelma leaned in to watch her closely and be in her face with an appropriate look of concern as soon as she awoke. As soon as Liv opened her eyes, Thelma asked, "Liv, are you feeling better now? You went to sleep, and I didn't want to disturb you. I thought it might be good if you could sleep your headache away."

Realizing her headache was gone, Liv responded, "I'm sorry, Thelma. How long have I been asleep?" she asked, looking at her watch. "Oh, my goodness! It's been over an hour! I'm *really* sorry. I hope I haven't been an inconvenience to you!"

"Not at all. I just hope you're all right, Liv."

"I *feel* fine," she said, rising. "I'm not dizzy at all, and my headache is completely gone, not a trace."

"That's great, Dear!"

Liv dialed Morgan's number before remembering his engagement and terminated the call without leaving a message. After thanking Thelma for her hospitality, Liv departed for home.

CHAPTER 6

COPING WITH THE SITUATION: A MUCH-NEEDED BREAK / OH, NO YOU DON'T!

A Much-Needed Break

Liv had not fully recovered from the shock of seeing that photo and was still in a somewhat dark place, even though they had a direction in which to go in getting to a resolution. She wanted, *needed*, a break. Morgan's mind was more at ease because of Liv's assurances that she had not been raped, and the fact that she was not as fragile as she appeared when first seeing the photo.

Nevertheless, his anger was revived, and he did not like the way it made him feel. He seldom became angry, and when he did, it was dealt with and short lived. That was not so when it involved anything related to this case. The rage he felt when he first received the photo had been stuffed so that he could function normally, but it was always just under the surface. He knew that the only way he could put it to rest would be to have a resolution. He also knew that there was a long row to hoe before that could happen, and he had to maintain his equilibrium.

Liv had *her* "go-to" place, her haven. They both had their prayer lives and faith. These resources were initiated, but relief, the relief Morgan needed, had not yet been realized. He turned to *his* "go-to" place that never failed to take his mind to a happy place, at least temporarily, away from any unpleasant current state or situation and provide complete respite.

He stood and took Liv's hands in his, compelling her to stand as well. He kissed her gently and said, "Come, My Shulamite woman. Your King Solomon detects we both need a long break." He picked her up and carried her upstairs to their suite.

The ringing of the telephone awakened them after a couple of hours from their peaceful sleep. Reluctantly, Morgan answered the phone as Liv checked the time.

"Hi, Morgan. This is Frank. Hope I'm not interrupting anything. I was just thinking about you two, and I wanted to let you know I'm planning on going to the Club tonight. I wanted to make sure Liv would be performing. I know sometimes she has a substitute, who is always good, but I especially want to hear Liv and see the two of *you* tonight."

Morgan hadn't thought about the possibility that Liv might not be up to performing after the trauma of that afternoon and wanted to make sure. "Hey, Frank. Let me check. I'll call you right back."

"Liv, Sweetheart, I didn't think about how you might feel having to go and perform tonight. Will it be a problem for you with this other stuff on your mind? That was Frank. He is planning to come to the Club tonight and wanted to see if you would be performing."

"That *is* my *job*, Morgan. I can't just call in a substitute just because I have a bad day. I'm supposed to be a professional, regardless. I may have to make a few changes in my song list for tonight. I have a couple of songs that will lend themselves well to these raw emotions that I know will still be strong. I'll make it work. Besides, we haven't seen Frank for a bit. It will be nice to see him."

"I'll call him back and let him know."

Morgan picked up his cell to call Frank, but a thought suddenly popped up into his mind. That thought was supplanted by yet another thought, and he called Frank back to say they would be looking forward to seeing him at the Club later.

When the call ended, Morgan began pondering the original thought he had vacated. Liv glanced in his direction and felt a vibe that concerned her. "What are you thinking that is making your brow furrow, Morgan? It looks serious. Is it Frank?"

"Well, yes, and no. What I am fudging on is whether or not the timing is right to do what I think we need to do soon."

"It's about the photo, isn't it," Liv stated. "You want to get Frank to find out who is behind it."

"You are so perceptive, Liv. I *am* anxious to get to the bottom of it, and Frank *is* the best person I know to do it. I *know* he will be discreet. I'm also thinking about how *you* will be affected by that photo being seen by him or anyone else. Personally, I hate the fact that it will be necessary, and I can't . . ."

"You are concerned about how *I* will feel having it seen by any other eyes," Liv interrupted. "If there were any other way, I know you would gladly take it. But there *isn't*. I have to *deal* with it. I *will*. I will start by dispelling my negative emotions in my performance tonight."

"Hey, Babe, I think I know the perfect song for you to sing to help you do that. Remember that song you wrote shortly after the ordeal with Casanova Adams and that insensitive jerk detective? I've only heard you sing it once, and you really *killed* it."

"Oh, do I remember *that*! I think I scared a lot of people that night, including myself! I only sang it that one time."

"What was the name of it?"

"Oh, No You Don't!"

"Yeah, that's it! Wow!"

"Maybe it is time to resurrect it. It's better than *killing* someone like I feel like doing about now! I'd better be sure to bring the charts for that one, just in case. I'll have to come up with a good setup so that people will understand. I'll have to think about it a while. In fact, I think I need to really *pray* about it, also. Well, it's time for me to start preparing for tonight."

"So it's okay if I have Frank over afterwards to get into it?"

"Yes, you might as well. Might as well get it over with sooner than later!"

"What about Mom and Pops?" Morgan asked cautiously.

Liv hesitated, knowing how awkward, if not downright painful it would be for her parents, and herself as well, seeing the photo in each other's presence. She thought perhaps it would be easier on everyone if Frank and especially her parents were briefed about it before actually seeing the photo as opposed to having it thrust on them "cold turkey" as she had viewed it.

"Morgan, I don't see how it can be avoided. I'll see if they are planning to come tonight, which I think they are, and I'll ask them to come here afterwards. I think they may have an inkling something is up after my performance, anyway."

"Okay, Sweetheart. I've got a couple of things to do myself before we get out of here. Say, why don't I just call them? And you know what I think I might do? While you are having your quiet time before you go on, I might brief them on our situation, you know, tell them about the photo. Perhaps Mom and Dad may opt not to see it. I will leave it up to them."

"I like that idea, Morgan. Thank you."

"Oh, No You Don't!"

(Liv's Supper Club and Lounge) Liv had given much thought to her performance that night. It was a typical Saturday night crowd with significant overflow. Liv wanted to give her customary opening set rather than come out swinging with her "anger" song. She made sure she was in the right character to evoke good feelings, mirth, and relaxing enjoyment. Her first set was so well done, even Morgan questioned within himself if she had changed her mind. His question was answered when she abandoned her usual routine and retreated directly to her dressing room following her standing ovation when the set was over.

When she heard her musical cue for the second set, Liv was ready. She walked out on stage amid the applause and signaled *pianississimo* to the band. She also held up her hand to silence the audience, something she had never done before. When the band's volume had dropped to the softest possible level and her expectant audience was totally still, Liv began her monologue.

"Friends, before I sing my first song of this set, I am departing from my normal practice of just breaking out in song, as you may have noted. You see, many times singing can be cathartic for me.

I can express emotions and feelings that may be hard to articulate in normal conversation, or that I can't, or don't want to hold in. I can share good feelings, which I love to do; I can express pain, or sadness, which sometimes is necessary; and I can even express anger or other negative emotions in a safe way.

"A few years ago, I experienced a situation that angered me greatly and caused very negative feelings. Consequently, I wrote a song to address and dissipate that unpleasant state of mind that my husband calls my *"anger"* song. Some of you may have been present that night and witnessed that performance.

"Today I was presented with a situation that caused me intense, negative feelings and emotions that I have not been able to dispel. I am talking about intense hurt, anger, and *rage*! I intend to release those emotions in my resurrection of that song.

"If I were to compare the level of anger I felt then with today, oh, my goodness! I would have to say on a scale of 1–10, *then* was a mere 2-1/2. Now it's 10 and climbing. That's why I am giving you this heads up." Just bringing up the subject was causing her emotions to surge to the surface, and Liv had to give up a nervous laugh to ward them off.

"So. I invite any of you who may have strong emotions of your own that you have been holding on to, to release them vicariously through me. Believe me. They are better let out than held in! The name of my 'anger' song is, 'Oh, No You Don't!'

"Hit it, Billy!"

The band took off, and it was on and crackin'! By the time they got to the song's bridge, almost everyone in the house was standing, going uncharacteristically wild. The tirade lasted a full six minutes!

After another full two minutes when things had finally returned to normal, Liv calmly smiled and said, "Thanks. I *needed* that!"

A patron in the crowd stood and shouted out, "We did, too, Baby Girl!" Everyone had a good laugh, and the set went on according to the usual tradition as Liv soothed everyone's spirits with some of her signature songs, continuing to weave her magic.

Liv was not in a hurry to face her parents or Frank and again retreated directly to her dressing room to shower and change before going home, something she did occasionally. She thought about donning a character to replace herself that would not be affected, but she had worn herself out with her "Oh, No You Don't!" rendition earlier. She resolved to face them head on, knowing she would be with not only the three people she knew loved her beyond measure, but also the one person who would surely be able to bring the situation to its resolution. She put on her happy, brave face and finally went out to join them.

Meanwhile, seeing the anxious looks on the faces of Lydia and Walter, Morgan realized Liv was taking longer than usual to appear and wanted to ease their minds. "Liv is probably changing. She must have worked up a sweat with that last set. She's probably taking a little extra time to get her head straight." He had just finished speaking when he saw her walking toward them.

Everyone stood as she approached their table. "Olivia, Honey," Lydia said as she embraced her daughter and held on longer than she intended to. She, as well as the others, wanted to make it seem as though nothing were out of the ordinary.

"Hi, Mom," she said, hugging her back. "I'm glad you came."

Turning to Walter, at Lydia's side, she hugged him as well. "Daddy," she said, avoiding eye contact.

"Hi, Frank. It is good to see you. It's been a while."

Frank gave her a hug. "Olivia, that was some show you put on! I've never seen your audience so fired up!"

"Well, tonight *was* a little unusual, Frank."

Morgan patiently waited as she greeted everyone. He came and stood by his wife's side, put his arm around her, and said, "Are we ready to go, Sweetheart?"

She looked him directly in the eye telegraphing that she was ready to do what was needed. "I'm ready, Morgan. Let's go."

CHAPTER 7

GATHERING THE FACTS / MORE TO DISCUSS

Gathering the Facts

The three cars caravanned to the Big House. Morgan told Liv that he had discussed the situation with Frank and her parents earlier before her first set and during her intermission. They had all been careful not to show any negative reactions, each one understanding and being sensitive to Liv's feelings and not wanting to add to any discomfort or embarrassment she may have still felt.

"How did Mom and Dad take the news?"

"Of course they were hurt and angry. I think your mom even cried a little, though she tried to hide it. Liv, I don't know if you noticed them, but they were right there with your audience letting loose to 'Oh, No You Don't!' You must know that that is a very powerful song and *very* effective, especially the way *you* deliver it."

"Well, it *did* help me a lot. I just hope I can keep it together and make it through tonight. I'm not worried about Frank. I know he is a professional and has seen a lot of things. Like you said, he is discrete. But for my parents, I think it will be difficult for them even though you have told them . . ."

"Liv, don't worry about your parents. They don't want to see the photo. They just want to support you in any way they can. They love you, and it's hard for them just knowing how *you* feel."

"It makes me feel much better knowing they *won't* see it. And, Morgan, I'm going to surprise *you*. I am going to be so strong and determined, you might think I'm faking it, playing a role. Don't think I didn't *think* about it, 'cause I *did*. But *I'm* going to be *me*! I am going to be strong. I *am* strong. I am also *determined*. Singing that song tonight really did something for me. I am ready to do *battle*. Woe to the person or persons who perpetrated this heinous deed when we expose them!"

"All *right*! That's my *baby* talking now!"

"And how are *you* now, Morgan?"

"Who, *me*? I'm good!"

"Oh, I *know* you *are*. I have to let you know, Morgan, I *saw* you up on your feet letting off steam with all the *rest* of those people with pent-up anger to dispel! Seeing you almost jerked me out of my character, I was so surprised!"

"Okay, Liv, we don't have to mention this again, do we?"

Liv knew he was embarrassed knowing she had witnessed him in that unnatural-for-him state "That remains to be seen," she laughed.

Once everyone was situated in the den at the Big House, they got down to the business at hand. Morgan handed the photo to Frank, who removed it from the envelope, viewed it briefly, and replaced it.

"Morgan, I will want to take this photograph, if you don't mind. I can see this guy has tried to disguise himself. I'm willing to bet he has on a rug and a fake moustache. The first thing I will want to do is run it through my facial recognition software. It is not fooled by makeup and props."

"Whatever you need, Frank."

"Walter," Frank continued, "I'm glad you are here. I think this situation may have implications for CECCA as well. In time, after we have more information, we may want to involve our security.

"Liv, Morgan has provided a thumbnail sketch, but can you describe to me everything you can? I understand you can pinpoint the date, probable location, and maybe even one of the persons involved. I can get that specific information later. But for now, Liv, please give me a detailed narrative."

With Morgan sitting next to her on the couch with one arm around her and holding her hand, Liv repeated the scenario she had given to Morgan in a very clear, decisive manner, omitting no important details. Listening carefully to Liv's account, Walter and Lydia were encouraged by her demeanor. She was taking everything in stride and appeared to be handling things well. They were able to relax.

After Liv had finished her discourse, there was a little more general discussion in which the music teacher's name was mentioned. Frank thought it had a ring of familiarity to it, but he couldn't quite recall anything specific. He didn't mention it, but he knew he would look into her background thoroughly. For now he felt he had enough information to begin his investigation. He was preparing to leave when Liv spoke up, stopping him.

"One more thing, Frank." She immediately got everyone's attention.

"Tonight, while I was preparing myself for my second set opening song, I was reminded of something that jerk of a detective said that awful morning way back when."

Frank was about to question her when Morgan spoke up.

"What, Baby?" Morgan said, trying to anticipate what she was about to say, but unable to do so.

"Remember when we were viewing the video of the attack on Mom and me and that detective made those awful, insinuating remarks? After you had laid down the law to *him* about what *he* could do, Morgan, he said something like, 'Rejection *can* be hard for some people to take,' or 'Rejection *can* be a powerful motivation.' I don't remember his exact words, but that sums up the gist of it."

With that explanation Morgan figured it out, but before he could speak, Walter spoke up. "Liv, who did you reject *this* time, and how bad *was* it?"

Liv couldn't blame him for suspecting her of causing someone to want to hurt her. Although it was not Liv who did the rejecting, she felt she *was* culpable because of what she *did* do. After all, it was her rejection, not to mention her sting of Casanova Adams, that caused him to attack the two of them.

Morgan didn't want his wife to be subjected to any further scrutiny in the matter and quickly came to her defense. "It wasn't Liv, Pops, it was *me*. *I* did it. *I'm* the one"

"You, Morgan?" Lydia questioned in surprise. *"You?"*

"Mom, it wasn't Morgan's fault." It was Liv's turn to come to her husband's defense. "This unmitigated wench shamelessly *tricked* Morgan and *threw* herself at him. He just stepped aside and let her behind hit the ground. Of course, I'm speaking figuratively, but she was a wonton hussy in *my* book! Morgan had initially thought of her, but he dismissed it because he thought it was unreasonable. But then, *she* is not reasonable, the wench!

"I think she should be checked out anyway. I think it is better to err on the side of caution in this case."

"Okay, Liv, I'll check her out, too. What is her name?"

"I call her 'The Wench Cavanaugh,' but her name is Camille."

"'The Wench'—I mean, Camille Cavanaugh? The social slut?" Walter interjected.

Everyone was surprised at his language, but not surprised that he knew who she was. After all, he was very influential and *did* know, or know of, multitudes of people. Frank also knew who she was.

"Isn't she the one who tried to strong-arm her way into the North Wing one day that Security had to eject?" Frank asked.

"Yes, that's the lady, to use the term loosely." Walter confirmed.

Both Morgan and Liv were surprised to hear this. They were unaware of any such incident occurring in their corporate offices.

"When was this, Walter? What happened? Why don't *we* know about this? In our offices? Walter, what happened?" Morgan asked all at once. He didn't realize that he had adopted Liv's propensity for stringing a barrage of questions in a short spurt without waiting for answers.

Walter responded, "Morgan, in hindsight, I think we *should* have reported this particular incident to you. There are things that happen on a daily basis that get handled routinely. We don't bring every little incident to your attention, not that there are many such incidents. In fact, this was the first and last time anything like this ever happened.

I think the fact that they had to involve security is significant enough to have reported it up the line. Even more so, as I remember, she was insisting on, in fact, *demanding* to see *you*, Morgan. They tell me she was madder than a wet hen!"

"When *was* this, Walter?" Morgan *really* wanted to know. For reasons of her own, Liv was anxious to find out when it occurred as well.

"I don't recall the exact date, but she told your secretary you had been to her house the prior Saturday, and that there was some unfinished business the two of you had. I believe she was referring to a presentation you made to a group she was involved with. She had called your office the following Monday and was told you were not available."

"None of us were available that Monday," Morgan recalled.

"Evidently, you had left word that you did not want to accept *any* calls from her, and she was not to be given an appointment to see you."

"Yes, that's right. We got to the office Monday, and Liv went into Holly's office to pick up the schedule for classroom auditing before she left for an appointment. You know how every month or so we officers audit classes, especially with probationary instructors and aides, and we communicate with faculty and students, you know, to keep up with what is going on in the classrooms and with the students. We want them all to know that we are accessible and interested.

"As I was going into my office, Jennifer casually inquired how my presentation had gone on Saturday. I just mentioned that it was a sham, that there *was* no meeting, and that I thought Ms. Cavanaugh had ulterior motives. I told her that I would not be accepting any calls from her and instructed her not to make any other appointments with this person. That's all there was to it."

"Evidently, that *wasn't* all that was to be," Walter announced. "That Wednesday, she came to the office anyway, again demanding to see you. It was about 11:30, just before lunchtime, and she was refusing to believe you were not there and refused to leave.

"I don't recall if you were in the Center at that time or not, but you certainly were not in your office. You *surely* would have been aware of her presence!"

"*I* must not have been there, either. Because *I* would have taken care of the situation *myself*!" Liv piped.

"Okay, Babe, simmer down, now," Morgan encouraged her. Deep down, he was appreciating the fact that his wife would gladly take on any woman who came after him with such designs. Liv resolved that she would ask Elizabeth and Holly about it, in case either of them had been present.

"Walter, I think this suggests that we need to re-examine some of our protocols and take a closer look at our communications policies. This can be a possible positive outcome of this whole, stinking situation!"

"To be sure, Morgan. We definitely will!"

Morgan sensed a vibe and momentarily turned his attention back to Liv. He was acutely aware of the pointed look in her eye. She didn't need to *say* anything. He knew her thoughts and that they would have a private dialogue later.

"*I* am aware because it was reported to me *after* the fact," Walter continued. "I know her family quite well. I don't know if Camille is aware, but her father is a member of the Network and a major contributor, not that it really means anything when it come to the misconduct of his daughter. I called and had a lengthy conversation with her father, Jesse. He assured me he would talk to his daughter, and I never gave it a second thought. I just assumed he would deal with her.

"Jesse Cavanaugh is a reasonable person, although he has always overindulged his spoiled daughter, giving her whatever she wants, especially after her mother succumbed to cancer when she was about 12. I was not aware, as it seems to be turning out now, that she had designs on *you*, Morgan."

"That is another story that might become significant at some point. We'll see," Morgan said, chancing another glance at Liv. He knew for certain they would have a talk about it. He realized more and more the probability that "The Wench Cavanaugh" could very well be behind everything, and it raised a different level of anger in him. He knew he would have to make amends to Liv.

Frank was taking all of this in as he glanced at his notes again. "Liv, I want to make sure I have the music teacher's name correctly. You did say her name was Thelma Olman, right? O-l-m-a-n?" he spelled out.

"Yes, Frank, that's right."

Frank looked deeply thoughtful for a moment. "My instincts are kicking in big time. I could possibly be wrong, but I definitely remember that name now, 'Thelma Olman,' and I'm thinking I will be able to tie her in with Miss Cavanaugh."

"It's quite okay, Frank," Liv was happy to tell him, "You can call her 'The Wench!' " Liv was not in a charitable mood concerning "The Wench."

"Morgan, I may need to get more information from you about your meeting with her at some point."

"No problem, Frank."

Armed with the photograph and the plethora of pertinent information he had received, Frank was confident he had everything he would need as well as the direction he would need to take to discover all there was to know about the situation. He was anxious to get started and took his leave.

More to Discuss

It was quite late by the time Frank left, and Morgan and Liv successfully entreated their parents to stay the night. They said their good nights, and Walter and Lydia retired to the guest room they usually used.

Lydia immediately began, "Walter, what do you think of all this? I think there is something Morgan and Liv still have to work out about this Cavanaugh woman. I saw the look she gave Morgan. And, Walter, you never said anything to me about that situation! Is there anything *else* I don't know? I know Morgan would never be unfaithful to Liv. I know how much he loves her. I think he would die before he would ever do anything to hurt her. They . . ."

Walter put his arms around his wife and kissed her silent, and laughed. "What's so funny, Walter? I'm being serious!"

"I know you are, Dear. But you're funny! For the first time since I have known you, you have now shown me the one thing I thought you did *not* share in common with your daughter."

"Really? What is *that*, Walter?"

"For a moment, I thought you were Liv. Did you *hear* yourself? Talking a mile a minute, not coming up for air, and asking questions without waiting for answers!"

Lydia had to laugh at herself, too, remembering how many times she has had to make her daughter slow down. "I'm sorry, Walter. I didn't realize I was doing that. I guess I'm still kind of upset about this whole thing. At least *now* I can see that she is getting a good handle on things. But . . ."

"Lydia, she and Morgan will be fine. They *are* fine. Let's just thank and ask the Lord for His blessings, and get some sleep. We'll probably have to get up at the crack of dawn to go home and get ready for church."

"We shouldn't have to do that. I think we both have clothes at Mom and Dad's place, and even here. We won't have to get up early to go home."

"Yes, you're right. I'm not anxious to get up early anyway. Let's just pray and go to bed."

Morgan and Liv retired to their suite, but each knew they would not be going to sleep any time soon. Neither would King Solomon be consorting with his Shulamite woman. There was other business to take care of. Morgan wanted to give it a little more time.

"Sweetheart, I know you have already showered, so I'll just take a quick one and join you, okay?"

"I'll be waiting right here, Morgan," she replied, still eyeing him steadily.

Morgan dallied in the shower as long as he could. He knew what was in store for him with Liv and he decided the best way to handle it would be to beat her to the punch. He knew he was partially to blame. He decided to eat crow, confess, and apologize before she could lay it on him. He wasn't worried about her and knew she wasn't really *angry* with him. He just wanted to delay to allow her to more fully process her feelings.

Morgan dried himself and came from the shower with a towel wrapped around himself. He eyed Liv suspiciously when he saw that she had removed her clothes and had *not* put on a "granny gown" or *anything*. He wondered what was up, if she had something sinister in mind! It caused him to vacillate on the plan he had devised. She was still eyeing him with that accusatory look. He wasn't sure how to respond, so he just stood there looking at her, waiting for her lead.

"Are you just going to stand there looking all sexy, which is probably what got you in trouble in the first place, or are you coming to bed?" Seeing the confused look on his face, Liv had to laugh. "Come on, Morgan, I'm not going to *bite* you—or maybe I just *might*!"

Morgan approached the bed cautiously. "Liv, Baby, are we straight? Are we cool?"

"You'll never know until . . ." she said as she snatched his towel away, "you get into *bed* with me!" She pulled back the sheet and patted the bed inviting him to join her.

"She is teasing me," Morgan thought. He was game, though! He slowly climbed in beside her, still watching her for a clue.

"Morgan, I *want* something from you, and when you *give* it to me, we will be straight. You *know* what it is, and you know *I* know what it is. So, give it!"

"Okay, Sweetheart. You're right. I owe you an apology. But you *know* I told you *everything* there was to tell. I *always* tell you everything."

"*Everything*, Morgan?"

"I *told* her that I wouldn't be coming back; that's why I left all of the information for her to disseminate to her group, if there really ever *was* a group. It was only after we went to the office that Monday when Jennifer asked how the presentation to Ms. Cavanaugh's group went that I told her I wouldn't accept any calls from her, and that I did not want another appointment with her. I didn't go into many specifics.

"But, Liv, it was such a little thing, I didn't even *think* about it until tonight when I learned that she came to the office that Wednesday! If I had known about the fiasco that happened *that* day, I would have known there would have to be more to it than the little note you sent to her when you returned her, what did you call it?"

"Her nasty cootie booty "floss!"

"Yes, I know you were just as surprised as *I* was. But now that we both *know*, don't you have something *else* to tell me?"

"Yes, Love, I do. I'm sorry for coming down on you so hard for what *you* did. I can see now that by itself, it probably *would* have been insignificant. But when you put it together with her obvious humiliation of having been thrown out of our offices, escorted by Security, no less, it makes sense that she would be motivated to stoop to the level she did. I have no doubt now that she is the one behind all of this. Frank will prove it. He will find the connection between the wench and the music teacher. A woman scorned is no joke!

"And, yes, Honey. I have to admit I have the lion's share of blame. What you did was miniscule. I'm sorry. Am I forgiven?"

Liv felt she had sweated Morgan long enough, and she was ready to let him off the hook. She gave him a devious look and winked.

"What is *that* look for?" he asked.

"Come here, My King, and let me *explain* it to you."

CHAPTER 8

"WHA' HAD HAPPEN WAS . . ."

(Liv's fact-finding Expedition) The following Monday morning Liv certainly intended to get a clearer picture of what actually happened that day when "The Wench" was kicked out of the North Wing, off the entire property. After dropping off the kids, Morgan and Liv went to their offices. Morgan went directly to his office, but Liv stuck her head into Holly's office and summoned her to come with her to Elizabeth's office.

Liv knocked on Elizabeth's door and stuck her head in. Elizabeth was on the phone and beckoned them to enter. They came in and sat down, waiting for Elizabeth to end her call, which she did promptly.

"Good morning, Ladies. How are things? It's too early to be having any problems, so what up?"

"I don't know, Elizabeth," Holly said. "This is Olivia's show. What's up, Olivia?"

"Right now, I am an ad hoc, fact-finding committee of one on a mission to find out exactly what happened in the North Wing on Wednesday morning, June 19, when, evidently, Morgan and I were both absent. Were either or both of you here that morning?"

"I'll have to refer to my calendar unless you can shed some light on what you think may have happened that day," Holly said, rising. "Let me go back to my office and check my calendar."

"My calendar is right here. Let me see . . . Oh, wow!" Elizabeth exclaimed. "We *did* have a difficulty that day!"

"Did it involve someone by the name of Camille Cavanaugh?" Liv asked.

"Why, yes. *She* was the *biggest* of the problems we had. There are *two* reasons for both of us to vividly remember *that* day!"

Just then, Holly returned with her calendar. "Olivia, you certainly picked a whopper of a day to inquire about! *That* day was a real *doozy*!"

"I'm mainly concerned about the incident involving the person *I* call 'The Wench Cavanaugh!' What happened with that?"

"I don't know what it was all about, do you, Holly?"

"No. Remember? We had our own problem with that other woman. I just came out to see what all the ruckus was about, and you had already alerted Security. This woman demanded to see Morgan and insisted she was going to wait right here until Morgan came, no matter how long it took. She was loud and belligerent, and Jennifer was at a loss. You know she's usually really good with handling people who are upset or are being difficult, but this was a *wild* woman, completely unreasonable and out of control!"

Holly continued, "I just remember thinking that it was a good thing *you* were gone, too, Olivia. I could imagine *you* handling it *yourself*! I think *she* would have been the one calling for security in that case!"

"Before all this happened, before she was thrown out, while she was just seething there in the waiting area, she was talking to the *other* woman, who was waiting to see someone else, someone who didn't look like *me*!"

"What do you mean, Elizabeth, 'someone who didn't look like *you'*?" Liv inquired. Elizabeth held up her hand and rubbed the back of it with two fingers.

"You mean she wanted to see someone who wasn't *black*?"

"Exactly! It was bad enough in *her* eyes that the person whose head she was insisting on going over was the Director of Human Resources, Charlotta Martinez! You can just *imagine* she didn't want to see *me*, either! I saw it as a bad omen that those two angry women were conversing together!"

"What was the problem with the *other* woman? What did *she* want?"

"She wanted employment, but she wasn't up to our standards on so many levels. I think even if she had been really qualified, had the appropriate training and experience, credentials, good references, or was even able to pass the rigorous background review, she *still* would have been inherently disqualified because of the reason stamped on the first page of her file—*'Adverse to Diversity!'* "

Holly put it into plain English. "That's a euphemism for 'racist!' "

"Diversity is the hallmark of CECCA! Without asking, I *know* you guys backed up Charlotta's action in denying employment."

"*I* didn't even *touch* it. *I* didn't want to waste *my* time with that old lady. I called and briefed Holly according to what Charlotta had told me so that she wouldn't have to spend time reviewing the file. I wanted that woman *out* of here as *soon* as possible. I carted her file and her butt right over to Holly's office"

"I didn't *need* to review the file. She had already been through the grievance procedure, and I saw and heard nothing that would make me want to change *anything*. Everyone did their jobs admirably, from the background and reference checks, psychological and personality testing, everything. She was unfit, pure and simple, in *every* respect!

"I didn't want her to feel that she had not been given a fair chance to state her case, so I did first invite her in to make her case and asked her to go back out and wait while I considered all the facts to make my decision. When I came out to tell her I was upholding the position that had been taken by HR, the other woman who was waiting for Morgan had gone berserk and was really giving Jennifer *and* Elizabeth a hard time. I had never heard such filth coming out of *any* woman's mouth!

"I expressed to the woman my regret that I couldn't take the time to sugar-coat my decision because of the on-going, difficult situation, which she could plainly see. The old woman herself became irate to add to the tumult; but after Security arrived and took over, there was nothing for either of them to do but leave, which they did—*with* the assistance of Security. The two new comrades left together."

Liv was grateful for all of the details Holly and Elizabeth provided. Still, everything didn't quite add up, and her gut told her a piece was missing. Than it came to her, and she inquired, "From what position was this woman disqualified? Also, and more importantly, what was her name?"

Holly responded, "She had a sad story to tell about how, because of our school, she had been left in dire straits—impoverished—and we owed her a chance to make a living. Her husband had died recently and she lost his pension. She was a senior citizen on a meager, fixed income. She lost practically all of her piano and voice students because of our superior, affordable music program. She said . . ."

"Oh, my God! Oh—my—*God*!" Liv interrupted her.

"Olivia, what *is* it?" Elizabeth asked, shaken by Liv's expression.

"Don't tell me—her name was Thelma Olman," Liv said, knowing that it *had* to be. It *couldn't* be anyone else!

Holly and Elizabeth looked at each other in surprise. "How did *you* know, Olivia?" Holly asked. "Do you *know* her? Did we make a *mistake*?"

"No, no. No, you didn't make a mistake. Not at all! I've got to go and tell Morgan!" she said as she hastened out, leaving her friends looking at each other in puzzlement.

She walked into Morgan's private office without first knocking, something she had never done. Seeing her, Morgan said into the phone, "Travis, I've got to go. I'll call you back!"

Liv just stood there, leaning against the door she closed behind her. Morgan was on his feet immediately at her side. "Liv, Baby, what is it? What is the matter? Come and sit down." When she was seated on the couch, he went to the door and told his secretary to hold their calls, and that they were not to be disturbed. In a flash he was back at her side on the couch.

"Okay, Sweetheart, take your time. Take a few deep breaths, relax yourself, and tell me what's going on."

Liv buried her face in his chest. Her body visibly relaxed as she took a few calming breaths. Holding her, Morgan patiently waited, stroking her hair. He couldn't know that Liv was extremely relieved having found out just about everything, or at least some very significant facts, to be able to resolved the most challenging issue they had to face since the Casanova Adams episode.

She lifted her face from Morgan's chest and gave him a lingering kiss. That made him happy and relieved his anxiety. "Thank you for the kiss, Baby. Now, what do you have to tell me?"

"Morgan, you won't *believe* it! I may have to open up my own PI office. You can call Frank and tell him that we have some more information for him. I have just tied 'The Wench Cavanaugh' to Thelma Olman!"

"Sweetheart, are you *kidding me*?"

"No, Morgan, it's true. It's really true. In fact, on the day 'The Wench' was thrown out of here, they *both* had been here, and they left *together*, *both* of them escorted out and extremely angry!

"They had both been in the waiting area at the same time, and they, evidently, were comparing notes, probably about their anger issues with CECCA. I can just see them cooking up a plan together to get even."

"How did you find this out, Liv?"

"When I knew that 'The Wench' had been thrown out of here, I figured Holly or Elizabeth might have been here, so I had a little conference with them as soon as we got here this morning. I *knew* that if they had been here, they would have to have been aware of the situation. The icing on the cake was the fact that the piano teacher was here at the same time appealing her denial of employment."

"I have said it before, Sweetheart, you're amazing!" Morgan kissed her and beamed.

"It's always nice to hear you say it again, though. You're pretty amazing yourself, you know.

"What's the next step? Do you want me to stay in the PI business?"

"No, Sweetheart. You've done an *excellent* job. I have *other* plans for *you*. I think we should just let Frank know what you have discovered. He will probably have more luck in finding and tying in the hairy ape."

"Oh, yes. You're right, of course. I have no desire to see *him* again, *ever*!"

Liv became quiet and Morgan knew why. "Liv, I know what you're thinking. I'm hoping you won't have to, but you *may* not be able to *avoid* seeing him when he is caught and prosecuted. I don't know, but what say we don't think about it for now?"

"Think about what, Morgan?" she asked, letting him know that she had already let it go.

CHAPTER 9

PUTTING TWO AND TWO TOGETHER / THELMA OLMAN

Putting Two and Two Together

Frank Bynum definitely had strong instincts that were leading him in a direction he felt was certain to result in resolving the issue of the photograph. Based on all of the information he was able to get from Morgan and Liv, he no longer believed it involved blackmail or extortion. He suspected that there may have been some details that Morgan and Liv withheld for some reason, but he was not going to press for it initially. His first step was to make a connection between the music teacher and "The Wench."

Knowing that it may take a while to process, he immediately employed his facial recognition software to try to identify the male in the photo. He next searched his personal database of all the investigations in which he had been involved, both before and after becoming a member of the organization's Network. He input the name "Thelma Olman" and immediately got a hit. When he reviewed his case notes, the wealth of information was more than enough to validate his suspicion that she was involved. The primary factor was his recommendation that she be disqualified for employment by CECCLA.

Thelma did not have a criminal record, but there was enough he found to severely question her ethics, character, and integrity, areas which were especially critical to CECCLA. She had substantially padded—falsified—her employment history, and the persons she listed as references were either deceased or nonexistent.

She indicated that she had worked as a substitute music teacher for several local school districts. It only took her being given one assignment at each of them before the determination was made that she was not employable, and her name was removed from the sub pools. This was even before it was determined that the teaching credentials she provided were bogus. That alone would have prevented her employment by any California public school district.

The proof that settled it in Frank's mind was the result of his review of each of their bank records. There were corresponding withdrawals and deposits of large sums from "The Wench's" accounts to Mrs. Olman's. There was initially a cashier's check payable to Thelma Olman in the amount of $25,000, purported to be full payment in settlement of a claim, although there was no readily available information about any kind of claim. Subsequently, there were five personal checks for $5,000 each, spaced a week apart, also payable to Thelma Olman.

Banking records for Thelma Olman reflected corresponding deposits of each of the $5,000 checks written by Camilla and included deposit of the $25,000 cashier's check with cash back of $7,500. Prior to any of these deposits, there had never been more than a $200–$300 balance in her account a few days after deposits of her social security checks, and the account was frequently overdrawn.

Frank's use of the facial recognition software produced the identity of the man in the photograph, Stanley Croach. Further investigation revealed that he had had previous arrests on drug charges, but there was nothing currently outstanding on him in the system.

There was nothing overtly telling about Mr. Hairy's bank records. He was still receiving nominal checks from occasional work as an actor, primarily from roles as an extra. The only significant change in the pattern was the deposit of two sizeable cash deposits equaling $7,000 following the incident in June. Frank surmised that it was from the $7,500 cash back from Thelma Olman's $25,000 deposit.

By Monday afternoon, Frank believed he now had identified all of the players and had all the pertinent information he needed, including a real picture of Stanley Croach without the rug, makeup, and fake moustache. However, he was not quite ready to report back to Morgan and Liv. He wanted first to determine the weaker link between the actor and the teacher in hopes of being able to induce one, or even both of them to give up "The Wench." He thought perhaps it would be the teacher, as she was a senior citizen and may not want to spend her remaining years behind bars.

On the other hand, Stanley Croach did have a criminal record involving drugs, and as Frank discovered, involved a date-rape drug conviction as well. Frank considered that he may be a candidate to implicate "The Wench" in order to get a lighter sentence or some other consideration. He would have to know he would be going down.

Frank decided to fill Morgan and Liv in on his progress that evening. However, he still wanted to find out anything else they may want to tell him that might shed more light on a possible motive.

Morgan's call to him that they had additional information to share with him was timely, and they made plans to meet later that evening at their condo after Liv's rehearsal. Liv had a shortened rehearsal that evening, and the band members all left promptly at eight. Frank arrived about ten minutes later.

"Come in, Frank. Liv will be in in a moment; she's clearing up the aftermath of her rehearsal. Can I get you anything? There is still some food left."

"No, I'm fine, Morgan. Good evening, Liv," he said as Liv came into the living room.

"Why don't we all get comfortable so we can get down to business," Morgan said, gesturing for Frank to take a seat. "Before you tell us what you have found, I first want to fill you in on a few more details that we really didn't want to go into earlier. We're sorry that if withholding this information made your job more difficult."

Morgan proceeded to relate exactly what had happened at the meeting he had with "The Wench" that Saturday and about Liv's finding her underwear in his pocket when he returned home. At that point, Liv intervened. "Frank, despite my shame, I feel *I* have to be the one to tell you what *I* did to additionally provoke 'Miss Wench.' Although Morgan told me to get rid of the thong, I was irked and mailed it back to her with a terse note that I am sure angered her even more. I didn't *sign* it, but I had to let her know that her little ploy did *not* work."

"Well, that's all very interesting, and I am sure in the totality of everything that happened, they all add up to the motivation I was looking for in putting all of this together," Frank admitted.

"But that's not all, Frank," Morgan interjected. "Liv questioned Holly and Elizabeth and was able to connect the two of them, Camille

Cavanaugh and Thelma Olman, both of them in the office at the same time on that day and leaving together."

"And, Frank," Liv added, "they were both angry. I think that is when, or soon after, they initiated their plan."

"Well, it looks like you two didn't need my help that much." Frank commented lightly.

"Oh, yes, we *did*, Frank. Had it not been for you, we may never have even *known* about the incident that prompted Liv to inquire and find out what happened, connecting the two of them together!" Morgan assured him. "You are the one who brought up the fact that there was the problem in the North Wing. Besides, we're *still* depending on *you* to identify the man they recruited to help them. Have you made any progress in that area?"

"Yes, indeed. That is part of what I had planned to share with you. Liv, you did an excellent job in linking the women together. I was able to link them through banking transactions with each other as well as with Stanley Croach, the man they hired to participate and who, I suspect, was the one to supply the drug. He is a two-bit actor with a criminal history involving drugs.

"I had contemplated speaking to either or both him and the teacher to determine if one or both of them would be willing to implicate Ms. Cavanaugh, possibly in exchange for consideration in their own cases. Now, however, I am having second thoughts. What they did is reprehensible. I think we have enough viable evidence through the financial and other records as well as contributory witness testimony to be able to get convictions for *all* of them without special considerations.

"It will be up to the District Attorney, but I would think they may be facing charges of conspiracy, kidnapping, assault, battery, and whatever else pops up. Hopefully, they can be tried together. That would minimize your involvement in their prosecution."

"Are we ready to file formal charges at this time?" Morgan asked.

"Almost. We're pretty close. But before we do that, I would like to talk to a few people in LAPD and the DA's office. I will also want to talk with Holly and Elizabeth, and the Director of Human Resources first, just to make sure of all of our facts.

"Well, I'm going to get going, unless either of you have any comments or questions."

Looking to Liv to give her an opportunity to add anything first, Morgan answered, "No, we're fine, Frank. As we expected, you have done another thorough, admirable job. Anything else you may need from either of us, just let us know."

"I will. Knowing you, Morgan, I am reminding you. I am working for and being handsomely paid by the Organization. This is not coming out of *your* pocket. Understand?"

"I got you, Frank."

Liv and Morgan walked Frank to the door where they said their goodbyes. They next went to check on the kids to find them all soundly sleeping. Grown-up Alex had volunteered to read her brothers a bedtime story, supervise their prayers, and tuck them into bed.

Thelma Olman

Thelma Olman had lived a comfortable life. Her husband had been a hard worker and a good provider, so she had never really had to work to supplement the household bottom line. Even after he retired, his pension, supplemented by social security benefits, was more than adequate for them to continue to live comfortably.

The couple had no children, mainly because Thelma had aspirations of being an entertainer and saw motherhood as a hindrance. Feeding her ambition meant she spent the bulk of her time and much of their income in pursuing a career. She had studied piano as a child, but was only average at best in skill. However, she did have an excellent grasp of music theory.

Thelma Olman began taking voice lessons as a teenager, but there was only so much that could be done to improve her inferior instrument and problematic ear for hearing her own singing voice, not to mention pitch. A career as a vocalist was just not in the cards for her. After many, many years of trying, she was finally convinced that she should focus on teaching piano and music theory and leave vocalizing to those that actually had talent in that area. However, she remained a great vocalist in her own mind.

Surprising to most who knew of her and her musical abilities, more accurately, lack of musical ability, she was extremely successful as a teacher of piano and voice to private students, although her methods were often questionable. At any rate, her private students who were able to overcome her unorthodoxy were able to excel, and each of them far surpassed her in ability and skill. Her success as their piano and voice teacher enabled her to command high fees for her services. Even so, she was a bitter and jealous woman because she could never achieve the level of proficiency she desired, even as a pianist, not to mention as a vocalist. She was not an unattractive woman, but she did not have an appearance that would allow her success in the entertainment arena without unprecedented talent, no matter how much good money she threw after bad.

Fortunately, she did enjoy the love of a husband who didn't begrudge her for wasting their money and squandering their savings in pursuit of a career she could never have. Unfortunately, though, everything changed when her husband died suddenly of a massive heart attack.

Since her home was mortgage free, even with the loss of her husband's pension after his death, with sensible spending and reasonable budgeting, she could have done okay with the exorbitant fees she charged those clients who could afford to pay them. The students she elected to teach were able to move on to bigger and better things musically.

Unfortunately for Thelma, aspiring musicians and their parents discovered the Calais Education and Community Center of Los Angeles, as well as other campuses that were springing up in other locations in increasing numbers. In a relatively short time, Thelma had lost so many of her regular clients to CECCA that she was forced to look for work. With no legitimate salable skills, in desperation, she obtained credentials as a music teacher from a diploma mill and applied for work as a substitute music teacher in surrounding school districts.

She was able to obtain letters of reference from the parents of some of her former students. Some had gone on to make really big names for themselves—a testament to her teaching ability. She used these references when being interviewed for the various positions. On formal applications, however, she gave references that were impossible to verify. Nevertheless, her career as a music teacher in public schools never got off the ground as her ineptitude and other negative qualities were quickly detected.

Although she felt much animosity toward CECCLA and blamed the school for luring away her students, thus impacting her livelihood, she was forced to try her luck in obtaining work in its music program. She could come off as very pleasant and motherly when she wanted to and intended to use that ability to facilitate her being hired.

She had not expected the detailed employment process, which was much more comprehensive and thorough than any process she had encountered with the public school districts. She was dismayed to learn she would have to go through a period of assessment *and* training, which included learning and subscribing to the Calais culture. Deluded, she thought she could fake all of that, but she had not counted on having to undergo performance testing.

The panel responsible for overseeing and judging the performance of applicants for positions in the Music Department was comprised of three members of the Department. The panel chair was Harriett Chase, also known as "Ms. C-PASS," who had joined the staff as a performance coach after subbing so successfully for Liv at her Brentwood Club when she took off for a month to prepare for her wedding to Morgan and during their honeymoon. She also had the enviable position of being hired to perform regularly at Liv's second club, which she opened in the South Bay area in 2015.

Harriett chose not to know anything about applicants' backgrounds or experience before their performance evaluations. She didn't want to be influenced by anything other than the actual performances. Since the position required teaching piano, music theory, and voice, Mrs. Olman was required to play from memory a piece of her choice as well as a piece selected for her to play from a cold reading. In addition, she was to perform a song of her choice *a cappella*.

Being the sensitive, kind-hearted individual she was, Harriett patiently sat through Thelma's torturous renditions without allowing her impressions to show. Her two co-evaluators were not so gracious; but since they were all viewing the audition from the darkened theater while Thelma was on the lighted stage, Thelma was, thankfully, unable to see their reactions.

After the performance, Harriett came up onto the stage. She was about to offer her hand, but Thelma's strong vibe and body language prompted her not to. "Thank you, Mrs. Olman, for giving us your time. My associates and I will evaluate your performance and make our recommendation to Human Resources."

"Well, are you going to recommend me for the job or not?" she said, finally overcoming the shock of seeing her black evaluator and finding her voice.

Being the tolerant professional she was, Harried replied, "There are many factors that are considered during the hiring process. Your performance evaluation is only a small part of what goes into the final decision. That is all put together by HR. I'm sure they will be in touch with you with their decision when they have reviewed and considered everything. Good luck to you. Can you find your way out?"

"I can manage that, thank you," she replied acridly, turning and storming off.

Thelma Olman received the registered letter the following Monday morning notifying her that her application for employment had not been accepted by the Human Resources Department. The reason was *failure to meet the requisite standards and guidelines in significant areas that were deemed necessary to maintain the level of excellence required of all employees of CECCA*. She did not receive the news well. Her desperation was, in fact, far exceeded by her fury.

Fuming, Thelma felt she was entitled to a chance to prove her capability and called the HR Department to complain and request reconsideration. She even went so far as to offer her services for a month without pay to demonstrate her ability. She demanded an audience with the HR Director and obtained an appointment.

On Wednesday, she arrived ten minutes early for her 10 a.m. appointment determined and armed with her letters of recommendation and anything else she thought might help her make her case.

HR Director Charlotta Wilson had reviewed her entire file before the meeting. There were many areas of deficiency, each of which alone was sufficient to deny employment. The list included falsification of information, submission of fraudulent credentials, psychological unfitness, demonstrated lack of integrity, lack of experience, and others, the least of which was lack of skill in her chosen field. The one thing that automatically disqualified her was the notation "*adverse to diversity*."

"Mrs. Olman, I am Charlotta Martinez-Wilson," she said from the doorway of her office. "Please come in."

Looking up, Thelma was shocked to see that the "Charlotta Wilson" who had signed her rejection letter was Charlotta *Martinez*-Wilson.

"Mrs. Olman, won't you come into my office, please," she repeated when the woman seemed to be frozen in place.

Thelma stood up and asked, *"You're* the Mrs. Wilson who signed the letter I received?"

"Yes, I am. Is there a problem?"

"Yes. I thought I would be speaking with someone . . . higher up, someone who had more authority, like a policy maker. I need to speak to an officer of the corporation—the president or vice-president. *Any* one of the *officers*. This is not right for you to just deny me employment. I demand to speak to someone who is *really* in charge. This is my livelihood you are denying me!" She was becoming more and more irate.

"Mrs. Olman, if you will please take a seat, I will call the corporate office and see if there is an officer available who can see you. You may have to come back another day."

Carlotta stepped back into her office and closed the door to call Morgan's secretary. She briefly describe the situation to give a heads up. Neither Morgan nor Liv was in the office, so Jennifer gave the call to Elizabeth, who reluctantly consented to see her after being briefed about the problem. Charlotta agreed to escort the woman to Elizabeth's office along with her file.

"Mrs. Olman, the Corporate Secretary will be happy to speak with you. Please follow me."

Thelma Olman followed Charlotta to the North Wing and sat in the waiting area while Charlotta took her file into Elizabeth's office.

CHAPTER 10

TWO ANGRY WOMEN / NEW BOSOM BUDDIES IN CAHOOTS

Two Angry Women

Camille Cavanaugh was seething in the waitingarea when Thelma came in. They made eye contact as Thelma approached to take a seat. It was obviousto each of them that they definitely had something in common—intense anger! Thelma was glad they had something else in common—they looked alike.

Recognizing Thelma's anger, Camille commented, "I thought *I* was ticked off, but I think you have *me* beat. What did they do to you?"

"This school has *ruined* me, reduced me to abject poverty!" I'm about to lose my *home* that my dead husband paid off. I had to mortgage it just to survive, and *they're* trying to tell me *I* don't meet *their* precious standards to be hired as a music teacher! I have been teaching piano and voice for over 38 years! I intend to speak to someone in charge! I'm *not* going to take this lying down!"

"Welcome to the club." Fuming, Camille complained, "I have been waiting and waiting for the head honcho to show up, and I'm about to go ballistic if I don't get satisfaction real soon! Nobody treats me like this and gets away with it!"

"Mrs. Olman, Mrs. Reynolds will see you now," Charlotta said, directing her to Elizabeth's office and returning to her own, glad to have been able to hand her off to Elizabeth. Thelma was in Elizabeth's office less than a minute when she stormed out and returned to the waiting area even madder than before.

"I take it things didn't go your way," Camilla said.

"*Hell* no! I *refuse* to appeal to anyone who doesn't look like *me*. I'm going to keep pushing 'til I get to the top dog! *That* one in *there* said she would *see* if the other officer was available to see me. I'll see how far *that* goes!"

"Well, if not, you're gonna have to get in line behind *me* to get to the top dog! I'm giving it ten minutes more before I go *postal* up in here!"

Following a call from Elizabeth, Holly went to retrieve Thelma's file and returned to her office. A few minutes later, she called from her office door, "Mrs. Olman?"

"That would be me," Thelma said, rising from her seat.

"Please come into my office."

Once seated in her office, Holly ventured, "Mrs. Olman, I can see you are very upset, and I want to give you an opportunity to explain why our Human Resources Director's decision should be overturned."

Holly had opened the door for her to vent, and she took full advantage of the opportunity, going on a wild, five-minute diatribe. When it ended, Holly asked her to wait outside for a minute while she made her decision. When Holly stepped out of her office to deliver the verdict, Ms. Cavanaugh was in full meltdown mode.

"Mrs. Olman, as you can see, we have a serious problem right now, and I regret that I cannot take the time I would like to sugar-coat my decision, but we cannot offer you employment. I'm sorry. Please excuse me." Holly went to see if she could assist with the other problem which was resolved when security personnel ejected the two from the property.

New Bosom Buddies in Cahoots

After their removal, the two humiliated outcasts were fuming about who was the more outraged at being escorted out, and who had been wronged the most. Camille Cavanaugh began to hatch an idea, based on what she had just learned about her new friend—that she was disgruntled with CECCLA, that she was desperate and needed money, and that she was a music teacher.

"Thelma is it?"

"Yes, Thelma Olman."

"Thelma, I can see we have a whole lot in common. I don't know about you, but *I* don't intend to let this go. I'm not going to take this treatment! You don't know me, but I am *very* well connected, and I pride myself in getting what I *want*. I don't accept being told '*No*!'

"I know you are financially strapped. I think I can help you. We can help each other."

"I want to get back at them for how they have treated me. Maybe I can sue them for age discrimination, even reverse racial discrimination!"

"What I have in mind will pay off much quicker. Care to have lunch with me and let me tell you all about it?"

"I have nothing *better* to do, as long as *you're* paying!"

"Of course. Follow me."

Two hours later, the duo had dined and discussed a tentative plan of action that involved a trip to a supper club in two days.

(Fast forward to Friday evening) The house band had just begun its first rendition when Camille Cavanaugh and Thelma Olman walked into Liv's Supper Club and Lounge. Since they did not have a dinner reservation, they were relegated to one of the smaller, overflow dining rooms with the closed circuit viewing of the performance.

"This is not acceptable!" Camille exclaimed to the host. "I demand to be seated in the main dining room!"

"I'm very sorry, Miss. As you can see, we are very crowded, and the main dining room is filled to capacity with reservation holders for both the 6 and the 8 p.m. shows," Aaron, the lead server working the reservation desk, politely explained to her.

"Surely you can set up a small table for two there! If it's a matter of *money*, that is no obstacle."

"I'm sorry, but it is a matter of law and safety. There is *nothing* I can do."

"Obviously, you don't *know* who *I* am."

"No, I'm sorry, I *don't* know who you are. Perhaps the general manager may be able to help you. If you will please wait over there, I will get him for you." Aaron said, happy to be able to take leave of her.

"I can't believe this! It's ridiculous!" Camille complained to Thelma as they waited.

The general manager approached them and asked, "May I be of assistance?"

"Yes, you certainly may. *I* am Camille Cavanaugh. *Jesse* Cavanaugh is my *father*. My friend and I require seating in the main dining room, thank you very much!"

"As much as I would love to accommodate you lovely ladies, that will not be possible. I can seat you immediately in the overflow room of your choice. The only alternative is to make a reservation for the next available opening in the main dining room, which may not be for a week or two. I'm very sorry. I will be more than happy to compliment your next visit. We *always* recommend advance reservations for the dinner shows."

Camille was not happy to hear those words. But she realized she was not going to have her way. It was more important for them to fulfill their purpose *that* night rather than a week or two later.

"Well, since we are here already, show us to the room with the best view of the show."

"Very good. Please follow me."

The women had been seated and had made their dinner selections when Billy, Liv's band leader, announced her entrance to the stage. Each of them had different areas of focus. For Thelma, it was the opportunity to see her own talent compare favorably to Liv's performance to reinforce what she believed in her mind, that she was as good as any of them. But before Liv had sung a single note, Thelma had already begun turning green merely from the tremendous reception Liv was receiving just by her presence!

It was all over but the shouting when Liv began to sing. There was no way Thelma could even *begin* to convince herself that she could *ever* hold a candle to Liv. She could see that Liv was the *complete* package—beauty, skill, finesse, class, talent, *everything*! For that she developed an immediate, intense hatred in addition to her energized jealousy.

For Camille Cavanaugh it was a completely different dynamic. *Her* main personal objective was to size up Liv, hopefully, to confirm her projection, her hope, that Liv's appearance, her body, would show typical signs of multiple births.

She had not followed Liv or her career and was not familiar with her in any way. After Morgan's initial rejection of her advances in June, she had googled Liv. She had to admit Liv was attractive, but she needed to credit photo shopping and manipulation of her online pictures. She was hoping that an up-close and personal scrutiny would give her the edge.

Seeing Liv's glowing radiance and beauty, she realized that the only possible chance she had of achieving what she wanted—to turn Morgan's attention from his wife to her—was to enact the plan she had devised.

By the time they left that night, they had worked out the plan to the tiniest detail, including selecting and making plans to commission a third accomplice/co-conspirator, a bit-part actor and extra known to Thelma by the name of Stanley Croach.

CHAPTER 11

THE RESOLUTION

Frank Bynum went about the task of bringing closure to Liv and Morgan by taking the steps he needed to take to have the appropriate charges levied against the three co-conspirators who had caused the pair so much trauma. He deposed and obtained records from Holly and Elizabeth as well as Charlotta Martinez-Wilson, the HR Director, to obviate their appearances in court. None of the three had any reluctance to appear, if needed.

Frank organized his records and gathered everything that the police and the DA would need. He reported the crime(s) to the police. He left it up to the DA's office to determine if there would be any plea bargains offered, and to whom. When everything was set, warrants were issued, and all three were arrested.

(A father's pain) Walter and Lydia had just finished with dinner when the telephone rang.

"Good evening," Walter answered.

"Walter, this is Jesse Cavanaugh."

Walter was not surprised to receive the call. He suspected that Jesse would call him, though he was hoping it would not be to ask him to intervene in any way on behalf of his daughter. He was not inclined to be amenable to such a request under the circumstances. He was doubtful that their last conversation, also about his daughter, had been fruitful.

"Hello, Jesse. How are you?" he responded perfunctorily.

"Not good, Walter," he said, pausing, and then continuing in Walter's silence. "I'm assuming you know about the charges against my daughter."

"Yes, Jesse, I know about that, and I'm sorry."

"Walter, I appreciate that you told me about her behavior at your corporate offices. I tried to talk to her . . . I *did* talk with her about it. Evidently, it had no impact on her. I would never have dreamed that she could do such an appalling, hurtful thing!

"Walter, I'm ashamed of what my daughter has done, and I have to bear some responsibility. It was just so hard for her after her mother died. I felt she had suffered such a loss, I wanted to do everything I could to make her happy. I failed all the way around. Maybe if I had paid more attention to her, spent more *time* with her instead of *money* on her . . ."

"Jesse, don't be so hard on yourself. Camille is a grown woman and knows right from wrong. She brought all of this on herself. *She* made the decisions she made and took the actions she took, not *you*. My question is, 'What are *you* going to do now?'"

"She is crying to me to bail her out and get her a top-notch attorney. She says jail is deplorable and degrading, and she deserves better than that. It's just like her to feel that way.

"Walter, she sees nothing wrong with what she has done, and she absolutely will not admit guilt. She seems to think that there is no direct evidence against *her* and she is not worried about a conviction. She's looking to *me* to take care of everything so that she can continue her carefree life—doing what she pleases with no ramifications and no thoughts about anyone she may hurt, as long as *she* gets *her* way.

"This *has* to stop, and it is *going* to stop *now*! It is the hardest thing I have ever had to do. I love my daughter, but I failed her by making it too easy for her. I know she will hate me. I won't ask any of my friends or colleagues to help her as a favor to me. She can hire anyone she can afford to hire. If she can pay thousands of dollars to fund this crime, she can pay thousands to defend herself.

"Walter, I'm sorry to take up so much of your time. I just want to apologize to you and your family. I am really sorry, and I hope our friendship is not impacted in any way."

"Don't worry about it, Jesse. You're a good man, and I know you've done the best you can. You can't hold yourself responsible for everything your daughter does. As I said, she is a grown woman. All you owe her is love and the chance to grow from suffering the consequences of her actions. Our prayers are with you. Good night, Jesse."

"Thank you, Walter. Goodnight."

(A lesson to learn the hard way) Jesse Cavanaugh responded to the collect call that he knew was from his daughter. He felt he had obtained the strength he needed to finally deal with her. "Yes, I will accept the call."

"Daddy, it's your little princess calling again. I *need* you, Daddy! It's worse than you know! You've *got* to help me. *Please*, Daddy!"

"Hello, Camille."

"Daddy, I can't *stand* it here. I'll never survive; I'll just *die*! I need you to post bail and get some of your friends together to make sure I beat these charges. I *can't* go to prison, Daddy! "You *know* I won't survive it!"

"Camille, do you realize the *pain* you have caused . . . the *harm* you have done? Do you even *care*?"

"Daddy, what are you talking about? I haven't done *anything*, really. *You* can fix this. You always *have* taken care of me!"

"Yes, as you say, I have always taken *care* of you, but I have not *helped* you at all. That is about to change. I am now going to *help* you—help you to learn to take responsibility for your decisions and your actions. You are a grown woman of 28 years of age. You are going to have to do what you can, what you must, to help *yourself*. All the help I can give you now is in the form of *advice*. That advice is to hire for yourself any attorney you can get. Admit your guilt and try to plea bargain."

"Daddy, you can't be serious! It's *me*, your little *princess*! You *love* me. If *Mom* were here, *she* would not let me suffer like this. She would make you take *care* of me!"

"Your mom is not here, and that tactic will no longer work on me. It is way past time for you to take full responsibility for yourself and your actions. I love you, although I don't like the way you behave, what you have done, and what you have become with my *care*. I will make your court date or dates, if you wish. I will continue to love you. That is all I can do, if you want me to. I have to go now. Goodbye, Camille."

(The final analysis) Stanley Croach and Thelma Olman were both eager to cop a plea to obtain some consideration in their sentencing. The District Attorney opted to give them less harsh sentences in return for their testimony against Camille Cavanaugh, since she initially was not of a mind to plead guilty. They felt the case against her was only circumstantial and would require direct, corroborating testimony from the other co-conspirators to implicate her as the mastermind in order to insure her conviction.

Camille continued to hold hope that her father would succumb to her cry for help. When she saw that his help was not forthcoming, on the advice of the attorney she had to hire, she gave in when she realized that her cohorts would be testifying against her for the State. Though she was conniving and despicable, she was not stupid.

CHAPTER 12

CALAIS CITY: A PLACE FOR ALL

Liv and Morgan continued silently sipping iced tea and watching the waves greeting the shore as children waded in the surf. The tranquil scene reminded them of happy events and many experiences they had enjoyed through the years.

A significant achievement for which Morgan and Liv were understandably proud was the project internally dubbed the CCP (Calais City Project). The Project was sponsored 100% by an anonymous group of The Network's most prosperous and generous supporters.

Theodore McCoy Henry and his wife, Eleanor, were truly visionaries with generous hearts. Theo, through his gift of knowledge of future events, was able to share with his wife a vision of the state of the country in which multitudes would be deprived of basic needs—food, clothing and shelter, medical care and other goods and services—with no real options or help. What he saw as most lacking was hope and charity. Those were the primary things they desired to provide for the benefit of the future forgotten multitudes while also continuing their on-going philanthropic activities.

Their vision for developing The Master Plan for change, known to all who subscribed to their vision, was comprised of a perpetually growing network of contributors known collectively as The Network.

For years The Network quietly went about the business of recruiting like-minded contributors, raising funds, implementing programs and systems, and making preparations for the time when the first phase of their labors would culminate in the opening of the Calais Education and Community Center of Los Angeles (CECCLA) and ultimately the opening of the Calais Education and Community Centers of America. The first Center was launched as planned following the union of Morgan Calais and Olivia Washington.

Unknown to most, an enormous parallel endeavor was simultaneously in the works. Also spawned by Theo and Eleanor Henry, a separate network with many overlapping participants existed. The purpose was to bring about the development of a viable community with the sole purpose of addressing the great unmet needs of the homeless, outcasts, and most blighted populations existing in the shadows, to the shame of the world's most prosperous nation.

This Project involved the purchase and donation of a contiguous area of unimproved land slightly larger than the City of Irwindale, CA. The area, approximately ten square miles, abutted Greater Los Angeles. With the goals and mission of the Calais Corporation in mind, select members of The Network pooled their resources, time, and energy and eventually brought the Henrys' vision to fruition some years after their deaths.

The first official order of business in the development of the land was to contract with the city and county governments to provide the necessary infrastructure. With funding provided by The Network, both governments were happy to oblige. Network planners had been busy mapping out a city blueprint from the beginning, even before the government became involved. Teams of architects had been busy designing the structures. These structures included, among others, a 200-bed general hospital and tower of medical office spaces, a 180-bed mental hospital, and several clinics.

Another campus complex for the Calais Education and Community Centers of America was designed, along with three libraries, two comprehensive cinemas, and four car washes. Three other major complexes contained retail outlets and multi-purpose facilities, several restaurants, and office buildings to provide opportunities for businesses and employment. A state-of-the-art convention center and adjacent major hotel ultimately attracted businesses and entities worldwide.

Provision was made for fire stations and churches as well as an artificial lake populated with fish, a major mall with a five-screen cinema, a bowling alley adjacent to a skating rink, and several park/play areas. There was infrastructure for a Metro link Sub Station connecting with Grand Central Station. Provision was made for a local city bus system that made transportation easy throughout the city.

Of prime important was planning for housing. Included were a multitude of single-family dwellings of various sizes, apartment buildings, senior housing complexes, duplexes, and three- and four-unit complexes. The land/housing was not for sale, but for rent or lease only. Rents or leases were based on income and subject to continued adherence to the criteria required for residence in the city. Financially able individuals leased or rented at current market rates, but were still had to adhere to the same criteria.

There were transitional facilities built to house the different states and needs of the people (mentally ill, physical ill, handicapped, addicts, alcoholics, etc.), the eventual inhabitants of the city during their evaluations. The criteria for the inhabitants was strict to ensure the successes of those homeless seeking refuge. Applicants were required to commit to drug rehabilitation if needed, mental and physical health evaluations, and education and training toward obtaining viable work, as applicable. Preference was given to families with children and to veterans, but all were vetted and welcomed.

A major goal was to reunite those who were estranged from their families because of their particular problems. They were provided rehabilitation and assistance with reconnecting through social services and counseling. It was not expected to be a quick fix and sometimes did not work at all. Nevertheless, approximately 35% of applicants were successfully reunited with their families. Another 28% transitioned out after being retrained in their former occupations or in new occupations and were able to obtain employment and relocate on their own.

Many were able to obtain work within the city and remained, being able to secure affordable housing. With the success of the endeavor, there was a steady incoming and outgoing of residents. It soon became apparent that certain individuals sought to capitalize on the generosity of the program.

A redirected vetting process revealed the reality that some people ineligible to receive the services provided were hiding or divesting themselves of their wealth (transferring accounts overseas, placing property in their children's names, etc.) to secure low-cost housing in Calais City, just as some have been doing for years to take advantage of goods and services designed to help those truly in need of them. This was seen as particularly egregious to The Network as more of an example of the rich getting richer off the backs of the poor when they were in positions to actually help.

The Network went so far as to routinely notify Medi-cal and Medicade when they were able to identify individuals taking advantage of those services in the same way. Members of The Network were vehemently offended by the rampant greed of these people.

The process of securing the various professionals, entrepreneurs, skilled workers, landscapers, medical personnel at all levels, and everything that was needed initially and ultimately to build and maintain a thriving, self-sustaining city was in progress from the beginning. All of the logistics, legal and otherwise, were carefully worked out so that the city would be viable, successful, and privately owned by The Network.

Above all, the Network sought to eliminate any social stigma attached to living in or coming from Calais City. That could not have been achieved without a population that included residents who were not from the ranks of the homeless or former homeless. Initially, most of the persons who worked in the schools and other establishments also lived in the community. That included the hospital and clinic staffs, and other service personnel.

County, State, and Federal entities were given 20-year renewable leases for the land and the buildings that they utilized. It was not long before people from elsewhere were looking to lease residences or facilities there and/or seeking work in the City.

As Theo Henry foresaw, The Program became the national standard for resolving housing crises among low-income and homeless people. The President became aware of the project in the middle of his first term of office and lent his personal support and influence. He was instrumental in the progress of the city. As did the planners, the President saw the potential for the replication of this project throughout the Nation. It was touted as a major accomplishment, the likes of which had never been achieved during any presidency before him. It certainly cannot be diminished, nor the credit taken by any succeeding president.

There were prominent welcome signs posted at the three major entrances into the city. The main thoroughfare was named President Barack Obama Boulevard. The City was officially opened in a ribbon-cutting ceremony that took place in April 2016. In attendance were residents and officials of Calais City, members of The Network, the Corporate Officers with Morgan and Liv front and center with President and First Lady Michelle Obama, members of the Advisory Committee, the current and former students of CECCA, Los Angeles City and County officials, and numerous State and Federal officials. There was a plethora of press that guaranteed extensive world-wide news coverage.

CHAPTER 13

REFLECTION ON THE FAMILY: ALEXANDRIA AKA (ALEX) (ALY) (BABY GIRL)

Morgan and Liv enjoyed a very satisfying family life. Even though they were celebrating their anniversary alone, thoughts of their children were ever present and were prevalent subjects of their reminiscing. Though their children were not perfect, they were so close to it, they were a joy to their parents, grandparents, and great-grandparents.

The pair had decided while they were on their honeymoon how they would raise their children. With insight from Birdie, Morgan's grandmother, they established their child-rearing strategy. They would primarily follow the dynamics of Morgan's upbringing as his was far better than hers had been. Liv felt she had nothing to offer as her formative years had been filled with abuse and violence. She felt her only input would be on what to avoid—everything that had been detrimental to her—and what to do, everything she had needed and wanted, but did not receive. Conversely, the results of Morgan's upbringing had produced a very well-adjusted, responsible individual with strong moral fiber. That was their goal.

They both modeled the behaviors they wanted to instill in their children. Taught by example, the children were eager sponges. Each had age-appropriate responsibilities and were disciplined with love.

The main thing Liv insisted on was that they never be disciplined physically—corporal punishment was not an option. Morgan, of course, had no problem with that. Their philosophy of child-rearing was carried over and inculcated to a great extent into what became known as the Calais Culture, the hallmark of CECCA.

Alex had been a dream child from the beginning. She had attached herself to Liv, and the feeling was mutual. They bonded immediately the very first day Morgan brought Liv to the Center to meet and speak with the children. Alex was smart as a whip, and with the love and attention showered on her by Morgan and Liv, even before they adopted her, she blossomed and thrived, showing no evidence of her abuse as a toddler that had left her withdrawn, silent, and unsociable, the state in which Morgan had found her.

That Alex would be a pediatrician was a well-established fact from the time she announced it at a very early age. ("I'm going to be a baby doctor and take care of all the little babies!") It was affirmed by Birdie, and it was soon evident that it would be so. That drive in her was accelerated when she witnessed the birth of her younger brother, Morgan II. Alex excelled in school and was placed into the independent learning program, where she proved to be unstoppable. Her parents had no problem in deciding what to give her in the way of presents, or where to take her on their mother-daughter, or father-daughter one-on-one dates.

Besides the obvious choices of books, teaching supplies, trips to libraries and science fairs, she loved to visit well-baby nurseries where she was, eventually, allowed to assist in their activities and supervise their play.

Alex read prolifically and had her own library in her room. When her room could no longer contain all the books, she was given her own section in the family library, where she spent much of her time. A natural gifted teacher, she enjoyed helping her little brothers and cousins, teaching them as well as setting good examples for them.

The most serious *problem* or issue they experienced with Alex occurred when she was eight years old.

(Alex's disconnect) Morgan and Liv had packed the kids into the SUV and were headed home from work and school. Four-year-old Morgan II was playing with his two-year-old baby brother, Randy, keeping him laughing and the ride far from boring. Alex usually spent the time to and from school in stimulating conversation with her parents. This day she was uncharacteristically subdued.

Morgan caught a glimpse of her in the rear-view mirror and noticed her pensive, almost sad expression, in addition to her taciturn behavior. "Hey, Baby Girl, excuse me, Young Lady, what's on your mind? You are awfully quiet back there."

"Nothing, Daddy," she replied listlessly.

"Nothing? Didn't anything *exciting* happen at school today?" Morgan asked, attempting to get her talking. It was so unlike her to be so quiet. Liv had noted the same thing and turned to look at her.

"Honey, are you not feeling too well?" Liv asked.

"I'm okay, Mom. I just don't feel like talking right now, please."

Liv thought perhaps asking about her project with would get her to talking, but after her response, she thought it better to leave it for now.

Morgan and Liv exchanged concerned glances, knowing that *something* was wrong, but not pressing further at that time. Once they were home, Alex went directly to her room and remained there until Liv called her for dinner. Her parents knew for certain that there was a problem, but they chose to wait for Alex to bring it to their attention.

During dinner, the boys ate heartily and talked about their day—Randy about the puppy that had been brought to school, and Little Morgan about the new boy that joined his class. Conversely, Alex only picked at her food and said nothing after Grace. She appeared to be lost in deep, troubled thought.

When dinner was over, the children did their after-dinner chores. In short order they were done, and the boys went to play in their room. Alex lingered a bit, and then retreated to her room, as well. Morgan and Liv went to the den to relax and contemplate how to help Alex with whatever was bothering her.

"I can't *imagine* what could possibly be causing her to *behave* this way," Liv expressed in frustration. "She was so *bubbly* this morning, really looking forward to working on her project with Lavana."

"Whatever it is, she is *definitely* concerned about it. I don't think we should press her into talking about it. It's probably best if we give her space and time to come to us. In the meantime, we'll just have to keep an eye on her and only intervene if it takes her *too* long.

"You know what, Liv, I had a certain feeling of déjà vu when I saw the look on her face this afternoon in the car."

"Really, Morgan? What do you think it was?"

"It was very much like the expression she had when I told her that you and I were going to get married and live together like mommies and daddies—a mixture of worry, sadness, and fear, I guess."

"Oh, Morgan, what could *possibly* be causing *that*?"

"I don't know, Sweetheart, but . . ."

Just then Alex came into the room, and immediately their attention focused on her.

"Mommy, Daddy, I have a problem," she announced solemnly.

When she didn't elaborate, Morgan probed, "Do you need to call for a family meeting?"

"No!" she stated adamantly.

Liv sensed that she wanted to talk about it but was reluctant to come right out and say what it was that was on her mind. She needed to have it coaxed out of her. "Is it a personal problem, a family problem, a school problem?" she asked.

"Yes, I think *all* of them."

"This seems rather important, Alex. Come and sit down," Morgan said, positioning the ottoman between Liv and himself so that she would be sitting between and facing them.

Alex sat on the ottoman with her head bowed peering up from one to the other and looking forlorn. As she sat there looking lost, Liv felt the need to embrace her. She shifted herself onto the ottoman and held and rocked Alex quietly for a few moments.

Finally, Alex spoke. "Mom, Randy looks just like *you*, except for his red hair and his eyes. His *eyes* look just like *yours*, Daddy. And Little Morgan looks just like *you*, except *his* eyes look just like *Mom's*."

Neither of them knew what to make of Alex's comments, which were totally unexpected! They now had a glimmer of an idea of her problem, but they still didn't know what was behind it. They knew she was expecting—*needing*—something from them.

Morgan answered, "Yes, Baby Girl, you are right. Is that what your problem is about?"

"I don't have *anything* that looks like *either* one of you. I don't *look* like *anyone* in this family. I don't look like I *belong*!"

"Alex, Honey, don't you *feel* like you belong?" Liv asked.

"I *want* to," she said as her eyes widened and began to tear. "I *used* to," she added after a pause, her tears now overflowing as she tried to blink them away.

"Oh, Sweetheart! My baby," Liv said, holding her closer. "You *do* belong. You will *always* belong! Don't you *ever* forget that, you *hear*?" After a few moments of holding her close again, Liv said, "I understand if this is how you *feel*, Sweetheart; but can you tell us *why*? What makes you *feel* this way? Did your Dad or I say or do anything to make you feel you *don't* belong? Did *anyone*?"

"Lavana said that *I* am not your *real* child because *I* was *adopted*. *I* didn't come out of your *stomach* like I saw Little Morgan and Randy do. *They* are your *real* children!"

Liv's heart was broken hearing those words from her daughter. It was so painful because she *knew* how it *felt* to feel unloved, or less than, or not belonging. She didn't want *any* child to feel that way. She *especially* didn't want *her* child to feel that way.

Morgan decided to take a different approach. He chose to appeal to her intellectual side rather than her emotional side. He knew how smart she was and mature beyond her years in so many respects. But the bottom line was that she was still an eight-year-old child emotionally.

"Listen, Alex. Your mother told me that you don't like to be called 'Baby Girl' because you're not a baby, you're a young lady.

I can understand that. But for starters, and just so you'll know, you *are my* baby girl, and you will *always* be, no matter *how* old you get—even if I'm still alive when you are a hundred years old! So, if I slip up and call you 'Baby Girl,' I'm entitled! You *are* my Baby Girl!

"Now, another thing! You said you don't *look* like anyone in this family. What color is your hair?"

"My hair is black!"

"Does anyone else in the family have black hair?"

"You, and Mommy, and Morgy all have black hair."

"Okay, you have our hair color. That's just one thing. Now look at your mother." Alex turned her head to look up at her mother. "She is beautiful, isn't she!"

"Yes, Mom is *very* beautiful. *Everybody* knows that!"

"Well, Baby Girl, that's what you have from your *mother*! *You* are very beautiful, *too*, and everybody knows *that* . . . especially when you *smile* that infectious *smile* of yours. So, come on, give it up!" Morgan said, lifting her chin.

Alex tried very hard and managed a semi-smile, but her heart wasn't in it, and she wasn't appeased.

"I'll accept that attempted smile for now, 'cause I know you're still not convinced."

Liv decided to follow in the vein Morgan had begun. "Alex, as a future *doctor*, a *pediatrician*, no less, you *know* what I am about to say is totally *impossible*. But if the fact that you didn't come out of my stomach is the *only* reason you feel you are not our *real* child, I would gladly have you surgically implanted into my womb—as big as you are—so that I could give birth to you, or at least have a C-section, so that you would feel you were our *real* child!"

The graphic visualization of that scenario was so ludicrous in Alex's mind that she had to laugh, and she did have to give up a genuine smile. It had an impact on Morgan, as well, as he wondered where Liv came up with some of the things that came from her imagination and out of her mouth.

"Are you feeling better now?" he asked, hopefully.

"Yes, sort of. But *Lavana* said that people *always* love their *real* children more than their *adopted* children."

"Okay, 'Dr. Alex,' the scientific term is 'biological' children, not 'real' children," Morgan corrected. "And just how many biological children has *Lavana* had, and how many has she *adopted* that make her an authority on the subject? Do you think *she's* smarter than *you are*? Is she in the independent learning program at school like *you* are?"

"Daddy, No! She is *my* age. How *can* she have all those children? And, no, she is in the regular curriculum. We just sometimes do projects with students in the regular program."

"Do you think Lavana is smarter than your *Dad or me*?" Liv asked.

"No, Mom, no!"

"If that is the case, wouldn't it be better for you to believe what *we* tell you rather than what *Lavana* says?"

"I guess that makes sense." Alex reasoned.

"Are you convinced now?" Morgan asked.

Alex was weighing everything that had been said against what she had believed and answered, "I have just one more question to ask before I can be sure."

"Okay, Baby Girl, what is it?"

Alex climbed off of Liv's lap and took Liv's former seat on the sofa.

"If our family was on a boat in the middle of the ocean and it started to sink, and you could each only save *one* of your children, which two would you save? Who would *you* choose to save, Daddy, and who would *you* pick to save, Mommy?"

Morgan could only look to Liv shaking his head, "Sweetheart, I'm going to leave *this* one for *you* to answer. *You're* so much better at this than *I* am."

"Alex, you've opened up this can of worms, so you will have to listen to my speech."

"Can of worms?" Alex questioned.

"Never mind that, Young Lady. First of all, it would depend on *when* this tragic accident *happens*. We *all* know how to *swim*, so if we are all adults, it's every man, or woman, for himself or herself!"

"Mom, you know what I mean! We are all children, like we are now!"

"Okay, Liv, let's see you get out of *this*!" Morgan grinned.

"Let me put it this way, Alex," Liv said in all seriousness. "In the situation you described—middle of the ocean, our family as it is today, boat sinking—if your dad and I can't figure out a way to save our *entire* family, we will all join in a group hug, and we will *all* go to Heaven together! End of story!

"Now, let me tell you this, My Daughter. I did *not* give *physical birth* to you. That is true. Better than that, though, I had the honor of *knowing* you in *advance* and *loving* you, knowing that I *wanted you* to be *my* child, to be *our* child. *You* were *chosen*! In fact, we asked *you* to *marry* us, and you said '*yes*!' You *do* remember our *wedding*, don't you?"

"Oh, yes, Mom! I *really* remember that," Alex smiled.

"Little Morgan and Randy *didn't* have weddings. They were just *born* into the family. *We* had no *choice*. We didn't get a chance to *pick* them like we picked *you*. We *love* them just as much, though, because God *sent* them to us. But before He sent *them*, He sent *you* to us. We would have been happy with just you, but God wanted us to have Morgy and Randy, as well. He wanted our family to be just the way it is—a daughter first, and then two sons."

Morgan marveled at the way Liv explained away Alex's misgivings, thinking all the while how blessed he was to have her and his children. A blessed life indeed. "Now do you know that you *do* belong, that you are an *integral part* of this family?" Morgan asked, assured of the answer he would receive.

"Yes, Daddy. I love you, and I love you, Mom. I love my brothers, too. In fact, I love my whole family—GranGran, Grandpa, MiMi, PawPaw, Uncle Kevin, Aunt Eleanor, Cousin Lydia, Cousin Kevin, Uncle Kyle, Uncle Travis—everybody in my whole family!

"And I'm going to tell Lavana that she is *wrong*!"

"You don't have to tell her anything, as long as *you* know the truth. But if she brings it up again, it's okay to tell her," Morgan coached. He swooped her up, "Come on, let's go and get ready for bed."

CHAPTER 14

REFLECTION ON THE FAMILY: MORGAN, II AKA (MORGY) (LITTLE MORGY) (LITTLE MORGAN)

Morgan II was born on February 11, 2015, weighing in at a healthy 8lbs. 7oz. and was 23" long. He had a batch of thick, black hair and was the spitting image of his father. When the doula presented him, his little arms were stretched upward, as if he were receiving thunderous applause, or had just finished a victory lap.

Liv returned to work with him after a week, and his first several weeks of life were spent in the North Wing in a temporary nursery that had been set up in Liv's office. Liv, and Morgan as well, talked to him continuously as they went about their day, giving descriptions of what they were doing and why. They always talked to the children in complete sentences, using correct terminology and using correct English. They never talked "baby talk" to them (e.g. "tah tah" for thank you, or "wah wah" for water). At about eight weeks of age, Morgy "graduated" to the nursery section of the day care center on campus, where he continued to develop and thrive.

It was soon evident that Morgy had the gift of gab. He showed an early interest in people, mostly in being helpful and in being everyone's friend. He was a natural-born leader and liked to organize and control, make and enforce rules, and settle disputes. He was the consummate champion of the underdog. More than anything, he liked to debate.

Morgan loved to watch documentaries about people in other countries and cultures. He was especially interested in politics and the workings of the government at all levels and in U.S. and world history. Amazingly, by the time he was in the equivalent of the second grade, he knew the capitals of all the states, when they were admitted to the Union, and the names of every president and vice-president and their dates and terms of office.

Shopping for gifts for Morgan, like his sister, was also easy. He like reading history books and biographies of influential people and historical figures. His ideal mother-son, father-son one-on-one time involved watching famous debates, attending public hearings, town hall meetings, and court proceedings. Visiting open council meetings was a real treat for him. At age nine, Morgy announced that he would be President of the United States and had decided to prepare by studying law.

In the Calais household, as well as CECCA, there was no tolerance for physical or verbal abuse. That meant there would be no physical fighting, no calling anyone out of their name, and certainly no profanity. The Calais children learned at an early age that they were to *communicate* their feelings orally. If there arose discord among any of them, they were expected to try to resolve it among themselves by *talking* it out. That included, if feasible, giving themselves a "cooling off" period.

If there were a breakdown in that process, the next step would be to call for a family meeting in which the entire family would assemble, and each party would have an opportunity to present his or her side. There would be discussion and perhaps suggestions posed to facilitate an outcome acceptable to each individual. If there could be no meeting of the minds, it was up to Morgan and Liv to settle any disputes, and it was understood their joint decision would be final.

This process was also utilized when anyone had a particular problem and wanted input, whether it involved a school issue, a classmate, a teacher, or any situation that was seen as a problem to the individual. Fortunately, in the majority of times a family meeting had been called, it was for relatively minor issues. No matter how insignificant it may have seemed, Morgan and Liv made it a priority to respect the feelings of their children. They realized that if a situation were perceived as a problem, it was *serious* to the affected individual. Therefore, no problem presented for consideration in "family court" was summarily dismissed, but received due process.

With the differences in ages between Alex and her younger brothers, Alex had an advantage of maturity and had little need to call a family meeting concerning either of them. In fact, *she* was sometimes solicited to mediate between them, obviating a family meeting altogether. They respected her as much as they did their teachers at school. She had been, in fact, their first teacher, teaching them both to read and write before they entered school.

There did come a time, however, when the process failed, and extraordinary measures were needed. Morgan, II, who usually could talk his way out of almost anything, had become infuriated with his big sister. He was angrier than he had ever been. Truth be told, he was not really angry, per se, but extremely frustrated and was not able to handle the situation any other way.

The previous Monday had been his first day in the independent learning program at school. His very first assignment was to assemble an intricate, 1,000-piece jigsaw puzzle. He had the entire week and weekend to work on it as it was not due until the following Monday.

He had been working diligently all week on the assignment. The puzzle was not necessarily expected to be *completed*. It was part of an assessment of his ability for the use of the instructors in initially plotting his individualized course. He was to photograph the result of his labor in whatever state of completion and turn the photo in on Monday morning.

Little Morgan had been primed for the longest by Alex. She knew how smart her little brother was, and she wanted him in the independent learning program with her. She was very proud of him when he was reassigned. Of course, Little Morgan knew what it meant, and he was happy to have achieved the same "status" as his big sister.

His parents were careful to make sure he knew that being in the program did not mean that he was any better than any of the other students, only that *his* way of processing some kinds of information was different than some of the others. They didn't want his ego to be inflated out of proportion.

Nevertheless, he wanted to be the best he could be, which he had been programmed to be. "As long as you know you have done your very best, you can be proud of whatever you achieve, no matter how it compares to what anyone else has done," are words that all of the Calais children, in fact, all of the students at CECCA had ingrained into them. Morgan always remembered that, but he wanted *his* "very best" in *this* instance to be the completion of the puzzle.

Sunday dinner was done, and the extended family members had all gone home. Little Morgan had just put the very last piece of the puzzle in place. He was so proud! He was anxious to show his parents his accomplishment. He had assembled the puzzle on a poster board, which was sufficient to assemble and photograph, but not sturdy enough to carry. In hindsight, he realized he should have either photographed the puzzle first, or brought his parents in to see it where he had assembled it. Oh, well.

In his eagerness, Morgan had picked up the puzzle and was carrying it when Alex unexpectedly turned into his path from another room, knocking most of the puzzle from his hands and causing substantial damage as a few hundred pieces went flying in all directions!

"Oh, Morgy, I'm *so sorry*! I didn't know you were there. Let me help you pick it up," Alex offered. She was devastated, knowing how long and hard he had worked on it and knowing it was due the next morning.

"You're not sorry, Alex!" he cried, in tears. "You did that on *purpose*! You just want to be the only one in this family to be in the independent learning program!"

"No, Morgy, it was an *accident*! I would *never* do that on *purpose*! Please forgive me, Morgy. I'll help you put it back together."

"Don't you touch it! I am so *mad* at you, Aly! You ruined my homework! I'm going to tell *Daddy*!"

Little Morgan dropped the remnants of the puzzle causing even more damage and ran crying to Morgan, while Alex ran crying to Liv.

"Daddy, I am *mad*! I am *so* mad at Aly! I don't know *what* to do. I think if she were a *boy*, I might want to *sock* her!"

Morgan could see that he was fighting mad. He didn't know the cause, and he wasn't about to tell him that he *shouldn't* be mad. "Yes, Son, I can *see* that you are very *angry*. I'm glad you can *tell* me how you feel. Everybody gets angry at *some* time. *I* have even gotten angry before. Do you want a family meeting?"

"No! I'm too *mad* for a family meeting. I'm too mad to *talk*! I just want to *hit* something!"

Without scolding him or raising his voice, Morgan calmly said, "Okay, Son, I *hear* you. Come with me, please."

Little Morgan followed his father to the gym where Morgan put a pair of boxing gloves on him. He stood his son in front of the punching bag and held it steady. "Okay, Morgy, show me how *angry* you are. You want to *hit* something? Now is your chance."

Morgan begin to punch the bag as his father held it. "Is that as hard as you can punch?" his father asked. You must not be that *angry*!" Little Morgan proceeded to punch the bag harder and harder to show how mad he was. "Are you still angry?" In response, Little Morgan kept punching the bag as hard as he could, over and over, until he was wiped out, at the point of exhaustion.

Breathing hard, he said, "Dad, I'm not *so* angry anymore."

"Oh? Well, I think you *still* need to punch some more."

After a few more punches, out of breath with his arms aching from the exertion, he stopped punching to say, "You know what, Dad? I'm not angry at *all* now. Can I stop, please?"

"Are you ready to talk now?" Morgan asked, knowing he was.

"Yes, Daddy, I'm ready now."

"Okay, Morgy, come and take a seat on the bench over here."

When they were both seated, Morgy still breathing hard, Morgan continued. Now. Let's talk. What did Alex do to make you so angry?"

"She made me drop my puzzle that I have been working on all week. I was bringing it to show you and Mom. She bumped into me, and the pieces flew everywhere! It's due tomorrow, and I'll never be able to finish it again in time!" Morgy had begun to sniffle.

"Surely she didn't do it on *purpose*. Do you think she would do that?"

"No, I guess not. She *said* it was an accident."

"Well, did she say she was sorry? Did she ask you to forgive her?"

"She *said* she was, but I was too *mad* to forgive her."

"How do you think *she* feels? Do you think she is *happy* about it?"

"No, Daddy. She wasn't happy."

"Well, what do you want to do about it?"

"Can I call a family meeting so that I can tell her I'm sorry for getting so mad, and saying the mean thing I said to her? I think I hurt her feelings."

"What did you *say* to her, Son?"

"I told her she did it on purpose because she wanted to be the only one in the family to be in the independent learning program at school," he said, truly sorry. He loved his big sister and looked up to her. For the first time he really felt the truth of a fact that had been stressed at home and at school: *"You can think what you want to think, but you need to think twice before you say what you feel like saying in a moment of anger. Once hurtful words come from your mouth and into the ears of the other person, they can never be unsaid!"*

"I'm *really* sorry, Dad. I know you are disappointed in me. *I'm* disappointed in me, *too*," he said, dejectedly. "I'm ashamed to face my sister."

"Have you learned anything from all of this?"

"Yes, Daddy. If I had been smarter, it would not have happened in the first place. Maybe I *don't* really belong in the independent learning program. I should have taken a picture of it *first* and then showed you the picture, or I could have asked you guys to come and see it. I should be kinder to people that I know love me, like Alex. I should . . ."

"Okay, Morgy, that's enough 'shoulds' for now. Let's go and have a family meeting."

Distraught Alex had run to Liv in tears. She was mortified, knowing how hard Morgy had worked on his puzzle. What hurt her the most was hearing him say that she did it on purpose to keep him out of the program. Nothing could have been further from the truth when she had been priming him toward that goal.

Liv knew Morgan would handle the situation from Morgy's standpoint. She consoled her daughter and assured her that her brother didn't really mean what he said, that he was just so frustrated, he couldn't respond correctly. "Give him a little time, Sweetheart. It will be all right. You'll see. Your brother loves you."

"But his *puzzle* is *ruined*. I offered to *help* him put it back together, but he didn't want me to *touch* it. It's still all over the floor. It's due tomorrow!"

"I'm sure that when your father gets through with him, he will have a different attitude. In the meantime, let's go gather the pieces and see how much damage is done. We can get it set up so we can start fixing it. It may not be enough time for *him* to put it all back together, but we can *all* work on it together and get it done."

"Okay, Mom," Alex said, feeling much better.

Randy had been relegated to picking up the single pieces of the puzzle that were not still connected to another piece, and they had everything set up in the den and had begun to work on it when Morgan and Morgy entered.

"We have a call for a family meeting; so everyone please stop what you are doing and gather around the table," Morgan announced. They each proceeded to the dining room and took their seats. "This meeting is called by Morgy, who first wants to make a statement. You have the floor, Morgy."

With his head bowed apologetically, Morgan, II began his statement. "I want to apologize to my sister for getting mad at her for making me . . ." he paused, rethinking his statement, "for *accidently* bumping into me and making my puzzle fall out of my hands and come apart. *We* accidently bumped into each *other*, so it was my fault as much as hers. It *was* an accident, I know, and Alex said she was sorry."

He raised his head and paused, looking to Alex for a response; but when no one said anything, he continued. "I said something I should not have said, because I know it wasn't true." He stopped and addressed his father, realizing the implication of his own words. "Dad, does this mean that I told a lie? I didn't *mean* to. I'm sorry. Can I ask God to forgive me when I say my prayers tonight?"

Everyone remained silent, allowing him to come to his own conclusion, which he did.

"I know, I have to forgive Alex first, and I do. Alex, I forgive you because you asked me to, and because I know you didn't do it on purpose," he addressed his sister. "I'm sorry I was not being a good brother to you. Will you forgive me, please, Alex?"

Alex smiled at him. "Of course I forgive you, Morgy!" I don't like it when you're angry with me. I'm glad you're not anymore."

"Is this meeting over with yet?" Randy asked impatiently. "I *still* have some more pieces to get." Everyone laughed.

"Just about, Randy, but not quite," Liv said. "Alex and Morgy, you guys hug each other to seal the deal." Alex and Morgy gave each other a hug, and that was settled.

"There is still the matter of Morgy's homework," Liv continued. "Now we are going to finish putting this puzzle back together so Morgy can take a picture of it to show his teacher. I can't think of a better way to finish a family meeting!"

"But Mom, *I* was supposed to put it together by *myself*. If we *all* do it, then it will be like *cheating*," Little Morgan said sadly.

"Son, you *did* put it together *once* by yourself, *didn't* you?" Morgan reminded him.

"Yes, I *did*, *didn't* I! So, it's not cheating! Relieved, Morgy's face lit up with a big smile. "Thanks, Dad. And thanks everybody for helping me put my puzzle back together again!"

Little Morgan was a happy camper!

CHAPTER 15

REFLECTION ON THE FAMILY: RANDY AKA (RANDY ANDY) (RANDY PANDY) (NEVER "RED!")

Born at home as was his brother, Randy made his debut on November 11, 2016. He was smaller than his brother at birth, but still a healthy 7 lbs. 9 ozs. and 20½" long. He had a thick crop of curly red hair and rosy, plump cheeks. A calm, happy baby who hardly ever cried, he was especially easy to care for. Though never a mama's boy, he was especially close to Liv, spending as much time with her as possible. Randy never had too much to say, but he was always busy in his head, paying attention to and watching people and things in his surroundings, much like his mother was prone to do—but for totally different reasons.

Randy loved to sit on the piano bench while Liv was singing, or writing music, or just playing the piano. It was quite a shock when the family realized how gifted he was. As part of their bedtime ritual, Liv sang her lullaby to them. She was about to do so one night when Randy, about 2 years old, unexpectedly, asked, "Mommy, can *I* sing the lullaby tonight?"

Everyone looked at him in surprise, and Liv responded, "Why, of course. *Yes*, Honey!"

To everyone's amazement, he sang the song perfectly with his youthful voice in perfect pitch. It brought tears to Liv's eyes. It reminded her of their wedding ceremony when Morgan unexpectedly broke out in song, surprising her and bringing her to tears. "Randy, that was *beautiful*!" Liv exclaimed, embracing him while the others applauded.

Randy, unaffected by the accolades, just looked at them as if to say, "Why are you making such a fuss? *That was nothing!*" They did not know what *he* knew, what he saw in his mind *and* his fingers. "I can play it on the piano, too, only not like *you*, Mommy. My hands are not big enough yet."

From the time he could walk, Randy could be found stretching up to reach the piano keys, but no one really thought too much about it. He pressed the keys with his fingers, as opposed to banging on them with his hands as often little children are prone to do. He never pronounced at a young age what he wanted to be or do when he grew up as his siblings had done. After he demonstrated his musical ability, Liv especially, and Morgan began paying closer attention. Liv knew instinctively two years later when Randy was sitting next to her on the piano bench as she worked on a new song.

"Mommy, I know you are busy, but can I show you something?"

"I'm never too busy for you, Sweetie. What do you want to show me?"

"You have to move over first."

Liv moved to the end of the bench and Randy took her place. He proceeded to play a very simple version of Liv's lullaby, playing in two-part treble harmony and a one-finger base line. Liv was speechless!

"Randy! When . . . how did you learn to do that?" she asked.

"I don't know. I just hear and see it in my head. I see lots of things in my head. I watch you playing, and I can just see the pictures all in my head," he said simply. "The song you were just working on that you were trying to make fit, I can see how I can make it fit."

"What do you mean, Randy? I'm just trying to work it out. It's not finished."

"I know, Mom, but I don't think you are hearing it—or seeing it right. Can I show you how to fix it?"

"Yes, Randy, *please*," Liv was curious.

"This is what *you* are doing." Randy played the melody line that Liv had been working on exactly the way she had played it. He had the meter and the melody line exactly. Liv just sat there open-mouthed, hardly able to believe her eyes *or* her ears. "This is how you can fix it." He played the same melody line again, making changes in the values of a few notes—changing a half note to a quarter note, and two quarter notes to eighths.

"Also, Mom, I know what you are thinking of naming the song, but I think I have a *better* name that you would like better. Do you want me to tell you?"

Wondering how he could possibly know what she was thinking when she had not mentioned any possible titles nor even sung the lyric outside of her head, she responded, "Well, *yes*, Randy!"

"Okay, Mom, you are thinking, ***'Should I Trust My Heart to You?'*** The better title is, ***'When I Can Trust My Heart to You.'***"

From that moment on, Liv knew that Randy's future would involve, at least to a large extent, music. To nurture his special musical talent, Morgan and Liv immediately arranged for him to participate in the music program at school where he seriously studied music theory and learned to play proficiently every instrument he decided he wanted to play.

Not only gifted musically, Randy demonstrated a real knack for poetry and creative writing, which naturally evolved into songwriting and composition. Randy was the total artistic package; his aptitude in the visual arts was manifested in his renderings in the various mediums and ultimately showcased in numerous art galleries.

One-on-one time for Randy included trips to concerts, art galleries and museums. Perfect gifts for him involved the various musical instruments in which he expressed an interest and went on to master. A huge thrill for him was to be allowed to sit in with the band at Liv's rehearsals. The ultimate, when he was old enough, was playing in the band occasionally at Liv's Supper Club.

There came a point in time when mother and son collaborated on songs and composed many songs together. By the time he was 12 years of age, Randy had taken over the job of preparing Liv's lead sheets and charts for all of the instruments in the band.

A significant income for Randy from the time he started publishing his compositions included royalties from the many songs that he composed for other artists and for those he recorded himself. His favorite recording was a CD of duets with his mother.

Though usually not as exuberant as his siblings, Randy was just as smart. He had a calmness about him that was much like his father's, especially when he became a teenager. As a child he was very easy going and could usually be counted on to fall in line with whatever the majority wanted. There were early signs of Randy's *other* major talent which went largely undetected for quite a number of years by his parents. Looking back, they could identify the first tangible signs.

(The campout) The family had planned a camping trip that was to last for a whole week. The kids were really looking forward to the trip, and excitement was rising as the departure date drew near. The night before they were to leave, Randy couldn't sleep and knocked on his parents' bedroom door at 2:30 a.m.

Morgan and Liv were immediately alert, knowing that could only be one of their children, and by the knock, most likely Randy. When Morgan answered, "Come in," Randy peeked his head in but did not enter.

"Randy? What's the matter?" Liv asked as she switched on the lamp. "Come in, Honey."

Randy came in and stood at the foot of the bed, but did not speak as he looked from one to the other.

"What's the matter, Son," Morgan asked, noting nothing unusual. "Are you so excited that you can't sleep? You know we've got to get up early and get on the road."

"I'm not excited, I just can't sleep anymore. I don't want to go camping tomorrow. I'm afraid!" he said, his bottom lip quivering.

"Oh, Randy," Liv said. "What's there to be afraid of? Come and get into the bed with us," she gestured with her hand.

"I'm not a *baby*," he said as he climbed on the bed and sat on top of the covers between them. "I was having a dream that frightened me, and I don't want to go camping. I just *don't* want to go. I don't want *any* of us to go!"

Morgan held him gently by the shoulders. "You know Morgy and Alex are very excited and looking forward to the trip. We talked about it in our family meeting, and we all voted to go," Morgan reminded him. "They will be very disappointed if we *don't* go."

"In that case, I want to change my vote!"

"You can change your vote, but it will still be four to one. We still have to go since the majority wins. You know how that goes," Morgan reminded him.

"We *can't* go. We will all die if we go!" he said and began to cry, his entire body shaking. Liv took him in her arms, but he continued to sob and could not be consoled.

"What was so scary about your dream? What was it about?" Morgan soothed.

"We were at the camp grounds sitting around our campfire. All of a sudden the fire got really big and spilled over, causing a bright lightning fire ball. I could see an old women standing by watching. She told me that we shouldn't be there and to tell you that we can't come there." Morgan and Liv shared a feeling of déjà vu.

Randy was more calm but still in tears. Morgan said, "Randy, tell me about the woman. Was she the one who scared you?"

"No, Daddy. She was a kind old Indian woman who seem to be friendly. In fact, she kinda looked like that lady in the picture in the den that Alex calls 'Birdie' and says she is our great-grandmother."

Liv looked at Morgan with the same thought as he when he calmly announced, "Okay, Randy, we won't go."

"Morgan?" Liv questioned without contradiction, "How can we do this?"

Morgan responded, "Randy, everyone is expecting to go camping for a week. I understand that you are very concerned, and I can see it is very real for you. I also don't want to disappoint your sister and brother. So, come and let me tuck you back into bed. On the way, I'll tell you what we will do so that everyone will be happy. Okay, Son?"

Confident that his father would make everything okay, Randy replied, "Okay, Daddy,"

At six a.m. the family piled into their previously packed mobile home and drove to a wooded area on their own property. They pitched their family-sized tent and began their seven-night campout a jogging distance from home. But having agreed that they would be roughing it on the real, there were no TV, radio, or cell phones—none of the comforts of home.

A week later when they returned home, Liv busied herself with supervising the children's chores and the cleanup while Morgan gathered the mail and the newspapers. A few moments later, standing at the kitchen door, Morgan called Liv's name. She turned at the sound of his voice, and the expression on his face immobilized her, sending a chill through her. Morgan merely beckoned to her and she approached slowly, maintaining eye contact, as one expecting to receive bad news. Morgan handed her the newspaper he held in his hand.

Liv's eyes slowly widened as she silently read the headline:

Camp Ground Death Toll Rises to 38.

Fire Only 44% Contained after Five Days

(Trip to the mall) Randy and his father were ending a Father-Son day visit to an art exhibit in the multipurpose center at the local mall. They made a rare stop at the mall's food court at Randy's insistence. While Morgan sipped coffee, Randy was enjoying a berry smoothie. He was drawn to a nearby table where he happened to catch the eye of a young girl about his age, six, seated there. He noticed she seemed to be afraid sitting there by herself, looking at him with anxious, sad eyes. Noticing a bruise on her arm, he stood and took a step toward her.

"Hi. My name is Randy. What's your name?"

After looking around, she timidly almost whispered, "Kylonne."

Seemingly out of nowhere, a rather large man carrying a bag of food he had just purchased grabbed her by the arm and said gruffly, "Come on!"

She maintained eye contact with Randy, fearfully looking back as she was hurried off. Morgan had responded to a call and had not witnessed the exchange. The urgency in his son's voice, however, captured his attention.

"Dad, I think that little girl is in trouble. She's afraid of that man who took her away. Can we follow them?"

Since the event several months earlier regarding the camping trip, Morgan was suspecting more and more that Randy had received "the gift." Given that, he was inclined to accept his son's assessment.

"Which way did they go?" he asked, looking around.

"Over there! Look! They're getting on the escalator. We need to hurry, Daddy!"

Hurriedly, they deposited the remnants of their beverages in the trash and proceeded to follow the pair through the mall and into the parking structure. Morgan had the presence of mind to take a few photos of the man and the girl and was also able to take a picture of the vehicle he was driving, and old dark blue sedan. They were able to get a good picture of the license plate as the car was backing out of the stall.

"Daddy, should we report them to the police before he has a chance to get away?"

Morgan finished sending the pictures and a text before responding, "Don't worry, Randy, I have already taken care of it."

Morgan had contacted CECCA security and turned the situation over to them. Within 24 hours, Kylonne had been returned safely to her parents, and a dangerous predator was in custody.

CHAPTER 16

THE CALAIS KIDS' REBELLION

As parents, Morgan and Liv were united in their main goal, to raise their children to be happy, independent, responsible, well-adjusted, productive, and successful adults with strong moral characters. Their philosophy and their methods to achieve their goals were carried over to their Centers in what had become known as the Calais Culture.

Essential to achieve that goal was to encourage financial responsibility and the virtue of delayed gratification. As Morgan put it, "Our kids are not going to be waiting around for us to die so that they can receive lofty inheritances in which they had no hand in amassing."

Morgan wanted to raise them as he had been raised, to be able to amass their *own* wealth and pass that legacy on to future generations. He believed that they would not appreciate anything simply handed to them, or that came too easily, without effort on their parts. He also didn't want them to grow up being selfish and feeling entitled. Liv had been in total agreement, but she also wanted to make sure they knew they were loved and that they received the love and care she felt she had not received as a child. Above all, she wanted them never to be abused or disciplined with corporal punishment. She wanted them to be able to feel safe in their own home and to feel free to come to them with anything, knowing they would be heard.

Of course, trust funds were established for each of the children that would not be disturbed until they were well into adulthood. They each received age-appropriate allowances that were not dependent on their performances. In other words, it had nothing to do with their chores, behavior, or achievements and was never withheld for any reason. They could always expect to receive their allowances. This was to teach them among other lessons the value of money, how to budget their income, and how to use it in responsible ways. It was for their use for whatever purposes they chose.

Their assigned chores and responsibilities were requirements. Failure to perform them had other consequences, but their allowances were never withheld for that reason. Any other funds they received for doing odd jobs or as gifts were also theirs to do with as they chose. However, they were always encouraged to be charitable and generous, to never spend everything they received, and to always save a part of their income for a rainy day.

To encourage them to save, Morgan and Liv opened joint bank savings accounts with each of their children, and they could deposit money into their accounts whenever they chose. To further induce their saving, their parents matched their deposits, dollar for dollar. If the deposit were $5, another $5 would be added. This prompted the kids to make frequent deposits to see their savings increase much faster. Although they could make as many deposits as they wished, they could not withdraw funds without consequences—another lesson to be learned.

The children had no real obligations that required their making payments from their own funds. They received meals and snacks at school, as did all of the students, and their parents provided for them very well. Their allowance and any other funds they received were their own disposable incomes.

To ensure that each of their children would have established credit histories, Morgan opened a few credit cards jointly with each one, as his father had done for him. He routinely made purchases with the cards every few months and paid the balances in two monthly payments. The children purposely had no awareness of the cards and, of course, had no access to use them. As they came of age, each was able to apply for a major credit card or two with no problem. By that time, they had been totally trained and competent to handle the cards responsibly.

One November Alex, Morgy, and Randy were discussing what they wanted to give their parents jointly for Christmas. Randy was easygoing and could be depended on to fall in line with whatever his big sister and brother decided. Each one wanted to give something really special and had considered several possibilities, all of them far from inexpensive for kids their ages to give their parents. Alex determined that their pooled available resources would not be enough for what they wanted.

There was money in their bank accounts, and if each of them withdrew $250 to add to the pot, they would be able to get what they wanted. In order to withdraw money from their accounts, they knew they would have to present to their parents a compelling reason for doing so. Alex, being the oldest, was to be the spokesperson for the group.

The three of them went into the den were Morgan was reviewing some proposals from the Physical Education Department, and Liv was editing a script she had recently completed.

"Excuse us, Daddy. Excuse us, Mommy." Morgan and Liv each looked up to see their three children standing together with determined looks on their faces.

"What is it, Alex?" Liv inquired.

"Morgy and Randy and I want to call a family meeting."

Morgan put his work aside, giving them his full attention.

"What is the problem? When do you want to meet?"

"We know you guys are busy, but we think it's kind of important. We want to meet now, if it's okay, please."

"Okay then. Why don't you guys take a seat. We can meet now, okay Liv?"

"No, Daddy. We want a formal meeting. We have to go to the dining room."

Surprised, Morgan raised an eyebrow and looked at Liv.

"Sure, Alex," Liv responded. "This must be important, and a formal family meeting in the dining room is the normal protocol. Let's all go there now."

With everyone seated around the dining room table, Morgan stated, "It seems to me that this is a joint issue. Who will be the mouth piece for your group?"

"Mouth piece?" Morgy questioned.

"Who will be the spokesperson who will present your case?" Morgan clarified.

"*I* will, Daddy. *I'm* the *oldest*!" Alex asserted.

"Okay, Young Lady, you have the floor. We are all ears."

"We each want to withdraw $250 from our savings accounts," she stated with determination.

"Oh, I see. That's a lot of money," Morgan expressed. "Are you sure you have enough?"

"Yes, we do," Morgy said, entering the conversation for the first time. "We each have much more than that!"

"Why do you want to withdraw so much money? Why do you need it?" Liv asked out of curiosity.

Knowing that it was to purchase a Christmas present for them and that they wanted it to be a surprise, Randy entered the conversation. "It's *our* money! Why can't we just *get* it? Why do we have to *tell* you why?" He was not trying to be sassy or disrespectful. Being younger, he was not as aware of the "rules" as his older siblings. Alex and Morgy tried to throw him cautionary looks. They *knew* the rules.

"So, your minds are made up? This is what you want to do, and you *don't* want to tell us *why* you want the money?" Morgan asked.

No one audibly answered, but Randy nodded his head in affirmation.

"Liv, what do you think about this situation?" Morgan questioned Liv.

"Randy is right, it *is* their money, after all. If they have their minds made up and are willing to accept the consequences . . ."

"Consequences?" Morgy and Randy asked in unison.

"Yes, of course there are consequences. If you have money in a *CD* and you *withdraw* it or a *part* of it before time, you have to pay an early withdrawal *penalty*. Your money is *not* in a CD, but for every dollar you withdraw, you will have to pay an equal penalty. You each want $250, so you each have to pay back the matching funds that your mom and I added to your deposits—$250 each," Morgan explained. "That means that $500 will be coming out of each of your accounts."

"Five hundred dollars!?" Little Morgan exclaimed as both he and Randy looked to Alex. Alex knew what the deal was. They had never withdrawn any money from their accounts, and she was secretly hoping her parents may have forgotten about that rule. She now knew they hadn't. She considered fleetingly that they might recant if they knew it was for presents for them, but they had wanted to surprise them. They had to rethink their position.

"Daddy, can we have a short recess so that my brothers and I can discuss this?"

"Sure, Sweetheart. We'll be right here waiting. Do what you need to do."

The three left the dining room and regrouped in the den.

"Alex, that's no fair!" Randy complained.

"I won't have much money left after $500 is taken out! What can we do?" Little Morgan asked his big sister.

"I have a plan, I think," Alex ventured. "In fact, I *do* have a plan, Plan A *and* Plan B. Listen. Here is what we can try to do," she said without much confidence in Plan A.

Alex proceeded to explain her plans to her brothers, who were listening eagerly, depending on her to have come up with the solution. When she finished explaining her plans, she asked, "What do you guys think?"

"I hope Plan A works. It will spoil our surprise, but I don't like Plan B that much at all, but it would be better than nothing," Morgan admitted. Randy just shrugged his shoulders in resignation.

"Plan B is our only hope if Plan A doesn't work. Let's just get this over with. Come on," Alex directed.

The three marched back into the dining room and took their seats. Group leader Alex presented her Plan A.

"We are hoping that if we tell you how we plan to spend the money, and you think it is for an important or good enough cause, you will waive the penalty."

Morgan and Liv looked at each other, both surprised by her use of the term, "waive;" but knowing how mature she was in many areas, they kept their poker faces. "Well, Alex," Morgan said, "you can tell us, but there are no guarantees. The penalty is there to serve an important purpose. Therefore, your reason would have to be even more important."

"We know we are the luckiest kids in the world 'cause we have the best parents in the world," Alex began. She had not initially planned to say that, but then she figured a little buttering up couldn't hurt. Morgan and Liv were not about to be buttered up into making a decision favorable to them.

"Thank you for the compliment, Honey," Liv said, "but you haven't told us what this important reason is. What is the money to be used for?"

"We didn't want to tell you because we wanted to surprise you. We wanted to put all of our money together so that we could get you and Dad a super cool Christmas present this year instead of homemade ones as usual."

"Yeah, Mom," Morgan interjected. "Don't you guys think that is a good enough reason?"

"Yeah, Mom," Randy echoed.

"Kids, nothing you could buy would be as valuable to us as something you made for us with your own hands!" Liv expressed, leaving the boom to be lowered by Morgan.

"Listen, Kids, what your mom said is true. I agree. But that is not the real issue here. If we let you withdraw $250 and *not* take back the matching funds from the account that *we* provided, it is the same as if *we* paid for half of the cost of our own presents. *We* might as well just buy them for *ourselves* and let *you* put *your* names on them. Do you think that's fair to us? When *we* give gifts to *you*, do we make *you* pay for half the cost?"

Alex remained silent. She understood what her father was saying and knew he was right. She was preparing to present her Plan B when Morgy, the lawyer/politician-in-training, tried to present his argument in favor of the waiver.

"But Dad, that is what parents are *supposed* to do. Parents are *supposed* to support their children! They are *not* supposed to make their children pay. They are *supposed* to give their children *money*. If you and mommy got a divorce, whoever doesn't get stuck with the kids has to pay money to the kids until they are grown!"

"Morg, where did you get *that* from?" Liv asked.

"You know Erice. He's in my class. His father doesn't live with his mother—just him and his sister. *He* gets money from his father every month, *sometimes*!"

"Okay, Morgy, now it is my turn to speak," Morgan declared. "I thank you for expressing it, and I appreciate your opinion. I think I can see how you might *feel* that way. However, as a future attorney, you have a little more to learn. Yes, ideally parents support their children. Many do, and some don't. And, yes, sometimes parents get divorced. I can *promise* you that will *never* happen with your *mom* and me.

"I want you to know that whoever gets 'stuck with the kids,' as you put it, is not *'stuck'* with the kids. They usually *want* the kids and often *fight* over who *gets* them. At any rate, they are called *'custodial'* parents. More and more, parents share custody of their children because children need *both* of their parents.

"And, yes, we know Erice. I don't know what he has told you, but the payments that his father makes, known as child support payments, do *not* go to *him* unless his mother gives them to him. His mother may *give* him a small portion if she chooses, but those payments are to *support* him and his sister. *He* doesn't support *himself*. His *mother* supports him and his sister. The payments are for his *benefit*, not for *him*. It is his *mother* who has to feed, and clothe, and shelter them. The payments his father makes go to *her* to help *her* do that. I hope you understand.

"Now, to get back to the subject at hand, our decision is final. If you insist on withdrawing your money, you forfeit the matching funds your mother and I have paid. The penalty will not be waived. Anything else?"

"Yes, Daddy," Alex spoke up. "I didn't think you guys would think that was an important enough reason, but I couldn't give up without at least trying, could I? And I wasn't just trying to butter you up to get you to waive the penalty. I really *did* mean what I said about having the best parents in the world. I hope you know that."

"Yes, we know, Baby Girl," Morgan said.

"But I *do* have a Plan *B*. Do you want to hear it?"

"Of course we do, Alex," Liv replied.

"We had decided that if Plan A didn't work, we will establish secondary accounts that we control that we can put money in and take money out any time we want to. We will take part of our allowances and any other money we get and put it into these accounts. *I* will be the banker. I will use three large envelopes to put our names on and to keep our money in the individual envelopes. Anytime a deposit is made or a withdrawal is taken from the envelope, a notation will be made on the outside of the envelope. There will be running totals on the outside of the envelopes so that the actuals totals on the envelopes will match the current balance inside.

"Morgy and Randy will be able to make deposits and withdrawals at any reasonable time, even weekends and holidays. Of course, our money in the bank savings accounts will not increase as much since we will be holding back a part of the money to put into our *own* savings envelopes, and we don't expect you to subsidize those amounts.

"That way, we can still get matching funds for *part* of our savings and also have access to some of our money when we want or need it. We are still saving money, Daddy."

Morgan and Liv were impressed with Alex's Plan B, taking note of her use of the term, "subsidize." They were reminded, again, how smart she was.

CHAPTER 17

THE CALAIS KIDS: THE MATURE, THE IMMATURE

Morgan and Liv were very proud of their children, and their considered method of parenting was extremely successful. They had always been affectionate with each other as well as with their children. It was not unusual for them to show their affection for each other in the presence of their children. However, they reserved their bedroom scenes for their bedroom when they were not home alone.

As it happened one Saturday afternoon in July, Morgan and Liv were alone on the patio. Liv was sitting on Morgan's lap, and they were sharing a tender moment. Liv kissed him with a little more passion than intended. Thirteen-year-old Alex, nine-year-old Morgan II, and seven-year-old Randy came out in their swimming gear ready to jump into the pool and could not help but see their parents so engaged.

"Eww! Don't you guys ever get tired of all that mushy stuff?" Morgan II asked. "I'm *never* gonna do any of that stuff!" he declared.

"Yuckee!" Randy agreed.

"Well, Son," Morgan said to him, "we'll just have to have this conversation again in several years when you are older and wiser. I suspect you will have changed your mind about that."

"No, I'll never change my mind about *that* stuff!" he said as he and his younger brother scurried off to jump into the pool.

Alex had crossed the aisle over to the adult side and was watching her brothers frolicking in the water. "Don't worry, Dad" she said. "They're just *too* young to understand. They don't *know* any better. Give them a little time. When they get about Christiaan's age, they'll see."

Liv and Morgan were somewhat surprised at her comment, and their antennae were raised at the mention of Christiaan. They knew the pair had been very good friends from the time he first came to the Center, even before Morgan and Liv had met.

"What does Christiaan know about it?" Liv asked. "Does he have any experience?"

"Mom, Christiaan is very intelligent. You *know* how he likes to do research and does experiments in many areas," Alex answered matter-of-factly as she turned and walked toward the pool with her dumbstruck parents watching her.

They sat in silence, reflecting for a few moments when Morgan voiced what they were each thinking. "Our baby girl is fast growing into a beautiful young lady. As her father, I'm thinking it will soon be time to put her under lock and key!"

"It's hard for me, too, to see her as a woman when I still see her as my baby girl, behaving as would be expected of a young teen in our family setting. We don't always see her as the matured scholar that she is, knowledgeable and wise beyond her years. I can see how as her father, you want to lock her away to protect her, but I think that may be a little extreme, don't you?"

"No, I don't. That's *my* baby girl. *Nobody* will be good enough for her. Do you think Christiaan has researched and experimented on *my* baby girl?"

"Simmer down, Over-protective Papa! Give our baby girl more credit than that! Give *Christiaan* and our *school's culture* more credit than that! Aly has a good head on her shoulders, she has high standards, and integrity beyond her years. I think we have done a great job in raising her *and* our sons. She deserves our respect and our trust. She has earned it."

They watched the kids a little longer. Shortly, Alex got out of the pool, donned her terry wrap, and returned to the table where she had left the pair and took a seat. "Mom, Dad, I think it's about time we had that talk."

"What talk is that, Alex?" Liv asked nervously.

"Let me take this conversation in another direction." Alex suggested, sounding much like her father. "We have always been able to come to you and Dad with anything, knowing that you will listen to what we have to say, whether we are on track or off track. I have to confess something about myself that I don't think you know or have realized."

"What is that, Alex, that you are growing up and are interested in boys?" Morgan reluctantly ventured.

"No, Daddy," she said, heaving a deep, patient breath at her father's obvious misunderstanding. "But I think I know why you are asking me that question. It's because of what I said about Christiaan earlier. Let me tell you how it is. I think the two of you are ready to hear what I want to tell you."

They *were* anxious to know, but *not* anxious to hear what they thought she might be about to tell them. They remained silent.

Alex continued, "You know about the left brain and the right brain that we all have, correct?" They nodded, wondering how it was related to the anticipated subject at hand. "Well, you see, probably unlike *most* people, *my* right brain and *my* left brain are each divided in half. There is the child, now the adolescent half, and there is the mature, adult half. Eventually, by my choice, when I am chronologically a full adult, I will still retain a portion of my 'child brain.'

"I try to always use my normal child portions when I am with my family and regular friends; and at school, I am usually using my mature, adult brain while I am in a learning mode. It helps keep things from getting too complicated for me, and the other kids don't think I'm weird. I also suspect it's easier for the two of you, as well. Remember when you were pregnant, Mom, and you guys told me about Randy and asked if I had any questions for you? You guys just started turning red and didn't want me to explain anything more to you."

Morgan and Liv each vividly remembered that day!

"You asked if I am interested in boys, Daddy. *Of course* I am interested in boys! What kind of pediatrician would I be if I were only interested in knowing about *girls*? Switching to my mature brain, I know what you are concerned about. Christiaan is very smart. He probably reads more prolifically than I do. We often have stimulating conversations, and we discuss many things. We have even had conversations about male-female relationships. We don't exist in a vacuum!

"We talk with our peers in both age and scholastic achievement. We have talked with students in the young teen parents program, both the teen mothers and the teen fathers. Although they are mostly, in fact, all are students who were not initially involved with the old Center, they have made some important decisions about their lives and their pre-marital sexual activity. We see the sacrifices they have had to make and know how being parents has affected their young lives.

"You know that Christiaan and I have been best friends forever. I love him just as much as I love my brothers. We are both alike. We want the same things. We accept it as a fact that one day we will get married and have a family. But we both know that there is so much more we want before that ever happens. We are both focused on our paths to achieve our goals. To remain focused requires that we eliminate and avoid distractions.

"We also want to preserve our friendship *and* our relationship. We have discovered through our research, mostly Christiaan's research, and we believe that nothing destroys a relationship like premarital sex. It can blind you to the real issues and muddle your thinking. We don't want our friendship to be jeopardized, and we don't want to have our focus taken off our goals.

"I hope I have put your minds at ease; so, if there are no more questions, I am switching back to adolescent mode and going back to have fun with my brothers! On second thought, while I am in adult mode, there is something I want to say to you, Mom."

"Do you want me to leave?" Morgan asked, not anxious to hear anything that might worry or embarrass him.

"No, Dad. You might as well hear this, too. You will probably appreciate the knowledge.

"Mom, I want to tell you how much I appreciate how you have always loved me and didn't want to hurt my feelings when I was younger. I want to let you off the hook."

"Of course, I have always loved you, Honey, just as your father has. Neither one of us would ever knowingly hurt your feelings. Just what are you referring to?"

"I'm talking about that atrocious pair of earrings that I made for you and forced you to wear in public! I didn't know how awful they were at the time, Mom. I wanted to make something for you, and I was just so proud that I had made them all by myself. You don't ever have to wear them again. In fact, you can just throw them away. I can't believe I thought they were more precious and beautiful than the Hope Diamond!"

Liv and Morgan looked at each other in silence on hearing Alex's candid confession about the earrings. It brought to their memory that dark period and the trauma associated with the events of the day Liv wore those hideous earrings. Against her will, a tear trickled down Liv's cheek.

Seeing the tear, Alex asked, "Mom, why are you crying? You don't *have* to throw them away. You can keep them if you want to."

Liv was thinking how because of those earrings they had been able to get through that horrendous ordeal with no permanent ramifications, and it was all because of Alex's earrings!

Liv embraced and kissed Alex. "Alex, I will *never* throw those earrings away! They are *more* precious, *more* beautiful, and even *more* valuable to me *and* your father than the Hope Diamond could ever be!"

"Okay, then. You don't have to throw them away," she said as she scurried off. Morgan and Liv just watched her, marveling at her maturity and her wisdom.

CHAPTER 18

CASANOVA RESURFACES

The calm, compliant exterior and the model behavior that exemplified his tenure as an inmate in the penitentiary belied the rage, hatred and anger that were consuming Tyrone "Casanova" Adams. He lived for one purpose—to exert revenge on the persons that he blamed for his sorry state of affairs.

Once the epitome of a charming, intelligent, successful Casanova, Tyrone Adams was reduced to the status of convicted felon serving out his time in prison a broken, dilapidated shell of the man he once was. Gone were his chiseled, Adonis good looks, his charisma, and charm that had been his pride and joy and had enabled him to be the 'dog' he was.

Thanks to "Ms. Liv," as he knew her, he was now impotent and legally blind. He also had her to thank for his disfigured face when her well-place, palm-butted uppercut broke his previously broken nose, rendering it irreparable. He was left with a face that would tie, if not take first place, in an ugly contest with the Medusa.

Unfortunately for him, his problems didn't end there. The final touches were added by Morgan Calais, who had arrived in the nick of time. Adam had crawled to the spot where his knife had landed after flying out of his hand when he jumped up to get into position to attack Liv when he heard Liv calling and coming to her mother's aid. Morgan pounced on him just as his hand was about to touch the knife. Morgan grabbed his arm, jerking and twisting it behind his back, unintentionally dislocating it, holding it in place with his knee as he delivered a debilitating blow to Tyrone's right ear.

Tyrone did not credit Liv for probably saving his life by imploring her husband not to deliver the next blow, which he was poised to do, deliberately aiming for his temple. Morgan was outraged that this man had dared to put his hands on his wife and his mother. Morgan's history as a champion of the underdog and the helpless included coming to the aid of a total stranger and rendering the attacker neutralized. How much more fury would he wield against someone doing harm to his wife and his mother!

Tyrone had years to stew over his losses which he directly attributed to Ms. Liv. In addition, the list included the loss of the effectual use of his right arm, the loss of his slave/wife and children, a major part of his income in child support, and the thousands of dollars Ms. Liv had charged to his accounts (with his consent). The most difficult for him to swallow were the facts that she had destroyed his most valued asset, his looks, and had delivered a deadly blow to his pride.

He believed his physical appearance was his most important asset as it accounted for his successes in his profession as a free-lance public relations specialist, which greatly facilitated his lifestyle as a womanizer. He had been paid handsomely for wining, dining and entertaining his clients' prospects and was quite the social monarch. It was in this role that he chanced upon dropping into a new hot spot known as Liv's Supper Club and Lounge in Brentwood, California.

From the moment he laid eyes on the proprietor, Ms. Liv, Tyrone was on a quest to add a notch to his belt in her honor. He chose Liv's place to bring his wife, Diane, and another couple to celebrate their ninth wedding anniversary in a random act of humanity toward her. Even so, he couldn't hide, nor did he even attempt to conceal his obvious interest in Ms. Liv. His many subsequent visits to the club were sans his wife.

It was neither his choice, nor was it his desire to be married, especially to Diane. She was no beauty queen, though she was not unattractive. Arrogant Tyrone had considered her a charity case when they were in college, as well as a convenient release when he had a lag in his schedule of "extra-curricular" activities. She also came in handy when he was in a bind with his schoolwork or was in danger of flunking out. In other words, he used her. Diane had been flattered by the attention this marvelous specimen of a man paid to her, and she saw being used as an acceptable alternative to being ignored.

Tyrone had only himself to blame for his shotgun wedding. He was the one who failed to put a cap on it. Being married did not prompt him to make any changes or adjustments in his lifestyle. His womanizing continued unimpeded.

Diane had dropped out of school, which was fine with Tyrone. He wanted her home where he could control her by keeping her barefoot and pregnant. In short order she was strapped with five kids all under the age of eight. He had quickly turned the situation into one that suited him. He had someone to dutifully do his cooking, laundry, housekeeping, and errands while being available to "service" him when he desired. He could also boast of his manhood as evidenced by his offspring. His domestic life was completely under his control.

The blow to Tyrone's pride was occasioned by his thorough humiliation and undoing at the hands of Ms. Liv. He had a healthy amount of intelligence, albeit not guided by wisdom. He considered women to be intellectually inferior, especially the beautiful ones that he saw as bimbos, to be used at his whim.

To have been so easily "used" by Ms. Liv in her grand scheme to teach him a lesson was hard for him to swallow. He may have been able to get passed it had it not resulted ultimately in Diane's gaining the courage to divorce him and take the kids and a large slice of his income. His attempt to even the score resulted in his total beat down by Ms. Liv as well as her husband and landed him in prison a disfigured, impotent convicted felon.

Nine years earlier, while Casanova Adam was still laid up due to his injuries, he was counseled by his attorney to decline the plea bargain deal that had been offered. His attorney felt that to see him in his current state, jurors may not be prompted to determine him to be a future viable threat to anyone in light of his many physical impairments. He was a pitiable sight, to be sure.

The prosecution had entertained the idea that he might receive a certain amount of pity from the jurors despite his actions that were clearly documented in the surveillance video. They didn't want to take that chance.

Tyrone was eager to accept the deal because it suited his ambitious plans for getting revenge on Ms. Liv and her husband. Were he to be tried and convicted of the myriad of serious felony charges he could have faced, he was certainly looking at 25 to life, more than likely without the possibility of parole. He had to be on the outside if he were to be successful.

With the beginning of his plans in effect, he now had a number of years to mastermind his take-no-prisoners scheme to the last, most minute detail. He was determined to be a model prisoner in every respect. He played his "handicapped" role to the hilt, which made his tenure behind bars more tolerable than most would have found it. It even worked for him in obtaining a "hands-off" status as he struck up relationships with a few of the hard-core inmates, a necessary component of his plans. After all, he knew he would need other eyes and able bodies to carry them out.

Tyrone was not idly passing the time in prison. He was busy keeping up with the events in the lives of his nemeses. He carefully followed Liv's career as she began releasing recordings and writing screenplays, even her acting career. He also followed Morgan's career—his published books and writings, speaking tours, news releases, and especially the progress and explosive expansion of the Calais Education and Community Centers of America, of which Morgan was President.

Thanks to his exemplary behavior and the overcrowded prison conditions, his release on parole was granted five months after he had served almost eight years.

Tyrone sought out and developed a relationship with the resident hacker, a computer genius by the name of Frederick Underwood, whose prison handle was "Hack." Frederick was a technology mastermind with an affinity for hacking, which greatly facilitated his propensity for orchestrating great heists with hired thugs to do the dirty work. He was not averse to physically getting his hands dirty on occasion.

During the four years they had served together, Tyrone had been able to appeal to Hack's intrinsic cravings for hacking challenges and opportunities to utilize his skills for insane profits to enlist his help. Dangling the carrot of a substantial monetary return for his efforts, Tyrone easily secured Hack's agreement to do part of the job he was planning. Just prior to his parole, Tyrone supplied him with the vital information he would need and assured him of a substantial return for his efforts. Frederick was the pivotal figure in the grand scheme devised by Tyrone.

Once paroled, Frederick went about his tasks, mainly hacking into accounts of the CECCA, and was thoroughly hooked when he was able to determine the massive sums that appeared to be up for grabs, his for the hacking.

For reasons that he was unable to determine, Frederick reached a point where he was prevented from going further despite all of his technological genius. He was even blocked from duplicating the success he had been able to achieve initially. He was, however, able to infiltrate some smaller targets, but he had to report to Casanova that he was hopelessly at a total impasse.

Tyrone did not receive the news well, but he was not deterred. He did have a backup plan and issued alternate instructions for its implementation. Admittedly, the backup plan would not be as lucrative, but the gains would still be substantial, and Tyrone could still achieve *his* main goal—revenge against Morgan and Liv. The alternate plan required other players—two fellow inmates scheduled to be released before him.

One, Bobby "The Butcher" Taggert, was a burly ruffian whose latest cause for incarceration was aggravated assault and battery, to which he plea bargained to simple assault. Truth be told, he was guilty of far more serious felonies, including a few homicides for which authorities had been unable to prosecute him due to disappearing potential witnesses and lack of viable evidence. Needless to say, he had the respect, not only of all of the inmates, but also many of the guards.

The other inmate was Marty "The Moron" Jankin. As his nickname implied, he did not have a lot going for him in the brains department. It could be said of him that his incarceration was for gross stupidity. Though a fright to see, Marty was more like an idiot in a hideous giant's body and could be bribed with little of nothing to do whatever he was told. He was the perfect flunky for "The Butcher," who led him around as if he had a ring through his nose.

As the time drew near for Bobby's release, Tyrone began prepping him for the job ahead. The first thing he had to do was to recruit his former charge, a young former inmate by the name of Victor Sterling. He delivered the clear message to Vic in no uncertain terms that it was now payback time for the protection he had enjoyed while in prison. The dire consequences for *not* complying were also made abundantly clear.

Vic was given limited information about what was planned and what he would be required to do. He had only to wait for further instructions, most of which he would receive two or three weeks before the job was to take place. Final detailed instructions were to be provided a few days before the event was to go down.

CHAPTER 19

VICTOR'S APPEAL

Kyle had just finished a lengthy conversation with a friend and was preparing to leave for an errand when his cell phone vibrated. He started to ignore it when he saw it was from an unknown caller, and he did not recognize the number. He thought about it a second and was prompted to answer.

"Who's calling?" he asked. When there was no immediate response, he was about to disconnect when he heard his name.

"Kyle?" the voice responded timidly.

"Yes, this is Kyle," he answered. "Who is this?"

"Kyle, it's me, Vic."

"Victor?"

"Yes, Cuz," Vic replied hesitantly.

"Where are you? You are obviously not in jail. I hope that you are keeping your nose clean if you're out on parole."

"No, I'm not on parole. I have served all of my time. It wasn't as long as it could have been, though."

"Are you okay? Do you need anything? You are sounding a little stressed. What's up with that?"

There was a moment of hesitation before Vic spoke.

"Kyle, I've been trying to keep my nose clean, to stay out of trouble—and jail. But . . . I'm in trouble now, but it's not like you think, Kyle. My life is in danger! I'm in a situation that I don't know how to get out of. Kyle, I need your help!"

"What kind of help? Have you committed a crime? I hope you haven't, 'cause I probably won't be able to help you. You know I am in law enforcement."

"I know, Kyle. That's part of the reasons I called you. I haven't committed any crime . . . yet."

"Okay, Vic. What do you mean, 'yet?' "

"Kyle, it's complicated, but you've got to help me. It involves someone you know. That's the other reason."

"What do you mean? Who?"

"Kyle, can we meet somewhere? I don't want to talk about this over the phone. I need to be face-to-face with you. *Please*, Kyle! It is *really* urgent! It's a matter of life or death!" Vic was close to tears, and Kyle sensed the urgency, especially since he knew it involved someone he knew, possibly a friend.

"All right, Vic. Where are you now?"

"I am right down the street from you. I was hoping that you would agree and that I could see you now. That's why I'm so close. I can be there in a few minutes, if it's okay."

"Okay, Vic. Come on."

Five minutes later Vic was at Kyle's door. It had been 18 months since the cousins had seen each other, and Kyle was glad to see him, even though it was under dubious circumstances. Kyle was four years older than his cousin. Growing up as the only son among three sisters, Kyle had always looked upon Vic as the brother he wished he had in place of at least *one* of his sisters.

The cousins were very close growing up, and Kyle looked out for Vic, trying to set a good example and keeping him on the straight and narrow. He had been very hurt to learn that Vic had been in the system as a juvenile offender. When Vic's parents divorced, his mother moved away with him out of state. Thus began his life of petty crimes as he acted out in response to his parents' circumstances.

After his release, the two did enjoy a few years of good relations as cousins before his incarceration as an adult. This was to be their first meeting since.

Kyle greeted his cousin with a fist bump and a cautious hug and invited him into the den. He had set out a couple of cold beers in anticipation and offered one to Vic.

"Well, Vic, it's good to see you. It's been a while. You are looking none the worse for the wear. So tell me, what is this all about?"

"Kyle, I don't know how well you can imagine what it is like to be incarcerated, for *any* length of time, never having been there yourself." Vic sat on the couch shaking his head. He took a sip from the beer Kyle had given him. Kyle just waited for him to speak.

"I have to tell you, Cuz. It's really rough, especially if you are considered 'fresh, new meat' and the cons are fighting over who gets you!"

The unpleasant memories resurfacing were mirrored on his face.

"Victor, I am sorry. I have an idea, and it hurt me to know that you were there. But what is this 'life or death' situation?"

"Well, like I said, it was rough, but I got lucky. The con who 'won' me was the biggest, baddest, meanest con of them all. He didn't *have* to fight. *No* one would go up against him. Whatever he wanted, he got! His name is Bobby Taggert. He was known as 'Bobby the Butcher,' or 'The Butcher,' for short.

"For some reason, he took a liking to me. He took care of me. He didn't hassle me, and he didn't let anyone else, either. He claimed that I reminded him of his little brother. The only thing, though, he said that in return for his protection, I would be in his debt on the outside. All things considered, he knew *I* would be out long before *he* would. I figured it was better for me to agree since I was there. I thought I'd let the future take care of itself. Well, the future is here, and I'm dangling by a hair."

"All right, what is the problem now? Is he out?"

"Yes. It's been just about a week now. He had already let me know what I would have to do and what would happen to me if I didn't. It's worse than being between a rock and a hard place. It's more like being between two flat stones that are closing in fast with increasing pressure!"

"What does he want you to do?"

"He wants me to participate in a kidnapping for ransom! I have to be honest with you. I *don't* want to get involved in crime again. I have been doing well so far. I *like* my freedom. I even have a girlfriend, Ohlisa, who I want to marry someday. If I *don't* do this, I'm dead; so it wouldn't matter. That's why I feel I have to go through with it. I'm not ready to die! The only thing that makes me want *not* to do it is *you*, Kyle. I don't want to hurt *you*! I'd *risk* dying for you. I *love* you, Cousin. You were always there for me. We're family, Man!"

"Vic! Get to the point! What role do *I* have to play in all this?"

It's not about *you*, Kyle. It's your best friend, *Morgan*."

"Morgan? They want to kidnap *Morgan*?"

"No, not *Morgan* . . . his *kids*—at least his two sons."

Kyle was stunned into silence. This was just too incredible to imagine. Kyle knew how much Morgan loved his family and the extremes to which he would go to protect any one of his family members, both immediate and extended. He knew he had to do something, the least of which would be to notify Morgan ASAP.

During Kyle's silence, Vic continued. "They promised me enough money to keep me comfortable for the rest of my life! Even so, I don't *want* to do it. That's why I've come to *you* to see if there is any way you can help me *out* of this."

Vic continued to silently beseech Kyle's help while waiting for his response. Kyle's mind was racing a mile a minute. Finally, he responded, "Listen, Vic, this *is* a dangerous situation. I'm stepping out on a limb by faith, but I will help you. When will you have all of the information you will need to do what you are being forced to do?"

"I'm supposed to meet with all of the players, at least *most* of them, tomorrow evening. I'm supposed to get all the information I will need. What should I do?"

Kyle reflected for a moment before speaking. "Go to the meeting and get all of the information possible, and then come back here to me about 10 p.m. Victor, I'm glad you came to me with this. Thank you, Cousin."

"Thank *you*, Kyle. I owe you my *life*."

The cousins embraced and Vic departed.

Kyle wasted no time in contacting Morgan.

"Hello," Morgan answered without waiting for the caller ID to engage.

"Morgan, this is Kyle, and . . ."

"What?" Morgan interrupted, "No 'How's my white brother from another mother?' " Morgan playfully chided his best friend.

"Morgan, this is *serious*. I need to see you right away!"

"Okay, Kyle, has Liv put you up to something? I know how she gets sometimes!"

"Morgan, please, Man!"

Morgan picked up on Kyle's urgency. "What is it Kyle? What's the concern?"

"I can't talk about it on the phone. Can you come over immediately? You know I wouldn't interrupt your family time unless it was extremely urgent. I don't want to go all dramatic on you and say it is a matter of life or death, Morgan, but it *could* easily come to that!"

"Okay, Kyle, let me say 'goodbye' to the family, and I'll be right there.

Just then, Randy came running in. "Daddy, Daddy, hurry! It's *your* turn!"

"Okay, Randy Pandy. I'm coming."

Morgan returned to the family game and took one last turn. "Okay, guys, you will have to finish this game without me. Sorry! I'll make it up to you, I promise. You'll probably be in bed when I get back, so give me your goodnight hugs and kisses now, before I leave. Mommy will listen to your prayers."

Liv watched with concern as each one hugged and kissed their father goodnight. She knew that Morgan would not lightly forgo their family time. She patiently waited until the last hug.

"Is everything all right, Morgan?" she questioned, trying not to sound anxious.

"Probably, Sweetheart. Kyle is having a problem and asked me to help him out. He knows it is our family time and hated to interrupt. He wouldn't do that unless it were urgent."

"What can *I* do?"

"Just stay here with the kids, keep the home fires burning, and be ready when I get back, my Shulamite woman!" he said, giving Liv "the look" and a wink.

Liv blushed, and Little Morgan asked his dad, "What's a Shulamite woman?"

Morgan subtly gave his wife a sensual kiss, in the way that only he could do, and said to his son, "Ask your mother—after I'm gone."

"Chicken!" Liv called out to his back as he headed for the door.

Morgan arrived at Kyle's condo a little over a half-hour later to find Kyle anxiously waiting. "What's up, My Brother?" Morgan asked as they fist-bumped and then hugged.

"Morgan, thanks for getting here so quickly. Come on in and sit down."

Morgan followed him into the den and they sat facing each other. "I'm sorry to be so dramatic, Morgan, but your family is in real danger! We've got to do something to . . ."

"What are you talking about, Kyle?' Morgan immediately shifted into protection mode. Who is threatening my family? Why? How?" he demanded.

"I'll tell you what I know right now, but it's not much. Hopefully, we will have many more details tomorrow night.

"You may not remember my cousin, Vic."

"The one who used to tag along with you sometimes until he was about fourteen or so?" Kyle nodded. "Yes, I remember him. I think he came to our wedding, didn't he?"

"Yes, he did; but he soon went back to prison for some time. He has been out a little while and is trying very hard to keep on the right path this time."

"Well, I'm glad for him, but what does he have to do with my family?"

Kyle proceeded to relate to Morgan the substance of his dialogue with Vic earlier. "Morgan, I know how these things can go sometimes, and I know that with you involved, we will get much further. I'm depending on you to be your usual calm, matter-of-fact self and just deal with whatever we find we are up against.

"I have a couple of general ideas, but we can't decide on any particular course of action until we know exactly, and hopefully, *who* we are up against. I haven't contacted anyone in the Department yet. There is time for that, I believe. I also have other resources, if need be."

All the while, Morgan had been calmly listening to Kyle's discourse while actively evaluating his options. He had decided to involve his father-in-law, Walter, first of all.

"Morgan, *you* now know everything *I* know. Can you be here tomorrow evening when Vic comes?"

"You can bet on it, Kyle. I'd better get going. And Kyle, I don't want Liv to know anything about this, at least until we know the threat is over. I don't want her to be worried about anything."

"Sure, Morgan. No problem. I will see you tomorrow evening."

(Meeting with Walter) Morgan sat a moment in his car before dialing Walter's cell. He knew Walter would be working on an important presentation to a group of potential benefactors on behalf of the Advisory Committee for the Calais Education and Community Centers as its Chairman. He regretted having to interrupt him, but he knew Walter would want to be involved and would be very displeased to learn about it after the fact.

"Hi, Son," Walter answered immediately. I was just about to turn off my phone. I'm almost finished with my presentation, but I am about to put together a key component and need to eliminate any distractions. Is everything okay at home? Everything fine?"

"Hi, Pops. Sorry to interrupt, but I knew you would want me to. No, everything is *not* fine."

Walter immediately put down his pen and took off his glasses. Morgan had his full, undivided attention. "What's the problem, Morgan?"

"Dad, our family is in impending danger! We need to talk immediately. Will you meet me at Liv's? I'm on my way there and should be there by the time you get there if you can leave now."

"I'm on my way, Morgan!" Walter went to the large safe behind the facade wall in his office and retrieved a package. Placing it beside the front door, he went to find his wife, Lydia, to let her know that he had to go to take care of some business.

Lydia was relaxing with a book on the chaise lounge in their bedroom. "I don't know exactly how long this may take, so you don't have to wait up for me. If you're sleep when I return, I'll wake you, if you want me to, Honey."

"Okay, that will be fine. See you later, Walter."

Walter kissed his wife and departed with the package he had left by the door. Once in his car, he made a phone call before heading to the Club.

CHAPTER 20

MEETING AT LIV'S SUPPER CLUB AND LOUNGE

Morgan had been waiting about ten minutes before Walter arrived and came into the main dining room. Morgan stood to greet his father-in-law and could discern his calm anxiety.

"Pops, perhaps we should go to one of the side rooms where we can have more privacy," Morgan suggested.

"Yes, I agree." To the server who had just walked up Walter said, "Zoe, we will just be having coffee in the smaller overflow room, please. I am expecting a gentleman to join us. Please direct him to us when he gets here."

"No problem, Mr. La Salle. Coffee coming right up."

The two men walked the relatively short distance to their chosen designation and sat in one of the out-of-the-way, four-person booths. Morgan noticed and was curious about the package Walter was carrying, but he did not inquire about it.

"Son, I have been needing to have a certain conversation with you, but circumstances were not quite where they needed to be. Now, however, I no longer have the luxury of time. We have a problem."

"We have a problem? You mean besides the one I called you about?"

"Yes. I suspect they could be related. I don't know. I have called

Anthony Davenport and asked him to come here with his files. You know he is now the Director of Security. He should be here shortly. In the meantime, tell me about this threat against our family."

"There's not that much I can tell you except that I know the situation is serious as well as imminent."

Just then Anthony joined them, followed immediately by Zoe with a third cup of coffee.

"Thank you," Anthony said to Zoe. "Morgan, how are you? Good to see you."

"I'm doing well considering," Morgan replied as they shook hands. "Walter, what is this about, and why do you think it may be related?"

"Morgan, we were not quite ready to bring you in on what has been going on because we didn't want you to be distracted by it."

"We?" Morgan interjected.

"The Advisory Committee, along with Security. You have not had to be concerned about the workings of the Organization's finances or detailed workings of many matters concerning operations, and rightly so. Everything has been working as it should. Our technicians and security personnel are the best possible. Our operations are more secure than the government's at all levels, even the military. We have *never* been compromised.

"In that our tech people are the absolute best and are always sprucing up controls and keeping several steps ahead of the most proficient hackers in the world, they have always been able to detect and thwart all attempts to hack into our most secured accounts. Someone was able to get as far as to be able to 'look' at some financial accounts and determine the where and the extent of some resources before the in-place checks were automatically initiated. They were never able to do anything but look.

"As soon as the alert was triggered, tech staff was able to neutralize and eliminate the threat by immediately initiating a fix which would not only disable the hack, but would also prevent its successful duplication. The hacker was not able to go further and could no longer even see what had been visible to that point. Anthony can shed more light on it for you, Morgan."

"Yes, Morgan. We figured since this hacker was able to get as far as he did, he could possibly keep trying and get closer. He, or she, is obviously very skilled, and we are interested in finding out who and where he or she is. We are in the process of backtracking using devices and protocols we have developed that have proven very successful in the past at identifying those who have made previous hacking attempts."

"Have you been able to identify this person?" Morgan asked.

"No, not yet, but we are very close. The process is in the works, but it takes a little time. We have been able to trace back far enough to know the general vicinity, somewhere in the southwest. It's pointing to here in Southern California. We expect to have the exact location and possibly identify the source in less than 24 hours.

"Walter, I was prepared to share this information with you when we met last week," Anthony said, "but in the process of dealing with this situation, we discovered that some unsuccessful attempts had been made to breach some of our principals' accounts at the Center. Consequently, we examined all of the computers in our systems.

"We suspected that attempts may have been made to breach the personal computers of the officers and some of the other higher-level administrators. Of all the ones we have checked, we only found a problem with Elizabeth's and Holly's computers, which we have neutralized. We determined they were only able to see innocuous personal e-mails. We believe your and Olivia's personal computers may also be involved, especially yours, Morgan. We would like your permission to examine your personal computers immediately, especially now that I understand there seems to be some sort of threat directed at you and/or your family."

"Of course, Anthony. You have my permission to do whatever you must do."

"Thanks, Morgan. The invasions to the computers were virtually undetectable under normal circumstances, and there would have been no way to know without employing the protocol established by our experts."

Walter continued, "We took a much more aggressive and proactive approach to protecting our assets, which includes our principals' assets, when Frank and I delved into the situation you presented to us regarding that music teacher a while back. At that time, we had considered extortion or blackmail, which wasn't the case; but as a result, we determined that it would behoove us to rethink our security strategies, safeguards and protocols, particularly for our principals, which we have done.

"Morgan," Walter said changing gears, "before we go further, tell us about this immediate threat to our family. You know how important you and Liv are to the organization, not to mention how important you are to *me* and *Lydia*. As you may be able to imagine, anything that affects the two of you personally could easily be linked to the organization."

Morgan then shared all the information he had obtained from Kyle, which, so far, wasn't that much. "I would like for you to be there with me at Kyle's house tomorrow evening when we will be able to get all available details.

"I will text Kyles address to both of you. Well, I supposed there is nothing more we can do here tonight. I'm sure Liv is waiting up for me. I know she was worried about why I had to leave, but I know she was trying not to show it. I don't want her to know about this, at least not at this time."

"I've got the home fires burning, too," Walter said, "and I agree that neither of our girls need to be worried about this, Morgan. I will see both of you tomorrow night."

(Informational meeting at Kyle's) Morgan arrived at Kyle's home about 9 p.m. to wait for the others to arrive, especially Victor, who was the key figure. Walter arrived with Anthony about 9:30.

"Walter, good to see you. Come in," Kyle greeted them.

"Hello, Kyle. This is Anthony Davenport, head of our security team. I see Morgan is already here. We're expecting one other person, who should be here shortly."

"Yes, Morgan is here. Mr. Davenport . . ."

"Please call me Anthony"

"Anthony, it is nice to meet you," Kyle said, directing them to the den where Morgan was deep in his own thoughts of possible plans. The one thing certain in his mind was that he did not want Liv to be worried prematurely about anything. "I have coffee all ready, unless you would like something else."

"Nothing for me right now, thank you. Maybe later," Anthony said.

"I'll have coffee, Kyle. Thanks," Walter indicated.

Kyle left to get the coffee while the others were exchanging greetings and getting settled.

The mood was understandably pensive and somber. Each one had been privately entertaining possible scenarios, preparing to share them, if appropriate, when the time came. It was impossible to do anything more than that until all of the facts were known. That could not happen without information from Vic.

Morgan noted that Walter was carrying the package that he had brought to Liv's the night before and inquired, "Walter, what is it that you have there? I noticed you had it last night, too."

"Yes, I did. I want to hold off on this for the time being. I have asked Frank Bynum to come tonight. Hopefully, he will be here any minute with information for us."

Kyle was just returning to the den with a cart containing chilled bottled water, coffee cups, and a carafe of coffee when the doorbell rang. "That might be Frank now," Walter added.

Kyle parked the cart and went to answer the door. "Hi, Frank. Come in. Haven't seen you for a minute. Everyone is in the den."

Frank followed Kyle into the den with a good-sized file folder under his arm. After the exchange of pleasantries, Walter was anxious to get down to business without delay. "Frank, I hope that file you're carrying has some answers for us."

"As a matter of fact, yes, it does, Frank affirmed. "We pinpointed the hacker source to an address in Torrance belonging to an individual by the name of Frederick Underwood. He has a prolific history which includes some pretty elaborate heists, the latest of which was about ten years ago. He was incarcerated, which may account for his inactivity, until he made the mistake of messing with us!"

Anthony added, "We had decided we would not take any action just yet, other than what we did in blocking and neutralizing his attempts, until we get to the bottom of this threat. At the appropriate time, we will deliver him to the police."

The doorbell rang about 9:55. Kyle opened the door to an even more shaken Victor. "Vic, Cousin, you don't look so well! Come in," Kyle said, giving his cousin a hug. "Are you all right?"

"I don't know, Man. I just don't know," Vic said, shaking his head.

"Well, come on into the den. There are some people you need to meet."

Vic followed him into the den with the bag he was carrying. Right away, he recognized Morgan. For no obvious reason, he had not expected to see Morgan there, and it caused him to feel very ill at ease, as if perhaps Morgan were blaming him and might be upset with him. Kyle proceeded to make the introductions. "You remember Morgan, I know."

"Yes, I do," he said cautiously, unsure of Morgan's reception.

"Of course you do!" Morgan said, ignoring the hand Vic extended for a handshake and holding out his arms for a hug. "A handshake is no proper greeting for old childhood chums. You look like you need a hug, anyway."

To Vic's relief, Morgan gave him a friendly hug. He was introduced to the other three men, and they all sat down to get to the business at hand. Kyle took the lead. He had earlier invited everyone to avail themselves of the notepads and pens he had provided, which they had used to make notes of their own while waiting for Victor. With pads and pens at the ready, everyone was poised to take notes.

"Okay, Vic, the floor is all yours. What do you have for us?" Kyle prompted.

Vic produced the notes he had taken during his meeting earlier. "I'm a little nervous . . . a *lot* nervous, so if I become incoherent, or leave out something important, I can respond to questions. In fact, it might be better if you ask *me* questions first, and I can fill in anything I remember that you didn't ask me about."

Frank spoke up, "That is a reasonable option. If everyone is in agreement, I would like to do the interrogation." As a well-established, successful private investigator, he was certainly the most qualified.

"I don't think anyone would object to your doing what you probably do better than any of us, Frank," Walter offered with no dissenting sentiments.

Frank began, "First of all, just who is to be kidnapped, and when?"

Vic looked nervously at Morgan and answered, "Morgan's two sons."

This was no surprise to anyone but Frank, whose professionalism kept him from reacting. He prompted Vic to continue, "And when is this kidnapping to take place?"

"As I just found out, it is scheduled for this coming Saturday at the theme park where the kids are supposed to be." It *was* a surprise to everyone that it was to take place so soon. That fact greatly increased the urgency of their need to act quickly in putting a plan into place. Vic offered a possible solution, "Why don't you just cancel the outing?"

Anthony suggested, "That is a possibility that could buy us more time to . . ."

Morgan immediately interrupted him with, "No! That would only give them an opportunity to come up with another plan, if they don't already have a backup, that we would have no idea about when, where, or how, without possibly going through this setup again with no guarantees. No, that is not an option I will agree with.

"Excuse me, Frank, for injecting myself into your lead in the questioning. I want Vic to tell us *exactly* what he knows, particularly about who is behind this. Who are the players, Vic, and how did they know my family planned to be there this Saturday?"

Because Morgan had retained his calm demeanor despite the circumstances, Vic was not intimidated and responded fully. "The only ones I know personally, who were in prison when I was there, is Bobby Taggert, the one who is calling in his markers on me; Marty Jankin, who was known in prison as "The Moron" because he's missing a lot of screws; and the one I understand is calling the shots, who wasn't there, by the way, is this guy named Tyrone Adams.

"The other person who was at the meeting that I *didn't* know was a guy they just called 'Fred.' I don't know his last name, but he is the one who got all of the information about the family's plans. I think he hacked into some e-mail accounts of several people who were planning the outing."

"Vic, thank you. That information is very telling and gives us even more information than you know," Morgan assured him.

"Yes, Victor. We know who this 'Fred' is. His name is Frederic Underwood, and we know of his shenanigans. We will definitely be able to tie him in on this attempted kidnapping and conspiracy. His days are numbered," Frank declared.

Morgan was not quite through with his interrogation of Vic. He wanted more specifics, if Vic had been privy to more details. "As far as you know, Vic, how do they plan to communicate their demands? How much are they asking? What is the time frame? Anything you can add will be very helpful. Most importantly, Vic, will the boys be safe? If they plan to harm them in any way, we will have to really rethink this whole situation."

"I don't *have* too many specifics. I believe the ransom is to be wired into a certain secure account outside the country. Fred will send a text message to your phone, Morgan, with instructions.

"Fred seemed to have some kind of scruples. He was insisting that the boys not be harmed, that they be released unharmed, or at least left where they would be okay until they are found after the transfer is complete and verified. I don't know how they planned to make contact with you to deliver the boys' location to you, probably by text message as well. I'm sorry, Morgan. I wish I could be of more help."

"Vic, can you tell us what *your* role is to be and give us as many of the details as you can?" Morgan asked.

"They showed me pictures of your wife and kids as well as some of your wife's friends and their kids so that I would be able to recognize them. I remembered Liv from your wedding. They were able to find out from the e-mails when and where they are supposed to meet—by the entrance to Kiddyland at 9:30. I am supposed to be at that location by 9 a.m. to identify and keep an eye on them until the boys are taken. I am mainly supposed to follow and keep the two boys in sight and to be on hand to help when Bobby and/or Marty grab them.

"They gave me this uniform to wear, that has a badge and everything," he said, referring to the bag he had placed on the floor beside him.

"They will have a navy blue van with handicapped license plates that will be parked in the handicapped parking area. They gave me a handicapped placard to use so that I would be able to park there, too, and hook up with them. There is to be another person who will be driving the van, and Bobby and Marty will be inside the rear of the van. I don't know who they recruited to be the driver, and I don't know what other role he will have. Once I know where they will be parked, I am to make my way back to Kiddyland. As far as I know, that is all they want me to do."

Frank asked, "Do you know where they plan to take them once they have them? Did they tell you that?"

"No, they didn't tell me. I don't know. Bobby said that once I did my part, I could go, and he would make sure that I got my cut of the ransom money. You guys, I don't want any *part* of this. I don't want to *do* this. Morgan, please believe me! I just want this to be *over*!"

"I believe you, Vic, and I truly thank you for coming out with this information. I'm not sure *how* just yet, but we *will* resolve this!" Morgan assured him.

CHAPTER 21

THE PLAN IS FORGED

Immediately recognizing the name of the instigator as the one who assaulted his wife just before they were married, Walter was experiencing a resurgence of his anger. Nevertheless, he knew he and Morgan had a job to do to protect their family as well as CECCA's interests. He remained on point. "Morgan, now we know for certain that this threat to our family is related, intrinsically related, to the situation with the hacking of our organization's accounts and computers. We will have to temporarily put that situation on the back burner for now and deal with our immediate situation."

"Don't worry, Cuz. Between all of us, we will come up with a plan. I think I have the beginnings of a plan right now. Let me take a look at that uniform you have."

Vic handed his cousin the bag, and Kyle removed the tan security guard uniform with the name of the theme park and a badge with Victor's picture on it. Holding the uniform up to himself, Kyle remarked, "Yes, I think I can fit this pretty well. Can you guys see where I'm going with this?"

"I'm on the same page with you, Bro." Morgan said as his countenance brighten with hope. "You will take Vic's place! We will have to come up with a good reason why Vic *can't* make it. There is a family resemblance. You do *favor*, but *they* will know you're not Vic."

"I may be a little thicker than Cousin Vic, but I'm just as handsome!

"Hey, I think I've got it," Kyle continued excitedly. "I think I know how we can get Victor out of the picture without getting him in trouble with Bobby, but we have to wait until the last minute to let them know he had to get a substitute. They will have everything in place and won't want to, or be able to change their plans at the drop of a hat.

"Vic, you are going to have your appendix removed Friday morning!"

"I am?" Victor asked, surprised.

"Yes! You are going to call Bobby from the hospital and let him know of your predicament. You will assure him that you have a trustworthy replacement, your cousin! Your cousin is out on parole and is the same size as you. He is more than qualified and has agreed to do the job in your place for a cut of the action!"

"Kyle, that's a brilliant idea!" Morgan exclaimed. "Have you been taking lessons from Liv?"

Kyle had to laugh, understanding Morgan's reference to his wife. "Do you know a better teacher?" he replied. Walter as well got the reference, but he was anxious to get things back on track.

"Yes, Kyle, I think you have come up with a great idea," Walter injected. I think we need to help Victor convincingly pull it off by scripting his conversation and giving him an opportunity to rehearse it."

"I agree," Anthony added.

Victor, despite his reservations that he could successfully pull something off like that, was visibly relieved. "Hey, I'll do *anything* I have to do. You guys, I can't tell you how much I appreciate what you are trying to do for me."

"Vic," Morgan immediately offered, "I appreciate *you* for making this plot known to us. We all have great stakes in doing what we have to do. I, for one, am happy that we are able to help you in the process."

"Now that we have a good picture of what we're up against," Anthony continued," we now need to put our own plan together. Since we don't know where they intend to take the boys, we have to be able to track them. I see two possibilities, both of which can be implemented for a double shot. Walter, I think it is time to brief Morgan and the others on what we have been planning. You have your package; I think it's time to bring it out."

Morgan's curiosity was revived as Walter reached for his package. "Morgan," he began, "Security and the Committee have been concerned about the safety of our principals and the possibility of situations such as this, though we had no idea this would arrive on the horizon so soon. At any rate, we had begun taking steps for such an eventuality. Personnel have developed, for lack of a better description, a tracking system for our principals and their family members. This seems to be an optimal time to put these tools into effect.

"Of course, we understand the implications of being in the position of having one's location tracked, thus our reticence. You would have to be in complete agreement, as well as Liv, and you would have full disclosure as to when and how this surveillance would be utilized, who would be able to have eyes on you, etc. This would be true for all of our principals. This is the exact time we need to be able to track the boys to insure that we know where they are taken."

"Exactly what is this, Walter?" Morgan asked his father-in-law. "Is it something that we can have control over when it is activated or active?"

"Let me explain how it works, at least at this stage and with the devices we are prepared to give you," Anthony volunteered. "I think the very first thing is to provide Kyle with a tracking device that he can place on the van itself when he meets with them in the parking area at the theme park. Agreed?"

Everyone expressed agreement. "Okay. Kyle, we will provide the device to you. For your family, Morgan, you can use them on rings, or pendants, or other ways."

Walter removed from the parcel the package with Morgan's name marked on the outside and handed it to him. "They can appear to be innocuous, inexpensive pieces of jewelry," Anthony continued. With a chuckle, he added, "I have to admit some of our people are avid fans of certain espionage movies and borrowed some of their ideas, but this is the real deal, no theatrics whatsoever. For right now, I propose for the boys, for *all* of the children, that the devices be worn as pendants around their necks, under their clothing. Theirs will be continuously activated so that they won't have to press anything or take any kind of action to activate them.

"For you and your wife, they can be worn on rings or pendants, and you can activate or deactivate them as you wish."

"How and where will they be monitored, and how will you know which signal belongs to whom?" Morgan asked.

"Without getting too technical, let me just say that the main tracking system is maintained in our headquarters with an offsite backup, and the monitoring activity will be handled by our classified personnel according to the protocols we have established and are continually improving.

"For our purposes this weekend, we will be deploying as many mobile tracking units as we determine are needed. We will have personnel and equipment all in place by Friday," Anthony explained.

"Morgan, I know that you don't want Liv to know anything about this yet, and I agree," Walter interjected, "but I am prompted to call an impromptu meeting of all of the principals Wednesday to explain our general concerns relative to the organization and provide them with tracking devices for themselves and their families. Holly, Eleanor, and Elizabeth will be able to equip themselves and their children for Saturday as well. They won't need to know anything about this particular situation, and Liv won't think anything of it if everyone is informed at the same time and will be utilizing the monitoring system.

"Anthony, will you be prepared to present the information to everyone then?"

"Yes, that will be no problem. Frank and I will have everything in order. I think at this point we need to concentrate on our tactics for Saturday."

"I can coordinate with the police department to . . ."

"Hold off on that, Kyle," Morgan interrupted. "Not that I don't have confidence in our city police department, but I want, if possible, for *our* security to handle this! Of course, *I will* be involved. I doubt if the city police would be amenable to my active involvement as a civilian, anyway, particularly since I'm the father of the intended kidnap victims. This is *personal*—this is *my* family at risk! Tyrone Adams terrorized our family once before. Now he thinks he's going to do it again? *I* think *not*!

"Anthony, do you agree that our people can handle this situation and then turn it over to the police for cleanup at the appropriate time?"

"Of course, Morgan! After all, we are a bona fide police department, just like the school police, the transit police, or the airport police. As a matter of fact, we have some of the best trained, trusted officers anywhere. I think we couldn't do better than to use our own people!

"Morgan, why don't you and Walter go home to you families and try not to worry. The three of us will work out the details for Saturday. Kyle, since you know your cousin better than any of us, why don't you work on a script for him to use when he calls his contact. You will be able, better than any of us, to come up with language that would be in keeping with his character and manner of speech."

"Sure, I can handle that," Kyle responded. "Cuz, plan on spending the night so that we can get a fresh start in the morning. I'll start working on the script. Actually, why don't you just plan to hang out here until all of this blows over?"

"Thanks, Kyle. I'm feeling so much better now. I'm not so nervous anymore. I'll just run by my place now and pack a little bag."

"Well, don't feel *too* good." Morgan teased. "After all, your appendix is about to burst!" That little spot of levity did wonders for the group's morale.

"Walter, I am going to leave this package with you," Morgan said, handing the parcel with the tracking devices to Walter. "I think it will be better if we all receive them at the same time when we meet Wednesday."

"That's a good idea, Son. Anthony, I'll just give them all to you. I will get mine and Lydia's Wednesday, as well. Come on, Morgan, I'll walk out with you."

The two said their goodbyes and walked to their cars feeling significantly more relaxed than when they first arrived, optimistic that everything would go well.

CHAPTER 22

BRIEFING IN THE BOARD ROOM

(Wednesday morning, (CECCLA)) Everyone gathered in the Board Room for the scheduled briefing. All of the corporate officers and principals and their spouses were present as well as the officers of the Advisory Committee. It was understood that the situation to take place that Saturday was not to be discussed. Everyone sat in the spectator section of the auditorium except for the presenters and Walter. Liv knew everyone, of course, and she was not surprised her mother, brother, and sister-in-law were there; but she *was* surprised to see Kyle.

There were greetings all around. When Liv greeted Kyle, she sensed an uneasiness in him. Kyle was, in fact, worried that he may not be able to act normally around her. He knew she had a way of reading him, and he did not want to give anything away.

"Hi, Kyle," she said giving him a hug. "I wasn't expecting to see you here this morning."

"It wasn't something I had planned on doing, but since I am here, I want to take the opportunity to apologize to you for dragging Morgan away from your family time earlier this week. I needed to follow up with him, and he said he would be here. So, here I am, in the flesh!"

Kyle was telling her selected versions of the truth. He knew she could spot, or at least suspect a lie from him, especially if he couldn't make or sustain eye contact with her. He made sure to look her squarely in the eye as he spoke to her.

"Well, Kyle, I accept your apology. As Morgan said, you would not impinge on his time with his family unless it were important. I'm glad he was able to help, whatever it was." Her tone and demeanor were such that Kyle correctly understood that she was seeking more information from him about his "problem." Walter saved him from further prodding when he called the meeting to order.

"Good morning! I want to thank everyone for being here so early in the morning. Up front, I want to assure everyone that what we are doing today is precautionary in light of what has come to our attention, a problem that we have been looking at and working on for several months. I am going to ask Anthony Davenport, our Director of Security, to explain everything to you. Anthony?"

"Good morning, everyone. I want to reiterate what Walter has said, that this is precautionary—there is nothing to worry about at this time. Some of you already know that a hacker has been busy and was able to breech some of your personal computers. You also know that we have taken care of that situation."

Anthony went on to explain about the failed attempts of a hacker to breach the organization's accounts and the fact that security is closing in on him and expects to apprehend him in a matter of days. He further explained in detail why the Advisory Committee had acted to implement a controllable tracking system for them and their immediate family members so that it would be in place in the event it becomes necessary to protect them individually and/or the organization.

He also explained how the device(s) would work, how they would be monitored, who would monitor them, the control individuals would have, etc. He and Frank answered questions and received feedback. Everyone understood the importance and was in agreement with implementing the system.

A major concern raised was the problems that could occur with the devices for their young children—losing them, tampering with them, even swallowing them! Staff had anticipated those and other possibilities. Various forms of the device were available for varying age groups. The tracking device itself was merely a small, wafer-thin computer chip that could be secured with a bandage, or with tape similar to that used to secure an IV needle, on a location such as the middle upper back of an infant or toddler.

For the sake of identification and tracking, each chip had a unique number linked to the assigned family and individual. Each principal received an envelope with the chips for their family members placed in individual baggies labeled with the individuals' names. (As families increased, additional chips would be provided.)

Everyone took their chips and prepared to get on with their day. Morgan lingered with Kyle in the Board Room. Liv said goodbye to her mother, and she, Holly, and Elizabeth walked toward their offices in the North Wing, joined by Eleanor, chatting on the way about plans for Saturday's outing.

"I guess we won't have to be so vigilant Saturday with these chips in place," Holly suggested.

"I don't know about that, Holly," Liv opined. "I don't think it is such a good idea to rely on devices and other aids, just because we *can*, without exercising our own common sense and good judgment. We shouldn't worry about it, but we still need to be diligent."

"Yes, I guess you're right, Olivia. I've invited Marlene to come along. She works so well with the kids in the preschool center. Patsy and Little Billy both like her. They think she's a lot of fun."

"That's a good idea, Holly. She babysits for me on occasion. She is good with all the kids," Elizabeth added.

The ladies entered the North Wing and were outside of Elizabeth's office. "Elizabeth, I just thought of something. Let's go into your office for a moment. Do you have anything pressing to do immediately?" Liv asked.

"No, not really. Come on in. Have a sit-down."

"What's on your mind, Olivia?" Holly asked when they were seated.

"If my calculations are right, we will have a lot of kids to deal with Saturday. That's too many kids of varying ages to be running amok while we try to keep up with them all wanting to go in different directions at the same time. With the grownups and Marlene, that's well over 25 people. I say we invite, that is, *hire*, two or three more of the teens to help chaperone and keep an eye on the kids."

"Oh, that's for sure!" Elizabeth said. "I can see them just scattering like cockroaches in the middle of the night when the light is turned on!"

"What a visual!" Holly cringed. "I like your idea, though, Olivia. I would suggest Lisa and Alicia, and possibly Rovelia, if they are available."

"You know," Eleanor suggested, "it might be a good idea to have at least one, maybe even two additional chaperones for the four-and-under group. They need more supervision and help with the rides and with the animals in the petting zoo."

"You're right, Eleanor. I hadn't thought of that. We will probably need one chaperone for every two tots. I'm thinking of Sheryl and Carlee.

"Maybe we can invite a few of Alex's friends so she won't have to be stuck with the younger kids. She will probably want her best friends, Christiaan, Lois, and Lavona and her twin to come. It might be good to have another male or two in the group so Christiaan and Joey won't be the only ones. Perhaps their pals, Miguel, Napoleon, and Carlos. I'll contact their parents.

"That's not quite all," Liv continued. "I want to use one of the medium-sized buses and hire one of the drivers to transport everyone at the same time."

"You want to make this a school function?" Eleanor asked.

"No, not at all. I will pay for everything myself. No one will be on company time. We will all be just private citizens on a friendly outing. We will be renting the bus, paying for the gas, paying the driver and the chaperones, and covering all the expenses for everyone!"

"Well, *I* personally like the idea of not having to keep up with *mine* all day. They never want to do the same thing at the same time. And I'm not that fond of driving, especially in the heat, even with air conditioning. The only thing, Olivia," Elizabeth added, "I think we should split the costs. *You* shouldn't have to pay for everything. So, with that caveat, I'm all for it! What about you, Holly, and you, too, Eleanor?"

"Works for me," Eleanor gladly agreed.

"Me, too," Holly joined in. "If we're done, I've got a parent group coming in shortly for which I need to finish getting set up. See you guys for lunch."

"Oh, I almost forgot. Barbara will be joining us with her three, the twins and Baby Luci," Elizabeth remembered.

"That's great, Elizabeth. There will be plenty of room on the bus if we get a larger one," Liv confirmed.

Meanwhile, Morgan and Kyle were still in the Board Room.

"Hey, Bro, I think Liv is suspicious. I think she wanted to know why I needed you Sunday, but she didn't want to ask directly."

"What did she say?"

"It's not *what* she said, but *how* she was *saying* it. You know better than anyone how she can be!"

"Fortunately, I do. Was she okay with how it ended?"

"Fortunately for *me*, I was saved by the bell!

"Morgan, I hope you don't mind my saying so, but I think it may be good for her to know what's up. It's your call, I know, and I'll follow your lead, of course.

"She has been through a lot in the years that I have known her, and she seems to have been able to meet all of the challenges in stride. She is witty, resourceful, and insightful. I will *never* forget how she invaded your bachelor party and how she got the best of *me*!

"But, like I said, you know her better than anyone."

"Yes, she is all that, Kyle. But now that she is a *mother*, I think she may become overly concerned and prone to worry about them unnecessarily. I can see her wanting to cancel the plans for Saturday. She is very confident about being able to take care of herself. She is fearless. But as a mother, when it comes to the safety of her children, she would worry and hover over them, probably *smother* them trying to keep them under her wing.

"Walter agrees with me about keeping this from Liv *and* her mother as well. We just have to make sure we keep on top of everything and not let anything happen to the boys. I feel what we have decided is the only way to keep these particular perpetrators from regrouping and trying again, and we won't know who or when. We have the upper hand right now. We can catch them in the act and put a permanent stop to them."

"Well, Bro, you *know* I'm going to do whatever is necessary to see that we take care of this."

"I know you will, Kyle. I love you for it."

Just then, Walter approached with Anthony and Frank.

"We need to go somewhere private and talk, Morgan. Is your conference room available?"

"Yes, but you *don't* want to go *there, believe* me! We want to be as *far* from the North Wing as possible!"

"Oh, yes. I get you," Walter said, shaking his head knowing that Liv would likely be in the vicinity and would want to know what was going on.

Morgan suggested they use one of the larger counseling offices that contained an adequate conference table and led the way there. No one spoke until the group was securely behind the closed doors of the conference room.

"Morgan, we have worked out a plan that we are confident will work. Kyle has a script for Victor that we think is good. He will be working with Vic until Friday morning and will be rehearsing and role-playing possible responses depending on what Bobby says, or how he reacts."

"He will be ready, Morgan. I'll see that he is," Kyle assured.

"I trust you, Bro."

"As you know, Kyle is going to take Vic's place," Anthony took over from Walter. "He is going to be there and make himself known to the perps and get up close and personal to the van, where he will be able to plant a tracking device. We will have people placed strategically in and around the areas of both Kiddyland and the handicapped parking areas, both men and women, some as couples. If Kyle is unable to get close enough to the van to place the bug, we will know, and another designated person in the parking area will know to place the backup."

"Kyle, Bro, I want you to be careful. I don't want anyone to be harmed in any way—that is, any of our people."

"Okay, My Brother. Relax. We are no longer the high-school duo where *you* do all of the hero work and *I* hang back and dial 911. I am well trained, and this will not be my first undercover gig!" Kyle asserted confidently.

"Undercover gig?" Morgan questioned. "I didn't know that!"

"You weren't supposed to know, Bro!"

"Okay, I won't be concerned about you. Handle your b-i-z."

Anthony continued, "No need to worry about Kyle. We'll be tracking him as well. He will be wired so that we will be able to hear anything in his earshot. We have had Fred Underwood under constant surveillance since we learned of his involvement. We will keep an eye on him through Saturday in case he is involved in any other manner with the actual kidnapping. That way, we will have more concrete evidence tying him to the conspiracy *and* kidnapping. If he is, hopefully, we may be able to apprehend the whole lot of them together. If we are able to ascertain in advance exactly where they will take the boys, we will have people on standby there as well. We are monitoring his phone, emails, and his online activity to see what else we can find out. We will keep everyone posted on anything even remotely significant."

"Here is a picture of Frederick," Frank added, passing out copies to everyone. "His booking photo was rather dated, but I was able to get his DMV photo, which is most recent. We will be able to recognize him if he shows up. I will have pictures of the other three—Bobby, Marty, and Tyrone Adams—sent to your phones."

Anthony went on to say, "For extra measure, we will also have personnel stationed along the anticipated path from Kiddyland to the parking lot as well as all possible entrances or exits in addition to the main entrance. Everyone will be connected and will be able to communicate with each other and our tracking vehicles. Morgan, I suspect you will want to be present in the vehicle that will be following the van with the boys?"

"Just try to keep me away!" Morgan stated. "Remember, this is *my* family, *my* sons that we are essentially using as bait by allowing them to be taken in the *first* place. And I'm warning you now, if Tyrone Adams is anywhere nearby and I get my hands on him again, they may have to arrest me, too. He will *not* have another opportunity to threaten *my* family again!"

Walter put his hand on Morgan's shoulder and said, "Come on, Son, let's get back to work." The group dispersed and they each went their separate ways.

CHAPTER 23

THE OPERATIONAL BASE

(Thursday afternoon) Anthony telephoned Walter to report that the monitoring of Frederick's online activity produced a promising result, the probable location of their rendezvous, a seedy motel in Valencia near the theme park where the boys would be on Saturday.

"That is good news, Anthony. Does Morgan know, or Kyle?"

"No, Walter. Before it goes further than Frank and the two of

us, Frank is going to follow through and find out who is going to be renting the room and for how long, etc. He expects to have that information by this evening. When we know more for certain, we will apprise everyone involved."

"Thanks, Anthony. That's a good plan. I'll wait to hear from you."

Morgan answered the call from Walter at 4:30 p.m. on his

cell phone. He wondered why he had not called his office phone, but understood when he knew the reason for the call. "Hi, Pops. I'm still here in my office. What's up?"

"Yes, I knew you would be. Are both of your cars here?"

"No, neither of us had anything on the calendar for this afternoon. We'll be packing the kids into the SUV and going home together. Why?"

"We have some new developments. Everyone will be here about 5. Can you ask Liv to take the kids home so that they won't have to wait until your impromptu meeting with me and a few others is done? I will give you a lift home."

"Do you know about how long it will take?"

"No, I don't. Just tell her not to hold dinner for you and that you will be home as soon as you can. That's what I told Lydia. After all, it's the truth!"

"All right, Dad. We can use my conference room. Everyone will be gone by 5. See you then."

Twenty-five minutes later, Walter entered Morgan's office. "Did you have any problem with Liv? I know how inquisitive she can be."

"No, she was fine with it. In fact, she already had plans. Evidently, Mom had called her when she knew I would be late with you and asked Liv to come and bring the kids for dinner. She suggested they could stay there until *you* got home with *me*, of course, and then I could drive us all home. That will work perfectly."

"Oh, here's Kyle. We may as well go and make ourselves comfortable in your conference room. I told Anthony and Frank that we would be here. They should be here any minute now."

They had barely sat down when Anthony and Frank arrived, ready to get down to business.

"Okay, folks," Anthony stated, "we're ready to roll. Frank has established that Frederick Underwood made a reservation for three for a three-night stay at the Dive-In Motel in Valencia beginning Friday night. That site was probably selected for is reputation as a shady, seedy place frequented by lowlifes, addicts, and hookers who only book rooms hourly. He paid the entire fee in advance, as required. No one cares what anyone else is doing, so they have somewhat of an expectation of a certain amount of privacy.

"Fred no doubt checked out the place in advance and would have been attracted to the more isolated position of the handicapped-accessible rooms and parking, which he requested. He, or somebody, is scheduled to check in late tomorrow night, around 10 p.m. He reserved room 114, where one of the two spaces reserved for handicapped parking is directly in front of the door. In addition, that is the only two-room unit in the whole place. The reservation was made over a week ago."

Morgan's heart began to beat faster, and his breathing quickened. He knew that he would be seeing Casanova Adams again. He controlled his strong feelings as he knew that he, more than anyone, needed to remain calm and in control.

Frank continued, "We contacted Kyle immediately because we felt he could be instrumental in gaining the cooperation of the manager because of his law enforcement credentials. We were able to book the adjacent room as well as one other room a short distance away and have already begun assembling personnel to do surveillance and to remain in place for whatever would be needed for Saturday and beyond, if it comes to that. A lot will depend on what additional information we can garner in the meantime, and what contacts we receive regarding their demands.

"In addition, Kyle was able to secure access to room 114 so that we could implant wide-range hidden cameras in each of the rooms.

"If we are able to ascertain that all of the players are in place whenever, we will be prepared to act. If we are lucky, we may be able to pick one or two off at a time leaving or returning to the room. We will be relying heavily on what we can hear from Kyle's feed, what he is able to communicate to us, and what we can see on video in the rooms."

"Bro, I want you to know," Kyle assured Morgan, "I *got* this! I will not allow a hair on either of those boys' heads to be harmed. You have been there for me many, *many* times during our long history as best friends—from elementary school all through college and beyond. I *know* how cool and collected you always appear, never worrying until you know for a fact there is a need to, but then you just go into action. But *this* is your *family*, and I won't blame you if you *should* freak a bit, though I know you won't. They are *my* family, too. Believe me, I *got* this!"

"Thanks, Kyle. I know you will handle your business. I'll be *your* backup with my ears and eyes wide open, just in case!" Morgan replied, still geared up to do whatever might become necessary for him to do.

"Just one more thing, though. Morgan, I know you don't want the police involved up front. But I do have some experience in these kinds of operations, and I have contacted a friend in the Bureau, a profiler who owes me and has agreed to profile the players in this game to help us to know what to expect from them. He has already been sent files on each of them to begin his profiles. He is flying in Friday and will be working with the teams that will be doing surveillance in the motel room. Trust me, Bro, his help will be invaluable."

Although Morgan and Kyle had been bosom buddies seemingly from birth, there was something Morgan never knew about his friend—his involvement with and ties to the FBI, the CIA, and the DEA! He knew that in the last several years, Kyle had been traveling frequently for extended periods of time, but they had always kept in touch. Morgan did not pay too much attention to that because he was involved with his own family, the Centers, and his writing and speaking engagements. He determined that he would ask Kyle about his activities at some point in the future; but not now. He had a more urgent matter at hand.

"Okay, Kyle, if you say so. I trust your judgment."

When the meeting was over, everyone was feeling much more optimistic. Anthony, Frank, and Kyle left, and Walter stayed behind as Morgan cleared his desk. Knowing they both had another important task to accomplish, Walter wanted to find out how Morgan planned to explain his absence on Friday night to Liv.

"Son, where will you tell Liv you will be tomorrow night and Saturday?"

"I was going to ask *you* what *you* were going to do. I was thinking that whatever we do, we should coordinate our explanations. You *know* how much Liv and her mother talk together, pretty much daily. If they compare notes and there is a contradiction, it could cause a problem. I can't, I *won't* outright *lie* to her!"

"Well, Son, I think between the two of us, we should be able to come up with a version of the truth. We don't have to lie. We can just leave out a few details. For instance, they both know that we have distributed the tracking devices to certain members of the organization and their families, right?"

"Right! I think I know where you're going with this, Dad! This weekend will be the first time we will be seeing it in action. We will be testing the system, although it will be a real situation, not just a drill."

"Exactly. We will be testing not only how the devices work, but it will also be a test of our security personnel in responding to the situation—our surveillance teams' operations, communications, and our undercover security personnel's effectiveness, for example."

"And it is only fitting that you and I as heads of the Advisory Committee and the Corporation are available to observe and critique the entire operation. Since it will be, basically, a 24-hour or longer operation beginning Friday evening, we're covered without having to fabricate anything. We will just be leaving out the facts that it is a real situation and that our family members, my sons and your grandsons, are the ones who will be tracked."

"Okay, Morgan, are we both on the same page? Are we clear on this?"

"Crystal, Pops! I will tell Liv this evening. She booked a substitute and won't be performing at the Club this weekend because of the outing on Saturday. We would have just been at home with the kids. Liv can handle them without me."

"Lydia and I were going to pick up her parents and attend dinner and a comedy show, but perhaps she may elect to just go and spend the time with her parents, or with Liv and the kids as well. I think she might prefer that. She is a little concerned about her father's health. Maybe they can all just relax with the family."

"I'll suggest to Liv that she have them all come over. We can even have your caterer prepare dinner for them."

Satisfied that they had come up with a good plan, the two departed for Lydia and Walter's home.

CHAPTER 24

ABOUT THE NIGHT BEFORE / MORGAN'S PRAYER

(Friday morning) Having been thoroughly prepped and rehearsed by his cousin, Victor felt prepared to make the call. Kyle took a cue from his experiences with Liv and even coached Vic on how to alter his voice to fit his pretended state of pain and weakness.

Vic knew he couldn't fail, that he had to deliver his message convincingly. After all, it was not just his life at stake. He was ready, even though he knew he would have to ad lib, to improvise in response to Bobby's reactions. Kyle could only suggest possibilities for him to consider.

Vic put his cell phone on speaker and dialed Bobby's number. Bobby had not been expecting his call, but he immediately answered when he saw that it was Vic.

"Vic! Why are you calling me? You know what the plan is! I don't want to hear 'bout no problems!" he said with more than a hint of irritation in his menacing voice. Victor was spooked, but forced himself to recover and go to his script.

"There is no problem, Bobby. I have taken care of everything. I . . ."

"What's the matter with you! What do you mean, 'taken care of everything?' Where are you?" Bobby demanded angrily.

"Bobby, I'm in the hospital, Man. I was in a lot of pain, but the medication they have given me is taking effect. I don't think I have much time before . . ."

"What the hell are you talking about, Vic? You know what's up! You . . ."

It was Vic's turn to interrupt. He had not been able to approach his script, and he knew he had to think and talk fast. "Just *listen*," he said as forcefully as he dared. "My appendix is busted or about to. They are rushing to take me to the operating room and open up my gut! I *told* you I have taken care of everything. My cousin Kyle is here with me now. He's agreed to take my place. I have filled him in on everything he needs to know to do the job. He has the uniform. It fits him better'n me! I *know* how you were depending on me, and . . ."

"Victor, you're a *dead* man!" Bobby was furious. "You . . ."

"Give me that phone!" Kyle demanded loudly, taking over. He could see that Vic was quickly losing it. He grabbed the phone and took it off speaker. He had to do what he had been coaching Vic to do, again using his experiences with Liv. "Look here, whoever you *think* you are! You may have been 'Mr. Big' in your little pen, but that's only because *I* wasn't there. You are *not* laying a finger on my cousin! If you want this job done, then you are stuck with *me*! I know *you* can't be the brains behind this operation. If it doesn't go down as planned, I'm sure it's *your* balls that will be caught in a vise.

"If you think you want to challenge or threaten *me*, that's your prerogative, if you happen to have a death wish. I will be happy to oblige you. If you would rather *live* and get *paid*, then I suggest you accept the help I am willing to give you so that we can *both* get paid.

Even in his condition, my cousin didn't want to jeopardize the job. That's why he called *me* right away. You should be *grateful* for that. So you tell me now if you want me to help you while I am still of a mind to do so!"

Vic was really amazed by the way Kyle took over with such intimidating authority and challenged The Butcher. He was also very relieved.

For *his* part, Bobby was caught off guard and thrown off kilter. He was not used to being challenged in *any* way. His very appearance was formidable and daunting, effectively discouraging anyone from even thinking about crossing him. Just as Kyle could not see *him,* he could not see Kyle; therefore, he had no way of knowing what he was up against. He wisely decided that the plan was more important at that time than challenging Kyle's questionable superiority. Besides, he figured that once the job was over—and he had had an opportunity to assess the threat in person—he could determine whether or not he wanted to take any kind of action. Still, he didn't want to wimp out, just in case.

"Okay," he said, "Kyle is it? You got the job. But just remember—if things go south, you and your cousin will *both* pay! I will expect to see you bright and early tomorrow morning in the handicapped parking area. My partner and I will be in the van. Come to the driver's window. Got it?"

"Yeah, I got it. I'll be there."

"And, by the way, *you* are coming with us in the van after we have both the boys!" Bobby abruptly ended the call. He was entertaining plans of his own to take care of Kyle once everything was under control.

This was a twist that had not been anticipated, but Kyle realized it could work to their advantage. He immediately called Anthony with the new development. Anthony also felt it could be advantageous.

(The surveillance Friday afternoon, Valencia, Calif.) The surveillance teams at the motel were in place by noon on Friday and had the opportunity to make sure all of the devices were intact and functioning properly. One team remained in the van that was parked further away, and another team occupied the room next door. Samuel Lang, the FBI profiler, worked from that adjacent room.

Morgan chose to remain in the van, so Anthony and Walter stayed with him. To lighten his mental load during the long hours of waiting, Morgan played one of Liv's CDs programmed into his cell phone.

Before about 9:45 p.m., they witnessed a van backing up to the door of room 114 and observed two men assisting a third man with a cane from the back of the vehicle. The men were recognized as Bobby the Butcher, Marty the Moron, and none other than Tyrone "Casanova" Adams. Except for Bobby's leaving in the van and returning shortly with a grocery store bag, they all remained in the room smoking, drinking, watching TV, and playing cards, until Frederick Underwood appeared.

The surveillance teams were videotaping and recording all communications, and watching their activities, especially with the arrival of Fred. The result of Fred's participation produced crucial information.

"Okay, Fred, do you have everything set up for me?" Tyrone asked.

"You know I'm taking care of business. I have the overseas account all ready to go. I am prepared to send Morgan Calais the text message with the instructions he is to follow and the account number he is to wire the money into. When we have verified the money has been successfully transferred, we will tell him where to come to pick up the brats. He'll have to wait for further details."

"I don't want you to text him until you know we have the boys here securely. Are you going to stay here tonight?"

"I think *not*, not in *this* dump!" Fred replied with disgust. I'll be back about 10 tomorrow morning. I'm out of here."

Fred was mildly surprised to see the number of vehicles in different spots in the motel's parking lot, but he dismissed it as probably typical of a late Friday night.

Once it was obvious that the motley crew was abed for the night, the surveillance teams also relaxed for the night, resting in shifts with one person in each location always on point manning the screens, just in case anything developed.

"Well, Morgan, we had better try to get a little shuteye"

"Pop, I think I am too revved up to be able to sleep. Just listening to these guys and knowing what they plan to do is working on my next-to-the-last nerve. I feel like I need to punch something to release my rising anger."

"Okay, Son, I understand how you feel, because I probably feel the same way. But we both need to be on our toes, at our best tomorrow. We need to be in total control of ourselves and our emotions. In order to do that, we need to be well rested and focused, not distracted by our emotions."

"Yes, I know. You're right, Dad. I'm too keyed up. I just need a little more time to unkey, to unwind before I can sleep, though, something else to occupy my gray matter."

"Hey, you guys, how about this?" Anthony suggested, reaching for the chess board contained in one of the van's many compartments and handing it to Walter.

"That's fine," Walter responded, reaching for the game. "How about it, Morgan? It's been a long time since I let you beat me!"

"All right, set it up," Morgan responded, accepting the challenge.

Morgan's Prayer

The spirited, fast-pace match did the trick for the two equally matched players and ended in a stalemate after an hour, leaving the two men more than ready for sleep, even in the van's semi-comfortable, partially reclining seats.

Walter readily succumbed to sleep, but Morgan was still unsettled. He was continuing to have mixed feelings about having allowed his sons to be used as bait in this plan. He began to pray within himself, "Lord, I thank and praise You for Your bountiful blessings. I thank You for the perfect wife You have given me and our wonderful children, two of which are presently in harm's way, as You know. I thank You for the friends and all of the people You have placed in my life to be a blessing to me and/or for me to bless. I thank You for Your leading and guidance as I try to serve You as I live from day to day.

"My heart is heavy as I prepare to face tomorrow, knowing that only You have the power to bring everything to a joyous outcome for me and my family, according to Your will. I sincerely trust and believe that You will bring it to pass.

"I am feeling regret that I have allowed my sons to be used as bait without first seeking and receiving Your guidance, for which I am now asking Your forgiveness. It is my prayer that I am never again presented with such a choice in the future; but if You in Your infinite wisdom should allow it, I pray that I will make decisions only after seeking and receiving clear direction from You.

"I pray that You will allow everything to go well tomorrow and that You will keep me in Your will, despite my strong feelings against the one who has perpetrated this present evil against my loved ones, as he has done in the past. May he never again prosper in evil doing.

"Before ending this prayer, Lord, I am compelled to confess what is in my heart, which You already know is true. I know what I want to do in my heart. I know what I must truly call this strong feeling I harbor for this man who has caused so much hurt to my family in the past—pure hatred. I want to destroy him with my bare hands. I am afraid that is what I may not be able to control if the opportunity arises tomorrow. I know it would put me completely out of Your will, a place I never want to be, for I know You are the source of all of my blessings. All of my help comes from you. I believe I can pass up any temptation when my focus is on You. I must confess that I am facing unprecedented temptation right now, to end this threat for once and forever, the only way I see how within myself.

"I know that people who think they know me see me as the calm Patron Saint of Patience. But, Lord, they don't know as You do the constant struggles I wage within myself to control forces that can rise up within me that try my patience to the core.

"I know the battle is not mine, but Yours, and I should do what I counseled my wife to do once upon a time, that is, to leave vengeance to Him to Whom it belongs—You, O Lord. I am asking You to replace the hatred I harbor for this man with forgiveness and with Your love for all mankind, whom You have made in Your own image. Help me to be still and know, as I do, that *You* are God.

"My final petition, Lord, is that You will not allow our sons to have any negative consequences as a result of what they may experience tomorrow.

"My Lord, My Savior, I humbly ask these blessings in the name of Jesus. Amen."

With his mind finally at peace, Morgan slipped into a deep, restful sleep to awaken only when coffee and croissant sandwiches were delivered to the crews the next morning.

(Saturday morning) Everyone was astir in the motel, and at 8:45, Bobby and Marty emerged from the room. Bobby took the driver's seat, and Marty climbed into the rear of the van with one of the motel pillows. The security teams on the theme park grounds and Kyle were alerted that the suspects were en route. Kyle was already in place and noted the van's arrival.

Kyle had arrived at the theme park about 8:15. He decided to wear dark glasses and a fake moustache in addition to the hat that had been supplied to go with the uniform on the chance that the boys might recognize him as their Uncle Kyle and somehow spoil the plan. The stakes were too high for that to happen. He felt his disguise would be sufficient since they had never seen him in a uniform, or a moustache.

He saw several parked cars, including two vans in the lot and knew at least two of the vehicles were there for surveillance. He communicated with them via his wire for verification. About 8:55, he noted the suspect's van pulling up and waited until he could verify the handicapped license plate when it was parked. At exactly 9 a.m., he walked up to the driver's side where Bobby was expecting him.

"Kyle?" Bobby inquired.

"Yeah. What the deal be?"

Bobby had scrutinized him closely as he approached the van, attempting to size him up. He was inclined to feel Kyle was no threat noting his smaller stature and the fact that he had an approximate 3- to 4-inch, 50-pound height and weight advantage over Kyle.

"You sure *sounded* tough on the phone. Now that I see you in *person*, I believe you were trying to sell me *wolf* tickets! Well, *I* ain't *buying*. When this job is done, we'll just see, won't we!"

"Don't be so quick to judge this book by its cover. I imagine Goliath might have felt the same way about David," Kyle responded in character. "You know how that turned out! Let's just get this job done."

Kyle had been expecting to see another person, the driver. He wanted to be able to provide information, at least to know this other person's whereabouts. He asked as he was about to turn to leave, "Where is your guy who's going to drive?"

"That's not your concern, *Boy*," Bobby said purposely to try to irritate Kyle, but Kyle didn't bite. "I'm electing *you* for the job. You will be my chauffeur. Go get in place! Marty is going to follow you in a minute or two and keep an eye on you so that you can point the kids out in case they don't look like the pictures we have. When he is sure, he'll let me know."

"You won't have trouble spotting the youngest boy. He's got the brightest red hair I ever saw according to the picture my cousin showed me! But I'll make sure, though."

"Wait a minute! You got a piece?" Bobby demanded to know.

"This is a security guard uniform. It didn't come with a gun. Vic said I didn't need one, but I can get my hands on one if need be. I don't see it as necessary for two small boys, do you?"

"Nah, but I don't take no chances. You just never know. For me, I'm like a boy scout. I am *always* prepared."

Kyle turned and walked back toward Kiddyland. When sufficiently far enough away, he communicated with the command post. "Did you get all that?"

"Loud and clear. You didn't give the signal. We didn't see you plant the device. Did you?" Anthony asked.

"Ah, that's the point. You weren't *supposed* to *see* me. Your people are geniuses. With that clear, thin, flexible adhesive device, I was able to place it where they would *never* expect or see it. Why don't you test it out now to be sure it's working properly? In the meantime, I'm going to choose my spot where I will be able to see everyone entering into Kiddyland through the main entrance."

"I'm curious," Anthony said. "Exactly where *did* you put it?"

"Right where he can almost touch it every time he opens the driver's car door. It's in the curve of the little recessed space behind the door handle!"

"Kyle, I would never have *thought*!" Anthony said. "We'll be standing by. Feel free to communicate with us any time. We will be monitoring you as well. We have already begun monitoring the boys. We will be able to see in real time exactly where they are on the grid once they are on the park grounds. We have even been monitoring the feed from the motel rooms."

"Kyle, this is Morgan."

"I know, Bro. What up?"

Though remaining calm, Morgan's emotions were active. "I just want you to know that I have complete confidence in you, and I really appreciate you and what you are doing. And, by the way, I can tell by your conversation with The Butcher that you have learned well from Liv. She would be proud!"

"Thanks, Morg. I'm going to try to get rid of The Moron as soon as possible so that he can take his place back in the van where you guys can keep an eye on him, too. Later."

CHAPTER 25

OFF TO KIDDYLAND

(Saturday, 7:30 a.m.) Liv had made all of the arrangements for the use of the school bus, for the driver, and for the students who were going to help entertain and supervise the kids. They each would gladly have volunteered for the job just to be able to spend the day at the theme park. Everyone met at the school on time and was ready for a day of fun and excitement.

Amid the din of shrill shrieks, laughter, and animated chatter, Liv's mind was on the devices she had taped to the middle backs of each of her children. She had never given particular thought to the safety of her family above the normal concerns of the average mother. But then, she was *not* the average mother, and her family was *far* from the average family. She was wondering if Eleanor, Elizabeth, or Holly were having similar feelings.

"Hey, You Guys, are your kids wearing their spy patches?"

"You mean the tracking devices?" Holly asked. "Mine are. Me, too. That's what we're supposed to do, right?"

"Well, yes," Elizabeth answered. I think it's a good idea, actually. Do you realize how many missing and exploited children there are? These devices could really come in handy, even if it's just a matter of a child who has wandered off and gotten lost for an hour or two.

"I taped them to my kid's backs. I thought they were too young to be trusted with a pendant or ring."

"I did, too," Holly added. "William was the one who suggested it. Did you guys say anything to them about what it was and why they were wearing them?"

"I didn't," Elizabeth offered. We felt they were too young to understand, and we didn't want them to worry about anything. They didn't see them, and they don't even know they are wearing them. I just put them on when I finished drying them after their baths last night. We will explain it to them in time."

"Kevin took care of our two. I think he put them on their backs, as well. I don't know what or if he told them anything."

"I didn't tell the boys yet, but we feel Alex is older and mature enough. Even so, we tried to make it seem like a simple safety device that could help us find them if they were ever lost. She accepted it matter-of-factly."

With their conversation over about the devices, their attention was drawn to their current situation and the typical school bus sounds coming from the excited children. "Oh, my goodness!" Holly exclaimed. "I had almost forgotten about how it was riding in a school bus!"

"Not me!" Elizabeth laughed. I have had many an opportunity to be reminded with all of the field trips I have had to supervise. I'm immune to all the noise!"

"The sounds of children's excited voices is not exclusively relegated to riding on a school bus, believe me!" Liv remarked, remembering her and Morgan's many experiences with their children in the pool, on outings, playing games, or even just roughhousing at home.

The excitement and chatter during the ride intensified tenfold when the theme park came in sight, and again when the bus entered the parking area designated for buses. Before leaving the school, the children were assigned to their chaperones and were given instructions about what was expected of them in the way of their behavior. Once at the park, before they disembarked, Elizabeth reminded them again for good measure.

When the group entered the main entrance to Kiddyland, Kyle was in place to see them and immediately recognized a potential problem. He was not concerned about Little Morgan or Randy and the possibility of their recognizing him. He felt confident that his disguise would be sufficient. However, Elizabeth, Holly, Eleanor, and especially *Liv* had been left out of the equation. They were all good friends of long standing and socialized often, whether it was a barbeque or pool party at the Big House, at Liv's Club, or any number of places they all frequented. He realized their seeing him there might be a problem that could compromise the operation.

He sagaciously opted to avoid them at all costs by remaining in hiding, as it were. Fortunately, they made it easier for him because they stayed pretty much together in the quasi lounge/lunch area while the kids went off in different directions with their chaperones. He noted that the boys were each in different groups and may not be in the same place at the same time. Though they were not terribly far apart, Kyle decided to shadow Randy, the six-year-old, while trying to keep track of the general whereabouts of Little Morgan's group. He was also on the lookout for Marty and spotted him near one of the several access points to Kiddyland.

He approached Marty and described to him the clothing the boys were wearing, each in blue shirts and beige cargo shorts, indicating that they looked just like their pictures except that Randy's mop of bright red hair was obscured by the baseball cap he was wearing. Kyle took note of his questionable mentality and wondered how effective he would be in relaying the message. Marty left to return to report to Bobby and to wait in the van for the boys to be brought there.

After about 15 minutes of staying with his group, Randy saw his brother and asked, "Miss Marlene, can I go over there where Morgy is? I have to tell him something important."

"Where is he?"

"He's right over there, see?" Randy answered, pointing in the direction where Morgan was waiting his turn in line for a ride. Marlene saw Morgan easily as he was not too far away.

"Well, okay, Randy, but come right back, understand? I have to keep an eye on you."

"I will," he said as he ran toward his brother. His big brother saw him coming and wanted him to hold the ball he had won so that he wouldn't have to take it on the ride with him.

"Hey, Randy!" he yelled to him. "Hold this ball for me." He threw the ball to his brother, but it went over Randy's head so that he missed it. It went rolling down the incline toward one of the access points to the regular park grounds, picking up speed as it rolled. Randy promptly ran after it. He looked up to his big brother and didn't want to disappoint him by losing his ball. He chased the ball as it rolled toward the place where Bobby had positioned himself.

Bobby saw Randy running toward him after a ball and easily recognized him from his picture and the description from Marty of his clothes. "Well, I'll be!" he said to himself, not believing his luck. The kid was actually coming to *him*, making his job that much easier. He waited until the right time and stepped into Randy's path, intercepting the ball with his foot and picking it up.

"Hey there, Li'l Fella. This *your* ball?"

"No," Randy replied. "It's my big brother's. He was throwing it to me, and it went over my head. I missed it. May I have it back, please?"

"Sure, here. Come and get it."

Randy advanced with his hands outstretched to receive the ball, which Bobby placed in his hand and immediately placed his left arm around Randy and chloroformed him. He quickly lifted his limp body before he could fall down, thus drawing attention to them. Holding Randy's body like a sack of groceries, his head resting slightly over his shoulder, Bobby began briskly walking away.

He was not conspicuous as Randy could easily be mistaken for a tired little boy sleeping as his father carried him. But the undercover surveillance team was following the actions and communicating the events as they occurred along the route to the parking lot.

Kyle had been watching as well and had already begun advancing in that direction and was almost at the spot of contact when he intercepted Morgan, who had witnessed his brother's kidnapping and had come running after him.

"Officer!" he shouted, crying wildly. "You've got to help me! That man took my baby brother! I've got to get him back! Help me, please! Hurry!"

Kyle wanted to delay a bit to give Bobby a chance to get closer to the van, but not long enough for anyone to start looking for either of them. "What's your name?" Kyle asked.

"My name is Morgan. He's getting away! We have to go!"

"Okay. Which way did they go?" he asked, using his cop voice that would be unfamiliar to Morgan.

"They went that way," he said, pointing toward the direction of the parking lot. Kyle took his hand, and they started walking.

"We need to hurry! I don't see him anymore!" He was obviously frightened and panicked, and Kyle wanted to assure him but could, obviously, not let him know what was going on.

"It's okay, Little Man. You are not as tall as I am. I think I see him. Is he wearing a blue shirt like yours?"

"Yes," Morgan replied hopefully.

"Okay, we'll speed up some, and I'll call ahead to another officer to be on the lookout."

Kyle communicated with Bobby on the walkie-talkie that had been supplied to him for that purpose. "This is me. It seems that a little boy in a blue shirt has been taken by a stranger. I told his brother that I would check with my partner to help find him. He is wearing a blue shirt and beige cargo shorts. I think he is heading toward you. I have his older brother with me now heading in that direction. Have you seen him?"

Catching the cue, Bobby responded, "Oh, yeah. There is a little lost boy in the parking lot. Says his name is Randy. You say his brother is with you?"

"Yes, he is. I'll bring him to his brother. I'm sure the little kid must be scared, lost and all. Let him know his brother is coming. Out."

Kyle was aware that Little Morgan would hear his communication and would be relieved knowing that his brother was safe.

Bobby had continued to the parking lot and had already placed Randy in the back of the van where Marty was waiting. Morgan, positioned in one of the vans that had made its way to the parking lot, was pained to see his son in that position and had to fight strenuously the instinct to go and rescue him right then and there.

Several minutes later, Kyle entered the parking lot with Little Morgan and approached the van. The back doors to the van were open, and only Bobby's legs were visible. When the two were in arms' reach, Bobby stepped from behind the door.

"Where is my brother?" Morgy demanded, recognizing Bobby as the man who had abducted him.

"He's here in the van. Come see." When Morgan looked passed Bobby into the van, he saw his brother apparently sleeping in the arms of Marty the Moron, who was tenderly holding him as if he were a beloved puppy dog. Immediately, Morgan was also gassed before he could react and was placed inside the van.

Looking around to see if they had been seen, Bobby ordered, "Okay, Kyle, you get up front and drive. I'll tell you where." Kyle opened the driver's door and got behind the wheel. Noting that the device was still in place, he drove off following Bobby's directions.

On cue, the first team departed ahead of the van heading in the direction of the motel to avoid any possible suspicion by Bobby that they were being tailed. Throughout the entire operation, communications continued so that everyone was on the same page and knew what was transpiring.

The lead surveillance team in the van with Morgan and Walter left the park parking lot following the van containing the boys at a safe distance to avoid detection. They knew where the van was heading, and they were not worried about losing it.

Once Kyle entered the motel lot, he noted that the first surveillance van had already taken its place. The team that had remained keeping watch over Tyrone was still just out of sight, where it had remained the entire period. The FBI profiler notified the command center that he had completed profiles of all of the players. For optimal success of the operation without avoidable injury to anyone, he wanted to provide his results for the value it would be to everyone involved. The best time, he felt, would be once everything was settled down inside. The team with direct view of the van was asked to be particularly vigilant and report the events in real time as the transfer was made from the van to the motel room.

Kyle backed the van as close as possible to the door, and he and Bobby both exited and came to the rear. Bobby first opened the motel door to find Tyrone anxiously waiting to get a glimpse of the boys, just out of curiosity. As one obsessed with physical attractiveness, and knowing that both of their parents possessed extreme good looks, he wanted to know how their offspring had turned out.

Bobby directed Kyle to open the van door and take one of the boys, while Marty was to bring the other. Kyle opened the door to see Marty holding on to both of the sleeping boys. He had been hovering over them like a mother hen over her chicks. He was reluctant to hand either of them over to what he suspected could be foul play. With some gentle urging from Kyle, he felt okay with at least releasing

Morgan II to Kyle's care. He exited the van holding Randy gingerly in his arms and quickly followed Kyle into the room.

Tyrone eyed the boys as they were brought in, and despite having his curiosity satisfied, he was angered even more by their resemblance to their parents, particularly Morgan II, who looked as if he could have been spit out by his dad.

"Get them out of my sight!" he ordered as he hobbled back to his seat. He took out his cell and called Fred, "We have the brats. Get back here so we can get this text message together."

Once notified that the boys had been removed from the van and everyone, including Kyle, was inside, the lead surveillance van entered the motel lot and took its former spot. Fred arrived in about 15 minutes, anxious to get his part in the plan over with so he could get completely out of that neck of the woods. Luckily, he was not as observant of the surroundings as he had been the night before.

"Let me see the boys," Fred said when he entered the room and did not see them. He wanted to make sure they were all right. Peeking into the other room, he saw Morgan II in the fetal position on the bed, and the little redhead sleeping in the arms of Marty. Satisfied, he closed the door and stepped back into the first room.

"Okay," he said to Tyrone. This is the text. All I have to do is press 'send.' and it's done. He handed the phone to Tyrone, who scrolled through the text and gave his approval.

"May I do the honors?" he said as he pressed "send," not waiting for permission.

"Looks like you already sent it," Fred retorted in disgust, snatching back his phone. "I'm out of here. I will let you know as soon as I get confirmation. I will text their father where they are. I expect you to be ready to leave immediately, leaving the boys here unharmed for their father to come and pick them up. Understood?"

"Sure! Now get out!" Tyrone ordered.

Once Fred had left, Bobby asked Tyrone, "You *are* going to let them go, aren't you?"

"What do *you* care?" Tyrone snorted.

"It's not my business. I just care about myself and getting paid what's due me . . . and one more little personal thing," he added, thinking about his score to settle with Kyle.

A text message with instructions had been expected, probably from a burn phone, so the team was prepared. When Morgan received it, the message was shared with everyone.

We got ur sons. Wire 7.5 mil $$ 2 account TX-949831072 by 12 2day. Whn $ is verified, we will tx u location of kids. NO COPS!

It was not very long after that Morgan received the call he expected from Liv.

CHAPTER 26

KIDDYLAND TRAUMA

Randy had just left his group to join his brother with Marlene keeping an eye on him when she was distracted by five-year-old Grace.

"Miss Marlene, Miss Marlene, I have to go potty!"

"Can you wait a couple of minutes, Gracie?"

Marlene didn't want her to go by herself and was hoping to wait until Sheryl, her co-chaperone, caught up with them.

"No, I have to go *now*!" she insisted.

"Okay. Does anyone else have to go?" she asked. Marlene wanted to take advantage of the situation and have all of the kids go at the same time.

With no other takers, she instructed, "I want you guys to hold hands and wait right here! Don't go *anywhere*, understand?" The children nodded and held each other's hands. Peeking out once or twice to make sure the other children had not budged, Marlene went into the ladies' room with Grace and waited there until she had finished and had washed and dried her hands.

"Thank you guys for staying in place," she said upon returning. "You don't have to hold hands anymore. I am very proud of you," Marlene complemented. She tuned to look in the direction Randy had gone and did not see him or his brother. Worried, she asked, "Did any of you see where Randy went?"

"He went to chase the ball, Miss Marlene," Joseph volunteered.

"Did you see Morgan, too?" she asked, on the verge of panic.

"Yes. He was running after Randy."

"Okay, Kids, we're going to play a game called 'Find Randy and Morgan!' " Marlene didn't want to alarm the kids, but she wanted to find Morgan's chaperones to see if they knew at least where Morgan was. "We have to hurry, and we have to keep together, so everyone hold hands again."

She said a silent prayer of thanks when she saw Sheryl coming toward them. She quickly briefed Sheryl, and they each took the hands of their charges, and they hurried in the direction of the missing boys' last known location. They had not gotten far when Marlene's cell rang. It was Lisa, who was chaperoning Morgan's group with Carlee.

"Marlene! It's Lisa," her frantic voice almost shouted. "Have you seen Little Morgan?"

"Lisa, where are you? I was just coming to look for *you*. I was hoping that Randy was with his brother and *you*! You're telling me that *you* don't know where *Morgan* is either? They're *both* missing?"

"Oh, Marlene, this is awful! What are we going to do? We've *got* to *find* them! Oh, God!"

"Where *are* you?" Marlene repeated.

"I'm by the Kiddy Roller where Morgan was supposed to be. When the ride was over, he didn't get off. He wasn't *on* it!

"Wait! Here comes Carlee. She went to check the little boys' room."

Carlee was visibly upset and trying hard not to upset the kids. As calmly as she could, she delivered the obvious news, "Marlene, he wasn't there! What are we going to do?"

"Marlene, Carlee couldn't find him. He's nowhere in sight!"

"Okay, Lisa, try not to panic. Keep all the kids together. We're coming there now with our kids. We have to go back and tell Ms. Liv! For all we know, they just might have gone to where the parents are. Let's hope!"

"And *pray*!" Carlee added.

The two groups met up and were about to head back to the lounge area where Liv and the others were leisurely relaxing and enjoying adult conversations sans kids.

"I want to play the game! You said we were going to play 'Find Randy and Morgan!' " Joseph said in disappointment, not realizing the gravity of the situation. "Isn't that like making a promise you *have* to keep?" he asked accusingly.

Marlene thought quickly. "Yes, you're right. We can all play. We will walk *this* way, and Lisa and Carlee and their kids will go *that* way, and we will meet back at where your mommies are. On the way, you keep looking to see if you see Randy or Morgan, okay?"

"Okay!" he said happily.

The two groups then headed in opposite directions circling their way and reaching their designation, the place where the adults were hanging out, in about five minutes. As they came together and approached, Liv was acutely aware that her boys were not among the children. The group that was being chaperoned by Alicia consisted of the oldest group of kids, among the oldest of which were Christiaan and his friend, Miguel. They had just recently checked in and were on their way again heading to an approved location outside of Kiddyland.

Liv's mother's intuition was heightened, but she tried to pass it off. The years married to Morgan had taught her much about worry and fear and the virtue of calm and patience. She chose to trust in that. "You guys are early checking in," she said calmly. Having fun?"

"Morgan and Randy are missing," blurted Sonny, a member of Morgan's group anxious to be the first to tell it. "We're just playing a game called 'Find Morgan and Randy!' "

"What?" chorused Eleanor, Elizabeth, and Holly. Liv remained silent, reluctant to react lest she should lose it completely. Remembering the tracking devices securely taped to her boys' backs, Liv forced herself to remain calm. Having failed in their missions to supervise and protect all of the children entrusted to them, the young ladies were obviously distraught, and Liv could clearly see that.

"Ms. Liv, I'm so *sorry*. I'm *really* sorry! It's all my fault!" Marlene admitted, on the verge of tears.

"We're sorry, as well. It's all of our fault, too!" Sheryl added tearfully.

Liv calmly embraced the girls in an attempt to comfort them. "Don't worry," she soothed. "It will be all right. Just tell us what happened. Maybe they are with their big sister."

Marlene composed herself enough to relate what had happened, how she had given Randy permission to go and tell his brother something. "I could see both of them; Morgan wasn't that far away, and I kept an eye on Randy as he walked toward his brother who was waiting in line. He was only out of my sight for a minute or two when I had to take Gracie to the bathroom. Joseph said he saw Randy running after the ball Morgan had thrown to him, and that Morgan ran after him. That was the last anyone saw them."

Liv felt a tinge of relief knowing at least that the boys had initially left on their own steam as opposed to being snatched.

Lisa added, "I was waiting for Morgan to get off the ride, but he must have left before his turn came. I called Marlene in case he was with Randy. That's when I found out Randy was missing, too."

"Okay, everybody. Let's just be calm for a minute," Elizabeth intervened. She remembered their conversation on the bus, particularly the part about being able to find children who had wandered away and gotten lost. "I know everyone is excited and worried. I think the first thing we need to do is pray. So everyone, please join hands, and let's pray."

With everyone in the group, adults and children alike, in a circle with heads bowed and hands joined, Elizabeth began her prayer.

"Dear Heavenly Father, we come to You with praise and thanksgiving for Your grace bestowed upon us. We know that You are all seeing, all knowing, all wisdom, all power, and all Love, ever present in our lives as we go day by day. We trust and know that You love and care for each of us, even the least of Your children.

"We are thankful for the guardian angels that You have encamped around each of us that make it possible for us not to be fearful, but to trust in You, Lord. We ask a special prayer for Marlene, Carlee, Sheryl, and Lisa, that You will give them peace and ease their minds from any guilt they may feel. Please let them know that You are the orchestrator of all things that you allow to befall on us, no matter how it may seem to us or to others.

"We ask that You remove all doubt and fear from our hearts, knowing that You love us unconditionally and that Your Will, according to Your dictates, will be done. We ask that you watch over all of us, especially Morgan and Randy, and keep us all safe, free from worry, and free from fear.

"These blessings we ask in the name of Jesus Christ, our Lord and Savior. Amen."

Following the communal "Amen," a more reassured Liv spoke. "Now that we are back on solid ground, I am going to call Morgan and let him know what has happened. I know that he will be able to tell us just what to do."

Remembering the tracking devices in play, Elizabeth, Holly, and Eleanor all knew what would be happening and waited for Liv to make the call. In the meantime, Holly called Alicia to make sure everything was still fine and that Alex was there, and Morgan II and Randy weren't.

Morgan recognized Liv's ring and answered immediately. Expecting her call, he was ready.

"Hi, Morgan, it's me, Liv." she began her ramble. "Of course I know you know it's me. You know my ring, so I really don't have to say, 'It's me, Liv,' do I. I mean, I just . . . " As she had always been prone to do in stressful situations, she had started her conversation with an onslaught of nervous chatter. Despite the prayer and all the assurances, Liv was still a mother whose sons were unaccounted for, at least by her.

Morgan interrupted her blitz as he had done so many times before.

"Slow down, my chatty baby! Sweetheart, I know why you are calling, and I want you to be assured that everything is under control. Believe me, Baby!"

"You know our sons are missing?" she asked in surprise as well as relief.

"Yes, Honey. But they are *not* missing. Remember the devices taped to their backs? They are working just the way they were designed to work. We have them in our sights. I just don't want you to worry about anything."

"What do you mean, Morgan? They are with *you*? Where are you, Morgan? Oh, Morgan, tell me, please, what's going on? What is happening?"

"Sweetheart, I need for you to just take a deep breath, calm down, and don't worry about anything. You will just have to trust me on this, Liv. You know how much I love you and our family. I will always protect my family."

"Yes, I know you love us, Morgan, and you know I love and trust you with my life. I realize that includes our children's lives as well. If you say there is nothing to worry about, I'll believe you, at least in my head. But now I'm working on my heart. Can you tell me anything else to help me?"

"If I know you and your cronies, especially Elizabeth, you have already done everything you need to do—you have prayed. Now as the Bible says, *'Be still and see the Salvation of God.'*" Will you do that for me, Love? I promise I will fill you in on every detail when I see you. We will all have dinner together tonight, I promise."

"Morgan, everyone is worried and upset, especially the girls who were watching them. What shall I tell *them*? What *can* I tell them?"

"Just tell them that I said the boys are okay, just out on a little adventure with their Uncle Kyle, and that none of you are to let anything spoil your day of fun, food, and games. Can you do that for me, please, Sweetheart? If you have to, transform yourself into one of your carefree, charismatic, ultra-convincing characters and pull this off. Will you do that for me, Babe, and for them?"

Admittedly, Liv felt much better, in fact more relieved. "Okay, Morgan, I will."

After the call was ended, Liv zeroed in on the mention of Kyle. She wondered what he had to do with anything. Her thoughts went back to the night Morgan had vacated their family night to see Kyle, and again earlier in the week when she unexpectedly saw him at their meeting in the Board Room. Her thoughts were crowding in on her, but she let go of those thoughts to deal with the situation at hand.

Liv had separated herself from the group to make her call, so she did not have an audience for her half of the conversation. She didn't return to the group immediately, giving herself time to conjure up an appropriate character. When she felt ready, she returned to the group that had been waiting somberly for news of what they should do next.

"Okay, everyone," she said brightly with a big smile on her face, "listen up! I just talked to Morgan, and he said not to worry about anything! He said the boys are on an adventure with their Uncle Kyle and would be home by dinnertime. They are perfectly safe and under supervision. So! Let's all just forget about this little episode and go on and enjoy the rest of our day!

"Ladies, I'm sorry for the obvious stress and worry the four of you were caused. I know how you must have felt. Don't blame yourselves in the least. You can be sure I will have plenty of words for their Uncle Kyle!"

"Thank you, Ms. Liv," Lisa said. "It's such a relief. You don't know how bad we felt losing them from our care like that. I'm just so happy to know that they are both safe."

Liv gave them each a hug and bid them on their way with their charges, happy to be able to continue with the fun, rides and games. Holly, Eleanor, and Elizabeth were not ready to let it go at that. They suspected there was much more than Liv was letting on. It didn't make sense to them that Kyle would just take the kids away from their chaperones without a word, at least to Liv.

"Okay, Olivia, what's going on? What is the *real* deal?" Elizabeth asked. "You're good, but I've known you too long, and I know you so well that I can often spot your performances. You really put on a good one this time. What did Morgan *really* say, and *no acting*!"

"Yeah, Elizabeth, you do know me better than probably anyone except Morgan, and maybe my mom, or my dad. I *was* trying to hide my true state of anxiety from everyone, including *myself*. But, honestly, I told you what he *told* me to tell you. He promised me that the boys would be home for dinner, and I trust him."

"But where *are* they?" Holly asked.

"I truly don't know. Morgan said they were under surveillance and that the tracking and monitoring systems are working as designed. I have the nagging feeling that my boys have been kidnapped, and I am trying very hard to keep it together."

"Oh, Olivia, how awful!" Hollie cried in support, feeling the pain as if it were her own.

"I hate to say it, Olivia, but you are probably right. Just think about it. Is it just a coincidence that the Advisory Committee and Security would call us in to get these tracking devices for ourselves and our families and for a kidnapping to occur within just days? I don't *think* so. Somebody knew something," Elizabeth said, throwing down the gauntlet.

"Elizabeth, if they already *knew*, don't you think they surely would have done something to prevent it from happening?" Eleanor asked.

"Well, Sis, if you're right, and you may be, we shouldn't worry about it. Our security force seems quite competent and certain of their ability to protect us. If Morgan says the boys are under surveillance, there must be safeguards in place. We have asked the Lord's covering. He is probably doing it through Security.

"Morgan didn't seem too concerned, did he Olivia?" Holly asked.

"He must be concerned, even though he is exemplary at hiding it. I *know* he doesn't want me to worry. I am choosing to trust Morgan. Let's all just try to go on and enjoy this time without having to wipe noses, kiss booboos, or settle disputes."

CHAPTER 27

HAPPENINGS AT THE MOTEL

Fred had left the room feeling uncomfortable about the fate of the boys. He had realized how unstable Tyrone was and really hoped he would not harm them. But as he was leaving the lot, his suspicion was aroused when he noted a couple of the cars that had been there before were still there, particularly the one he specifically remembered from the night before.

Based on what they were hearing and observing, command gave the signal to intercept Fred after allowing him to leave the area of the motel. They would approach him from the front as he came toward them rather than from behind as he might expect. He was busy looking back and did not have an opportunity to issue a warning before he was apprehended without incident and turned over to an awaiting police unit.

Back in the motel room, the only thing to do was wait until notified that the transfer of the money had been made, so Bobby made his move.

"Okay, Kyle, you're finished here. Get in the van and drive us back to the park so you can get your car. You and Cousin Vic will hear from me about your cuts. Thanks!"

Though reluctant to leave the motel with the boys there, Kyle knew he had no choice. He knew surveillance was outside and next door, and he had a more comfortable feeling about Marty after seeing how he interacted with the boys. He got into the van with Bobby and drove away, knowing that security would take this opportunity to apprehend Bobby once they cleared the motel.

Samuel Lang was eager to share his profiles with the rest of the good guys. When given the go-ahead, he began, "First of all, Fred is not prone to violence. In fact, he shuns it. He *does* have some scruples and is opposed to seeing the children harmed in any way. However, he is not aggressive in even that and will not intervene to protect them, thus his eagerness to depart.

"Bobby, on the other hand, is the polar opposite. *His* only concern is *himself*. He *is* prone to violence and takes pride in asserting his physical dominance over anyone. It is surprising that he sought to protect the young man who served with him in prison. As it turns out, he did have a younger brother that he protected from their father growing up. His brother was quite a bit younger and often received the brunt of their father's violent abuse. Bobby was ultimately unable to protect him from being beaten to death by their father.

"I would describe Marty as the 'Gentle Giant.' He sees the boys as his friends, just as he would beloved pets. I see how protective he is of them and he would probably fight to the death anyone who tries to hurt them or take them away from him. I would use extreme caution where he is concerned. I think if it comes to that, Morgan would have the best chance of convincing him that he is no threat to the children. The uncanny resemblance of father and son would go a long way toward convincing Marty that he is part of their family and means them no harm. He should be handled with kid gloves and kind, soothing words. Don't rush him by any means!

"Tyrone Adams is completely another story. He is self-absorbed and extremely angry. He has a vendetta against the family, and I believe he intends to harm the kids just to spite their parents. I am familiar with his story and the interactions he had with their parents. His self-absorbed, narcissistic personality causes him to be perpetually enraged due to his present state of disfigurement, for which he blames them, taking no responsibility for the decisions he made and the actions *he* took. *He* is the one to watch out for, and I would recommend neutralizing him as soon as feasible once you are inside.

"I recommend taking out as many of the players as soon as safely possible, and end this without delay at the first opportunity.

"Morgan, I would like an opportunity to speak with you privately, if I may."

"Certainly. I'll be right in."

Morgan exited the van through the back doors and made his way carefully to the surveillance room next to 114.

"Thanks for coming in, Morgan. I don't usually do this, but for some reason I was prompted to profile you as well. I see from what I reviewed from Tyrone's records, from what I know about you from your public records, and from what I have learned during this surveillance, you are a very dedicated, driven man and mindful of everyone. I can see you are a devoted husband and father, and I perceive that you will go to any extreme to protect your family. I also see and understand that you have very strong feelings for this Adams guy. You are very angry, but you are a man of great self-control. I can see it is being sorely tested about now."

Morgan admitted, "I can't say that you are wrong about me."

"I can see your wanting to take Tyrone Adams completely out of the picture, though I know that's not what you would choose to do under normal circumstances. My advice to you is to allow the professionals to do their jobs in taking him down. I know you have confidence in them. Let them do *their* jobs. *Your* job is to talk Marty into letting your sons go with their father. Thank him for the care he has taken of them. You'll know what to say and do instinctively."

"Thank you for telling me this. You have told me just what I needed to hear. Thank you."

As he turned to go back to the van, Morgan thought back to his prayer the night before and said, "Thank You, Lord, for answered prayer!"

Reluctantly, Kyle climbed into the driver's side. When Bobby got in the passenger's side, Kyle observed him place his gun just under the floor mat. Wanting the surveillance teams to know he was armed, Kyle remarked, "I see you brought your piece. Do I need one?"

"Don't worry about what I have. Just attend to your own business, which right now is driving back to the theme park. Just shut up and drive, *Boy*!"

"Whatever you say, *Boss*!"

About a half-mile from the motel, they saw stopped up ahead a van Kyle recognized as one of the black surveillance vans seemingly pulled over by two black-and-white units. Seeing one of the officers flagging them down to stop, Kyle began to comply. "What ya think ya doin'? Don't stop!" Bobby forcefully ordered.

"What are you, crazy? I *have* to pull over. There's another unit coming up behind us. We haven't done anything. If I don't stop, they will pursue us. "Man! I'm not up for that."

Bobby tried to relax and look blasé, but he was breaking out in a cold sweat. He reached down and got his gun to have it handy inside his waistband, just in case.

"What's the trouble, Officer," Kyle asked when the officer stepped up to the window.

"It's just routine. We're stopping all dark-colored vans with handicapped license plates. Mind showing me your license, proof of insurance, and registration, please?"

"Sure thing, Officer" Kyle slipped his license from his wallet. "Here is my license. This is *not* my vehicle, so I don't know where the registration is," and turning to Bobby, "do you Bob?"

"It's probably here in the glove compartment. Let me see," he said, reaching for the handle.

Not knowing where the gun was, the officer immediately ordered, "Hold it a minute! For the safety of everyone, please keep your hands where they are. We'll check the glovebox. There has been a kidnapping in the area, so if you gentlemen will step out of the vehicle and open up the back so that we can take a look, you can be on your way." To Bobby he said, "I'll need to see your drivers' license as well, Sir."

Bobby had been focusing on the officer at Kyle's window and did not notice that another officer had come up to the passenger door. Noticing through the window the butt of the gun poking from Bobby's shirt at the waist, the officer drew his weapon and yelled "Gun!" as he was about to yank open the door. Bobby kicked the door while reaching for his own gun, causing the officer to fall backwards and his gun to discharge, fatally wounding Bobby.

Knowing that the situation with Bobby would be handled by the officers on the scene, Kyle joined with the team in the van and returned to the motel to be of whatever assistance was needed. He was anxious to see how his friend was doing and sought out Morgan.

"Hey, Bro, how you holdin' up? Anything you need me to do?"

Though the ordeal was not entirely settled, Morgan was very grateful to his friend and just wanted to embrace him.

"Thanks, My Brother. I'm really glad you're here. I'm out of words at the moment, forgive me, Bro."

"Isn't that what brothers are for? Anytime, Bro, anytime! Anything you need from me, just name it."

"There *is* something you can do for me once I get my sons to a safe place. The teams are about to go in, and we will be transporting the boys by ambulance to the hospital. When that happens, will you go and bring Liv to us?"

"You got it, Morg."

Having received notification that both Fred Underwood and Bobby Taggert were neutralized, the surveillance team was preparing to enter room 114 and take custody of the other two co-conspirators. They were in no great hurry and wanted to make sure that everything was in order, knowing that they had a bit of time before Tyrone would be expecting the call from Fred confirming that the wire transfer was completed. What they couldn't know was that Tyrone Adams had become anxious to carry out his pre-planned execution of the boys and was not planning to wait for Fred to call, as expected some time after 12 noon.

By the time they realized what he was up to, Tyrone had emerged from the bathroom, something he had done a few times before, but he did not return to his usual position. Instead, he opened the door to the second room and was standing there with his gun, calling out to Marty.

"Okay, Marty, move out of my way. It's payback time!"

Seeing the weapon in Tyrone's hand, vigilant Marty went into action immediately. He jumped up, placing himself between Tyrone and the boys. "You are not going to hurt my friends!" he asserted.

"Get out of my way, you stupid moron!" Tyrone shouted.

His face suddenly darkening in anger, the gentle giant balled his fists and held his stance, ready to pounce. "You shouldn't call me names. That's not nice!"

In a flash, Marty grabbed Tyrone and swatted the gun from his hand, taking him by complete surprise. He pounded his massive right fist with full force into the left side of Tyrone's head, snapping his neck and leaving a visible dent in the side of his head. Tyrone crumbled to the floor like a wet towel, bleeding profusely from every orifice in his head.

The alarm sounded when Tyrone was seen advancing to the room with the gun in his hand. By the time everyone rushed in, it was all over but the shouting. There was nothing for them to do at that point. Marty had stopped the threat.

His heart racing, Morgan came to the front of the pack, paused momentarily, and walked slowly to the door now blocked by Tyrone's unconscious, bleeding body. He could see Marty sitting on the side of the bed watching over the boys. He looked cautiously at Morgan, but made no move.

Morgan looked for signs of life in Tyrone and summoned the emergency personnel that were on standby. They came in, placed Tyrone on a gurney, and took him away.

Morgan continued to stand in the doorway, remembering the caution given to him by the profiler. He smiled genuinely at Marty, "Thank you, Marty. Thank you very much for watching over my boys. I know they are your friends. Their mother and I appreciate the way you didn't let that bad man hurt them."

"Yes, they are my friends." Marty smiled, and then frowned, "Are you here to take them away from me? I don't want them to go. I'm just waiting for them to wake up so they can play with me." Morgan's heart was filled with compassion and gratitude.

"Yes, Marty, I know you want to play with them. That's what friends do. They play together. I know they would want to play with you, too. But you know what, Marty, they won't be able to wake up by themselves because those bad men, Bobby and Adam, they did something to them so that they won't wake up without help."

"Oh, that was *not* a nice thing to do to my friends!" Marty's displeasure changed to hope. "Can you help them? I think you look like one of my friends, this one here," he patted Morgan II gently on the head.

"Yes, you are right, Marty. That's because I am his daddy. I am both of their daddy. I need to take them to the doctor so the doctor can help them wake up and be happy again. They will be able to play again, too"

"They will? You promise?" Marty smiled.

"Yes, Marty. I promise. Will you let me take them to the doctor now, please?"

"Well, since you are their father, and since you talk to me like I am a regular person and you don't call me names, I'll let them go with you. They haven't eaten anything. Will you get them some food? They like pizza, I know. I do, too!"

"Thank you very much, Marty. Are you hungry?"

"Yes, I'm hungry for pizza," he said enthusiastically.

"I tell you what. I have some friends waiting outside who will take you with them, and I'll tell them you are hungry for pizza. Will you go with them now, please?"

"Okay, but first, will you tell me their names? I call this one, Red," he said softly smoothing Randy's hair, "but I want to know their *real* names."

"Sure, Marty. The one you call 'Red' is Randy, and his older brother has the same name as me, Morgan."

"You know, Morgan, I know I am not as smart as a lot of people, but I am not as *us-smart* as some people *think* I am. I know we were not supposed to have these kids here. They are not ours. I think the people you have outside are police who want to put me back in jail, but that's okay. I get along better when I am locked away. I don't have to think about anything, just do as I'm told. I just don't like it when they call me names, though. Okay. I'm ready to go back now. Say goodbye to my friends for me when they wake up."

Marty walked through the door and into custody without incident. Walter came in and picked up Randy while Morgan picked up Little Morgan and carried them to the waiting ambulance.

Kyle returned to the theme park and headed for Kiddyland, where he found Liv and the other parents, in the lounge/lunch area.

Of course, while they knew that Randy and Little Morgan were on some kind of adventure with their Uncle Kyle, they were all surprised to see Kyle there without the boys—and in disguise!

Liv, as he expected, was the first to address him. "Kyle, where are my boys? Do you know? Why are you wearing that uniform? Why didn't you . . ."

"All right, all right, all right, Sis!" Kyle said, holding up his hands in the shape of a cross in front of his face. I deserve all of the bad thoughts you must have been, must *be* having about me. I take full responsibility. You can let me have it."

"Kyle, we were just so worried! Please tell me where they are!" Liv implored.

"They're *fine*, Liv. They are with Morgan. Everything is fine. He asked me to come and get you and bring you to where they are. He thought perhaps Alex could stay with her aunt and go home with her and you guys could pick her up later in time for dinner. He figured she might like to stay longer with her friends here at the park. The day is still young."

The ladies did not know of the happenings at the motel. Kyle knew his familiar casual manner would seem normal to them and would not add to their already heightened anxiety.

"That's okay, Sis," Eleanor assured her. It will be no problem. I'm sure Alex will be happy to come with us."

"Okay, Kyle, take me to the rest of my family. I don't want you to tell me *anything* about what has been going on. I *know* something *has*. I think you had a chance to tell me Wednesday, but you chose not to. I don't think I want to hear it from you right now."

Once they were in his car, Kyle called Morgan to find out his status. He knew they would have left the motel by now. They had already agreed he shouldn't bring Liv to the motel.

"Hey, Bro, where you at? I have your wife. She's anxious to see you."

"Is she upset?"

"Affirmative, Bro. Where are *you*?"

"We're at the hospital. They had a room for us and a team of doctors waiting. The boys are still out. They're being tested and evaluated now. What's your ETA?"

"We should be there, I'd say, in about 25 to 35 minutes."

Liv had remained silent and was trying to concentrate on anything other than the events of the day and what was happening at that moment. The fact that Kyle had appeared so unaffected gave her a degree of confidence that everything *was* fine, but she was still perturbed. She closed her eyes and tried not to think about anything.

When the car finally came to a halt about 30 minutes later after several quick turns, Liv opened her eyes and was alarmed to see they were in the hospital parking lot. "Kyle, what are we doing here at the hospital? Who is hurt? Is it one of my boys? Morgan?" she demanded, with increasing panic.

Kyle got out and was walking around the car to open Liv's door when he spotted Morgan walking toward them. He breathed a sigh of relief. Opening Liv's door and helping her out, he said, "Here is Morgan, Liv. As you can see, he is fine—a little grungy and unkempt, maybe, but perfectly healthy. You may not want to hug him until he has had a chance to clean up," he added in an attempt to distract her focus.

Liv just stood there relieved, in constant eye contact with her husband as he neared her and put his arms around her, just holding her as she melted into his embrace.

"Oh, Morgan, I was . . ."

He silenced her with a kiss. "Hush, now, Baby. Let's go and see our boys. They have been asleep. I want our smiling faces to be the first things they see when they awaken. Let's hurry now. I will fill you in on *everything* that has happen once we get settled down, I promise. Okay, Sweetheart?"

Liv smiled faintly as he kissed her on the cheek and took her hand. With Kyle following a few steps behind, they walked into the hospital and on to the room where the boys were in stages of awakening. Walter had remained in the room while Morgan left to meet Liv and Kyle so that a friendly face would be there if the boys woke up in the meantime.

Little Morgan was the first to awaken. He opened his eyes slowly and blinked several times before focusing on his mother's anxious face, and then on his father's. "Mommy? Daddy?" he said as the fog cleared from his head. His eyes reflected that his last memory had come into focus. "Mom! Dad!" he almost shouted excitedly. "Where's Randy? Where's my brother?" he cried, frantically looking about.

"He's right here, Son," Morgan said, taking his other hand. He's right here."

Morgan moved aside so that Little Morgan could see Randy, who was beginning to wake up as well. Satisfied at seeing his brother was safe and sound, he relaxed, "I must have been dreaming. I thought he was being kidnapped! He was . . ." He stopped midsentence, remembering. "No, Dad, I *wasn't* dreaming! We were at the park.

I threw my ball I had won to Randy, and it was too high! I saw this policeman, and I. . ."

Noticing the brown uniform on Kyle who was standing nearby, he looked more closely and recognized Kyle for the first time. "Uncle Kyle! Uncle Kyle! That was *you*? Was I *dreaming*? Wow!" Seeing Walter, he was also surprised.

"Grampa! You're here, too!"

"Yes, I'm here, too, Little Man, Walter replied, relieved that Morgy seemed to have no ill effects.

Little Morgan resigned himself to the fact that he didn't understand any of what was happening, and he decided that he didn't need to know anything except that he and his brother were safe, and their parents and grandfather were there with them. He gave his mind up to rest and watched the attention that was now shifted to Randy.

Morgan continued holding Little Morgan's hand while Liv went closer to Randy, taking his hand. "Randy, Honey, it's me, Mom."

"Mom?" He relaxed and smiled, seeing his mom and his dad nearby. When he saw Little Morgan, his last memory was triggered, and he looked worried. "Mom, do you have Morgy's ball? I don't know what happened to it. I don't want him to be mad at me for losing it. I'm sorry. I'll use my allowance to buy him another one just like it, I *promise*!"

He was on his knees on the bed by now. Liv put her arms around him and kissed him gently on the cheek. "Don't worry about that ol' ball, Randy. Everything is all right." Though close to tears, Liv didn't want to show any signs of worry to either of her boys lest they might react negatively.

Looking around, not recognizing his surroundings, and noticing he was not wearing his clothes, Randy grabbed his flapping hospital gown in an attempt to cover himself. "Hey, why am I wearing this *dress*? Where are my *clothes*? Where *am* I? What's the big idea?" he demanded.

"Sweetheart, it's okay. You are in the hospital, both of you. You . . . "

"In the hospital?" he repeated with unexpected jubilation. "No way! I've *never* been in a hospital before!" he said, jumping out of bed unmindful of his flapping gown. "Where's the button you push to make the nurses come in?"

Everyone was happy to see he wasn't upset, but they weren't prepared to have him running amok. "Hold on, Randy," Morgan said, swooping him up in one arm. "Back into bed you go!"

"But I'm not sick, Dad. I feel *fine*—just a little hungry!"

"Maybe you're not sick, Randy, but you still have to mind your manners. Here the doctor is now. He'll let us know if you can get up. Now simmer down."

"Mr. and Mrs. Calais?" the doctor seemed pleased.

"Yes," Morgan answered.

"I am Dr. Mazer. Looks to me like these young men are anxious to *leave* us. Can't say as I blame them. You have some fine specimens here, both in tip-top shape, no residual effects of any kind. I'd say they are ready to go. They weren't formally admitted, so everything that is needed has been taken care of. It was a pleasure seeing to your sons, Mr. and Mrs. Calais. Take care."

"Thank you very much, Dr. Mazer," Morgan said taking the doctor's hand.

"Don't we get to taste some of the hospital food?" Morgan II asked.

From the doorway, the doctor turned and laughed, "I think you'd better leave well enough alone!"

The boys each looked puzzled while the other's laughed as well. "Okay, boys, we'll go and get some real food. First let's get you two dressed. Come on," Liv prompted.

The men stepped into the hall while Liv helped the boys to get dressed. "Kyle, I owe you big time." Morgan said sincerely, Thanks for all you have done. You know I appreciate you, more than you can possibly know. I hope Liv wasn't too hard on you. I know she'll come around when she knows the whole deal."

"No need to thank me, Bro. You know we're always cool. I'm not worried about Liv. I know she loves me. She knows she can dump on me all she wants, and I will still love her, too. We are all just one, big, giant, happy family!

"I'm going to get going now. I've got a load of reports and paperwork to do, and I know Vic is beside himself waiting to find out how everything went. He'll be happy with the result, I know. Later, Bro."

CHAPTER 28

THE AFTERMATH

(Kyle and Victor) Kyle arrived home to find Victor frazzled with worry.

"Kyle! Is everything okay? Are the boys safe? Is this thing all over? What happened?"

"Victor, just relax! Everything is fine, thanks to you, Cuz. It's all over but the shouting! Have you eaten?"

"How could I even *think* of eating under these circumstances! I have been too consumed with worry to eat! I think I can even feel gray hairs growing out of my scalp!"

"Well, you can stop worrying now. Like I said, everything is fine. *I* am certainly hungry. I'm going to take a hot shower and get myself cleaned up. If you want, we can go and get something to eat. I will fill you in on everything that happened. I can tell you one thing for sure—you will never have to worry about The Butcher ever again!"

"For *real*? Are you *sure*? I won't have to deal with him again?" Vic dared to ask, desperately wanting to believe it could be possible.

"Not ever again—that is, unless you both happen to end up in the same place in the hereafter, Cuz!"

"Kyle, are you telling me that he's *dead*? You're not joshing me, are you?"

"It's for real, Vic. Let me get myself together. I'll fill you in on all the gory details, okay, Cuz?"

Feeling the tremendous relief of the knowledge of Bobby the Butcher's demise, Vic sank down into the armchair on the brink of shock. At that moment he wasn't even concerned about the how or why of it all. While waiting for Kyle, he dared to let himself think about the future he wanted with the young lady he had been dating and wanted to marry. One thing was for certain; he planned to keep himself so far on the right side of the law that he would *never* be looking out through bars again!

(Walter and Lydia) Lydia had spent Friday evening at the Big House with her parents, Liv, and her grandchildren. She returned home after spending Friday night with her parents. She had not thought too much about the fact that her husband and son-in-law would be gone overnight on business relating to the Organization's security system. It was not until a few things that Liv had said the evening before made her think more of it. She planned to get specifics from Walter.

She returned home about noon to be home when Walter arrived. She thought nothing of his calling to let her know that he had offered to host the Sunday family dinner that week. So as not to spring it on her at the last minute, he also suggested she contact their caterer so they would not have to scramble to prepare. Lydia had no problem with that arrangement. She loved cooking for her extended family, but she appreciated the opportunity to have a carefree evening with her husband that night following his absence.

Lydia was engrossed in the book she was reading and didn't hear Walter when he entered the house. "Hi, Love!" he said, startling her.

"Oh, hi, Honey. I didn't hear you come in. I missed you last night," she said, as she stood to be embraced and kissed.

"I missed you, too, Sweetheart. I'm feeling seedy about now. Let me get out of these clothes, shower, and clean up. Then we can talk. I need to fill you in on a few things, to tell you all about our adventure last night and today, okay, Sweetheart?"

"Sure, Walter. I think I'll go on the patio and do some stretches. I don't feel much like reading anymore."

When Walter returned, Lydia had returned to her book, but she had lost focus on the story that had been so intriguing before. Walter relieved her of the book, placed the bookmark on the page she had been reading, and put the book aside. He embraced and kissed her.

"You look tired, Honey. Are you sure you don't want to relax a bit first? It must have been taxing, whatever was involved. I can wait." Lydia was not sure she was ready to hear anything that might be disturbing. She wanted to delay it as long as possible.

"No, I'm fine. I want to do this while everything is fresh. Come and walk with me," he said taking her hand. As they walked through the gardens, Walter related the events that had occurred, pausing only to respond to questions or to allow Lydia to react to the various elements.

Lydia had mixed feelings, but the paramount ones were gratitude and relief that their family members were all safe and sound. "Walter, thank you for telling me. I'm glad you didn't let me know about it beforehand. I think I would have been out of my mind with worry. I suspect Olivia didn't know, either?"

"No. Morgan and I both felt it would be better not to let either of you know."

"That was certainly the right call for me; but I'm not so sure it was the right call for Olivia. I believe she strongly suspected something. She was not quite her usual self, though I couldn't pinpoint anything specific. Mother's intuition, I suppose. Knowing Olivia, I don't think she will appreciate not having been informed up front. My daughter is strong, much stronger—and braver—than I ever was. I hope there will not be any negative repercussions from this. I will try to feel her out tomorrow at some point after dinner."

"I'm glad *you're* okay, Lydia. Walter kissed his wife.

"Yes, I'm fine. We'll just have to pray for our family."

(Morgan and Liv) Morgan and Walter each had rental cars delivered to them at the hospital so they would have transportation home.

Morgy and Randy were happily playing and talking to each other. Liv was unusually silent, at first just trying to keep her mind devoid of anything but her thanks to God for the fact that her sons were safe in the car with her. To her they seemed to be none the worse for wear, whatever they had experienced that day. Breaking the wall of silence between them since leaving the hospital, Morgan asked his wife, "Liv, are you okay?"

"That remains to be seen, Morgan," she answered in a listless tone. I'm not sure at this moment if I even *know* how I feel. At any rate, I am not ready to talk, or even think about how I feel."

"Okay, Sweetheart, I'll leave you to your thoughts. Whenever you are ready, just know I am here."

Morgan was regretting more and more that he had kept her out of the loop and that he had not listened to Kyle. He had to admit to himself that he had not been truthful about the plan he and Water had devised in the name of protecting their wives. He knew deep down that a lie is not in the words one actually uses, but in the intent of the heart. Their intent was to hide the fact that their family members were an integral part, in fact, the main focus of the operation.

He resolved that as soon as she was ready to hear him, he would tell her everything there was to know. He knew that, at the very least, she would be disappointed in him. But he hoped that once she knew the whole story and the intent behind the planned course of action, she would be able to see it from his point of view and be okay enough to at least forgive him.

As they continued in silence, Liv had begun to try to connect all of the disjointed elements swirling around in her head concerning the period from that past Wednesday until then. There were just too many missing connectors for her to make sense of what made no sense to her. From their conversation Friday evening regarding their husbands' absence that night, Liv realized that her mother knew even less than she did.

She decided to give it a rest and just wait until Morgan told her everything as he said he would. He had promised that they would all have dinner together that night, and that would be happening shortly. She would wait.

Taking Morgan's suggestion, Liv called Eleanor to ask her to bring Alex home and for her entire family to come and stay for dinner. Morgan thought that his cooking dinner for everyone would give Liv more time with the boys and to, hopefully, relax a little.

Showered and dressed, Morgan began to prepare dinner. Liv quietly sat on the patio watching the boys playing. Everything was ready to go on the table when Kevin and Eleanor arrived with Alex and her cousins. After everyone had washed their hands and taken their seats, Morgan blessed the table, and everyone began to eat. Little Morgan and Randy were ravenous as they had been taken so early and had not eaten since breakfast. Contrariwise, the other children had consumed so much during the day, they were not very hungry.

Morgan noticed Liv merely picked at her food, barely consuming anything. He didn't take it personally. He knew how much she relished his cooking. Given the day's events, he understood her not having an appetite and didn't comment about it.

Kevin and Eleanor didn't stay long after dinner. She and the kids had had an eventful day, and Eleanor was spent. She wanted to get home, get the kids to bed, prepare for church Sunday, and get some rest herself. Kevin helped by supervising the kids' baths.

It was about time for the Calais bunch to do the same. By 9 the kids had all had their baths, the family evening prayers were done, and all three kids had been kissed good night and tucked into bed.

While Liv lingered in the boys' room reading them an unsolicited second bedtime story, Morgan went to their suite and started a warm bubble bath for her. He had just turned off the faucets when Liv entered the suite. Looking at her, he couldn't get a sense of where her head was. He couldn't know that she didn't know where her head was either. She seemed resigned and lost as she just stood there looking at him.

Morgan walked over to her and cautiously put his arms around her. Liv surrendered into his arms and held on to him as she laid her head against his chest. "Liv, Sweetheart, I have filled the tub for you. Do you want to get in now, and just relax?"

"By myself?" she asked, pulling back and looking up at him. The COW was beginning to make preparations, but Morgan wasn't sure. "Do you *want* company, Liv?"

"Morgan, I don't know if I want company, or if I *need* company—or *both*." She sighed, releasing Morgan and hugging herself. Looking up at him, she confessed, "I feel lost, as if in a strange place. I'm a little tangled in my head, and my stomach is in knots."

Liv rested her cheek back on his chest and returned her arms around him tighter than before. Morgan lifted her chin and kissed her gently on the lips. She didn't resist. He kissed her again and began to undress her. She began to undress him, as well. Before they knew it, they were spooning in the warm water just relaxing. Liv closed her eyes and surrendered to the warm water and the comfort of her husband's arms around her.

Morgan closed his eyes as he held his wife and contemplated how he could best explain to her the events that had unfolded. He had always loved her and always wanted to protect her from the day he first laid eyes on her. They had experienced bumps and potholes in their road together, and they always managed to thrive through them; but it had always been a team effort. Morgan was censuring himself for not relying on the practice that had worked in times past. He was praying for God's help.

Liv could feel her tension and apprehension melting away as she accepted the comfort she always found in Morgan's arms. She was reminded how much she loved him. She also knew how much he loved her and his family. She knew they would not sleep that night until all of her questions had been answered. In the meantime, she would continue to enjoy just being with him in the frothy water.

The water had become lukewarm bordering on cool, and they knew it was time to get out. Morgan got out first, toweling himself and holding up a towel for Liv to wrap in. When they were both dry, they climbed into bed.

"How do you feel now, Sweetheart?" Morgan asked.

"I am all relaxed and ready to listen to you expound on everything I need to know, Morgan."

"Are you going to put something on first? 'Cause if you don't, I don't know if I will be able to concentrate on anything else."

"Well, Morgan, to tell you the truth, I *love* you, as you know, and I really *missed* you last night. On the off chance that after I hear what you have to tell me, I will want or need space from you, this seems like a *good* move on my part."

"Sweetheart, I'm praying that it won't come to that and you will still love me."

"Oh, Morgan, you *know* I will still *love* you, *whatever* it is. Besides, what's to stop a repeat performance later?"

Hearing those words, the COW that had been cautiously waiting at the ready was Johnny-on-the-spot.

Twenty-five minutes later, Liv announced, "Okay, Morgan I'm ready. Let me have it."

"I *thought* I just *did*!"

"Morgan! I'm *serious*!"

"I know, Sweetheart. I couldn't resist!" Morgan said with a tender smile.

Morgan related everything that had transpired from the initial telephone call that prompted him to vacate their family night and take off for Kyle's place up to the time he walked out of the hospital to the visitors' parking lot to meet her when Kyle arrived with her. Throughout his discourse, Liv was listening very attentively, never interrupting, even when her roller-coaster emotions were at a peak.

"Liv, I want you to know that I am *deeply* sorry for the stress you had to endure not knowing the truth of what was transpiring. I should have listened to Kyle when he offered his opinion that I should let you know what was going on. He said that you were stronger than I was giving you credit for. He was so right."

At the mention of Kyle, Liv was reminded how negatively she had responded to him at the theme park when he came to get her at Morgan's request. She now knew he was helping to protect their family. "Morgan, I have to apologize to Kyle. I wasn't very nice to him. I *didn't* know. I hope he will forgive me and accept my apology."

"I know he understands, Liv. I wouldn't be concerned about him. He loves you like a sister."

There was a lot of data for Liv to process, and she had not had time to fully digest everything. She needed more time, and Morgan realized it. He put his arms around her when she laid her head on his chest.

"Morgan, I love you, and I know how much you love us. I appreciate knowing the lengths to which you will go to protect us. I just need you to hold me while I try to process everything."

"Whatever you need, Baby. Let's just sleep on it," Morgan said, holding her as they both drifted off to sleep.

It was about 4 a.m. when Liv woke up in a cold sweat. She had awaken from a nightmare. This was the first one she had experienced since that day Morgan had given her a tour of his home before they were married. Seeing Morgan sleeping peacefully beside her, Liv was comforted. When her breathing returned to normal, she put her head back on his chest. Without awakening, Morgan instinctively put his arms around her. Nevertheless, Liv was still shaken by her unpleasant dream and unable to return to sleep.

She didn't get up and do her laps that morning, but everything else was typical of their usual Sunday routine—church services and their Sunday extended family dinner, hosted by Walter and Lydia. Walter had suggested having it at their home, wanting to give Morgan and Liv more time after their traumatic Saturday. He was happy to see that everyone appeared to be adjusting.

CHAPTER 29

A NIGHTMARE FOR LIV

Two weeks had passed since the ill-fated outing to the theme park, during which time Liv and Morgan had been trying very hard to return their family to its former state of normalcy. The children were sure to be fine. Alex was old enough, and mature enough to understand what it all meant. She was also provided a little more detail of the events of that day. The reasons for and use of the tracking devices were explained to her in more detail as well, and that, along with the assurances of both her parents, went a very long way in maintaining and enhancing her feelings of security that they would always be able to protect her and her brothers.

Little Morgan and Randy were only able to recall events up to the time they had been gassed. That was perfect for Randy, who knew only that at one moment he was about to retrieve his brother's ball from a stranger, and the next moment he was looking up into the faces of his mom and dad from a hospital bed! The only explanation he received, which seemed to be sufficient for him, was that he had been in a deep sleep for a few hours. There would be time years later to let him and his brother know about everything that transpired.

It was not quite as simple for Little Morgan. He had seen his brother being taken away and had pursued him. He also saw his brother's unmoving body in the back of the van with his abductor, which had been *his* last memory. His parents talked to him at length, giving him every opportunity to express his anxieties and fears, and then reassuring him. They told him about the device he was wearing that enabled him to be watched the entire time, expressed the fact that he would always be able to be found, and that he would be safe. He had no reason to doubt that that was true, and he had no negative repercussions from the experience whatsoever.

It was *really* not quite so cut and dry for Liv. Morgan noticed that she had not readily been able to return to her usual self, despite having everything explained to her and indicating she understood he did what he thought was best. After a week, her behavior prompted Morgy and Randy to privately petition their father to intervene on their behalf. They didn't want to call for a family meeting, which was the normal procedure when anyone had a problem with another family member, or when they wanted the family's input on a problem *not* regarding a family member.

Being the oldest, Morgan II was the spokesperson when the boys came to their father with their problem.

"Dad, we have a problem that we want you to help us with. We really need your help bad."

"You need my help *badly*?" Morgan corrected.

"Yes, Daddy," Randy asserted.

"Does this problem involve another member of the family? Do you want to call a family meeting?"

"*No*, Daddy! We *know* we're supposed to try to work it out with the other person first, but we couldn't do that," Little Morgan explained while Randy agreed, nodding his head vigorously.

"So, why not call for a family meeting?"

"Because. *Mom* is the *problem,* and we don't want to hurt her feelings. If we have a *family* meeting, *she'll* be there. We want *you* to talk to her!" Little Morgan explained. "We don't want her to think we don't *love* her anymore!"

Morgan realized that he wasn't the only one concerned with his wife's behavior. He inquired, "Okay, just what *is* the problem?"

"Dad," Morgan said, "We *love* Mom. We know *she* loves *us*." He hesitated.

"Well that's a good thing, isn't it? What is the *problem*?"

Randy answered, calling it the way he saw it, "She loves us *too* much, Daddy! She is always hugging us, holding our hands when we are walking on the trail, kissing us, a lot of *mushy* stuff. *Alex* doesn't *mind*. *She's* a girl, and girls *like* mushy stuff! We're *men*!"

"Yeah, Dad," Morgan agreed. She hugs too long and too tight. It's like maybe she's afraid something is going to *happen* to us!"

Randy guessed, "Maybe she thinks we're going to go to sleep again and wake up in the hospital!"

"Okay, guys, I think I see your problem. I'll talk to your mother for you. But I want you to give her a little more time. Sometimes mothers get that way. They tend to be over protective because they love their children so much. Don't worry about it. I'll take care of it."

"And, Dad, *please* don't tell her that we *told* on her. She didn't *mean* to," Randy cautioned.

"You can trust me to handle it the right way. You guys run along. Leave your mom to me."

Liv *had* been a bit withdrawn, subdued, and pensive. At times Morgan saw her as being melancholy, and at other times, shying away from eye contact with him. For no apparent reason as far as *he* knew, she booked Athene to cover for her that Friday and Saturday night. Although Morgan was always happy to spend time with her on such occasions, this particular timing was a concern for him.

With their evening family prayer done and all of their children tucked into bed, the pair retired to their suite. Liv was lingering in the bathroom and Morgan was in bed thinking about his wife's atypical mood, her behavior. While he contemplated what he would do, he did something that had been practically obviated once they had been married—he was prompted to dialogue with the COW.

"Okay, Big Guy," the Chairman of the Board initiated, "You know how to deal with this, Mighty King Solomon! Just give her *'the look'* and command your Shulamite woman. You know how she just melts into your arms!"

"You know we never use them to settle any difficulties we may face from time to time, trfling as they may be. This is, obviously, *not* insignificant. She *needs* something from me, and it's *not you*, Little Man. I am going to get to the bottom of it tonight, so you and your boys might as well turn in."

Hearing the bathroom door open, Morgan turned his attention toward Liv as she emerged wearing a long, non-revealing nightgown, sending a non-verbal cue letting him know he had made the right decision in overruling the COW. Liv climbed into the bed and reclined beside him on her back with her arms crossing her chest, holding her arms firmly, motionless and silent. Morgan turned on his side toward her and watched her profile as she slowly inhaled and exhaled with her eyes closed.

"Sweetheart, "what's on your mind?" Morgan asked. "A penny for your thoughts."

"My thoughts are not even worth a penny," she said in a monotone, moving nothing but her lips.

"Liv, Sweetheart," Morgan said, raising up on one elbow to look down at her. "Baby, I know something is bothering you. You haven't been yourself lately, and it really concerns me that you took this entire weekend off from your club. It's not *like* you to do that. *Please*, Sweetheart, can't we at least *talk* about it? You still *love* me, don't you?" he asked, knowing she did, but hoping for a rise out of her.

Liv reached up, drew him to her, and gave him a reassuring kiss. "Morgan, you don't have to ask me that. You *know* I love you. I'll *always* love you. I'm sorry you felt you needed to ask me. Have I been acting that weird?"

"Yes, Honey, I'm sorry. I know how much you love me—almost as much as I love you. I just hate to see you like this, and if I don't know what is bothering you, there is nothing I can do, and I feel so disconnected, so helpless. And I have to tell you, Liv, you are *smothering* the children. I think *I* understand, but *they* don't. You can't tie them to your apron strings, Baby.

"Please tell me *something*. What are you *thinking*? How do you *feel*? What's in your *head*? If it will make it easier for you, you can use a character who will just tell me like it is."

Liv looked at herself through her children's eyes and through Morgan's eyes and realized he deserved an explanation. She was prepared to tell him. "Morgan, I have no character that can make it any easier. This is me, Liv. Morgan, for almost the entire last two weeks I have been thinking more and more about a recurring dream I had as a pre-teen and teenager. It has resurfaced with a vengeance in the last two weeks and has recurred six or seven times."

Morgan wanted to ask if it were a dream or a nightmare, but he decided to let her characterize it however she would. He continued to listen to her actively, taking her hand and stroking it as she spoke.

"In this dream, I am suspended midair, dangling from a very high altitude by an extremely thin, fragile thread. I don't know what is *below* me, I don't know what I am *hanging from*, and I don't know how I *got* there, just that it is very high up. I am feeling very unsafe, very vulnerable to anything that might cause the thread to break, including the strain of my own weight, probably sending me to a horrible death.

"Then, it happens," she continued in a voice trembling with the strong emotion she was experiencing merely speaking about the dream, "I am falling . . . and falling . . . and *falling* . . . and *still* falling. I *keep falling*, forever, and ever, and *ever*, and I *never* hit the bottom! The worst part is that the entire time I am falling, my mind keeps visualizing and imagining all of the terrible, horrible, *dreadful* things that might happen to me when I *do* hit bottom! That unknown, unknowable fear is sheer *torment* to me, Morgan. Can you even *imagine* how much?"

"Come here, Baby. My Baby, just relax a moment," Morgan said. He reached for her and pulled her on top of him, holding her in his arms and gingerly stroking her back. Morgan was deeply pained hearing those words coming from his wife and not knowing what he could say or do to alleviate any of her pain. Ordinarily, merely being in that physical position was a call to arms for the COW, but even the Committee, sensitive to Liv's state of being, stood down.

When Morgan felt enough time had elapsed, he spoke, "Liv, I can see how such a dream could be disturbing, especially when you were a child. I think it can rightly be classified as a *nightmare*. Can you imagine *why* it would be coming back now, and so prolifically? Or why you are being so affected by it, making you act, as you described it, weird?"

Liv released herself from Morgan's arms and sat up facing the edge of the bed, looking away from Morgan. Morgan immediately raised himself up and turned her around to face him. It was then that he saw the tears overflowing the rims of her eyes. "Baby, Sweetheart, what *is* it? *Talk* to me, *please*, Liv," he said as he returned her gently into his arms, brushing away her tears with his fingers.

Liv leaned back to look into Morgan's eyes. "Morgan, that awful, tormented feeling is the way I feel *now*, the way I have *perpetually* felt for the past two weeks, ever since, ever since . . ."

Morgan embraced and continued to hold and rock her as she cried. "It's okay, Love. You're doing fine. Keep talking to me. We'll figure this out. Come on." Morgan understood now that her behavior and the recurrence of her falling nightmare were resulting from the stress and trauma of their family ordeal. It was easy to see that the children may have been negatively impacted due to their tender ages and to take action to deal with them to help them get over it. Morgan was even aware of his *own* attitude and how he had been affected, even the extremes to which he would go and would have gone to safeguard and to protect his family. How much more so would Liv have been impacted as a mother!

"Liv, can you tell me in specific words just what it is you fear, how you feel?" he asked her.

"I'm sorry, Morgan, for being such a cry-baby drama queen. I am in dread *expecting*, but not knowing *when* or *what* awful thing is impending, but knowing, *believing* that the next phone call, or the next knock on the door, or the next text message, or the next email could be bringing the devastating news, right out of the blue. I will be caught off guard without an inkling of trouble and not having an opportunity to prepare.

"And, please, Morgan, don't tell me that I have to have faith and rely on God, and pray, and all of that dialogue! I *know* all that. I *believe* all of that. I pray 24/7. I have seen the power of God in my life, *many* times! I *know* His role in my life, in our lives, in our *children's* lives. I know all about the guardian angels that are encamped around us, and I know the sovereignty of His will.

"I *don't* believe the fact that I *know* all of this and have complete faith in the promises of God, and that I *still* feel the way I do in this instance is a contradiction of my faith. I *have* asked Him for peace in this situation, and I *know* that He will bring it to pass. What I *also* know is that *He* knows the heart of a mother when it comes to her concern for the safety and well-being of her children, and that for it to sometimes be overly concerned is intrinsic. I *believe*, in fact I *know* He has given me the answer, but it is *not* within *me*. I need *you*, Morgan."

"Oh, Love of My Heart! I would gladly lay down my *life* for you and our family. *Anything* that is within my power to give you, it's *yours*. Tell me, Sweetheart, what you *need* from me. *Anything*!"

"Morgan, it is simple enough. All I want, all I *need* from you is your promise to me that you will never again withhold the fact that our family is in danger, or that we are facing a serious problem, or any situation that you know of for fear that I won't be able to handle it. I am *not* that fragile, Morgan. In fact, I'm *not* fragile at all!

"I know we have said that we won't keep secrets from each other. I know I have violated that promise in the past; now you have, as well. Can we both renew that pledge here and now and adhere to it from this moment on?"

"Liv, Sweetheart, you have my solemn promise. There shall be no more secrets between us. What *I* know, *you* will know, almost as soon as *I* do."

"I solemnly make the same promise," Liv said, relieved, looking into his eyes and smiling the first typical, truly genuine smile Morgan had seen on her face in two weeks.

"Are you happy again, Heart of My Heart?" Morgan asked, expecting to hear the response he always hears when he asks that question, "I couldn't be happier!"

"Well, yes, Morgan. I am happy," she said unconvincingly, lowering her eyes.

Morgan knew by her unspoken words and her shrinking from his gaze that all was *not* as it should be. "Liv, could you be any happier?" he queried.

Glancing up and quickly away from Morgan's scrutiny, she responded, "There is *always* room for *more*, Morgan."

Morgan knew for certain that things were not as they needed to be, and he wanted to get everything out into the open. "Okay,

Love. We've got to *end* this! *Please* tell me *exactly* what it is that you want or need from me that you are reluctant to ask for. You know in your heart that I will give you anything, *anything* within my power to give. I just need you to *tell* me what it *is*. Will you *do* that, *please*?" Morgan implored.

Liv knew that he would give her anything, and therein was the problem. "Morgan, I need another *promise* from you. Please listen before you say anything. I *know* how much you love your family and what it means to you as a man to protect us from all hurt, harm, and danger. I can only imagine the lengths to which you would go to do so. I am reluctant to ask for your promise because I don't want to tie your hand by making you promise something that circumstances may in the future require you to break. Besides, I don't believe, *now*, that this promise as originally conceived would add to, but take away from my happiness, our happiness.

"I don't want to prolong this unnecessarily, but I have to choose my words *very* carefully so that I can realize the desired outcome. Understand?"

"No, of course not. You can be a complete enigma sometimes, Sweetheart, but I love you to my soul. Don't worry, just take the time you need. It's okay!"

Liv sat up cross-legged in the bed facing Morgan. "I need to know that you will never again use any one of your family members as *bait* in order to protect us. The caveat is, *unless* you *first* seek the Lord's guidance, and in your wisdom—which I trust—feel certain that it is the *only*, or the most *viable* recourse. The judgment will be all yours, Morgan. So, if it ever comes to that, whatever you decide to do, you will not be breaking your promise to me."

Morgan was relieved that it was as simple as that, and he appreciated how she had given him the freedom, rendering the promise easy to make. Besides, unbeknownst to Liv, he had already resolved that issue when he was in prayer in the van outside the motel room on the eve of the kidnapping. He pulled her to himself and kissed her passionately on the lips. "Sweetheart, no words can express how much I love you. You have my promise." For good measure, looking deeply into her eyes, he added, "My Love, *now* are you happy?"

"Morgan, absolutely nothing could make me happier!" she smiled.

As they remained lock in their mutual gaze, Morgan slipped the straps from her nightgown over her shoulders. She put her arms around his neck and whispered, "Hello, my King!"

CHAPTER 30

A TIME FOR RECOVERY / A RETURN TO NORMAL

A Time for Recovery

The entire Calais family was striving to get completely back to normal after their family's ordeal. Although they seemed to be doing well enough, Morgan was not completely satisfied. He prayed for guidance, and he believed he had received direction. He shared his thoughts with Liv, and they both prayed together for confirmation.

Early on, in collaboration with the Advisory Committee, the officers had designed and instituted an on-going program to benefit all of the students in their schools. It was initially required that each student graduating from high school be proficient in both English and Spanish, and functional in at least one other foreign language of choice. State of the art language labs and the most highly qualified instructors were in place from the beginning.

An integral part of the program was immersion. Students, families, or groups of students participated in travel to certain countries to be immersed in the language(s) of the land. Funding for these trips came from various sources including grants, corporate sponsors, income generated from programs at the schools for that purpose, families who had the resources, scholarships, and others.

Morgan and Liv personally sponsored 10 to 15 students per year in addition to their own children.

Since participation was a requirement, no student was denied the opportunity because of a family's inability to pay. In addition, travel time was allowed during the regular semester as parents could withdraw their child(ren) as long as certain criteria were met, although this was not encouraged as the most ideal timing. The use of summer and other recess periods was encouraged.

Though the Calais family had traveled extensively, exposing the children to many things educationally, culturally, and historically, Morgan felt an urgency, because of their recent family trauma, to pull them out of school and take them on a trip without waiting for a recess. Liv was in agreement, and they immediately began clearing their schedules and making the necessary arrangements. They polled the children in a family meeting to determine where they would like to go. They unanimously chose Hawaii.

The entire family was eagerly looking forward to the Hawaii trip, especially the children. Their enthusiasm was not diminished by the fact that they would still be required to keep up with their studies. They had plenty of motivation to tackle their studies expeditiously to be able to avail themselves of all that was there for them to explore and enjoy.

Following the family's successful two-week hiatus, life at the Big House had definitely returned to business as usual. Morgan was certain of it when Liv announced, "Morgan, don't you think it time we hosted another patio party? Holly and Elizabeth have been dropping not-so-subtle hints for several days!"

"Are you up to it, Sweetheart?"

"Why wouldn't I be? *You're* the one who does all the work! All *I* have to do is be the consummate hostess and play the role of social butterfly! Besides, I haven't had a chance to really talk with Kyle to express my thanks to him and to apologize for being so curt with him when all he was trying to do, all he was *doing*, was helping you to protect our family."

"Liv, Kyle understands. I had a conversation with him and let him know that he was right when he suggested that you should have been told what we were doing. He loves our family and considers all of us as *his* family. Nevertheless, I think he would appreciate hearing from you how you feel."

"I have already checked the master calendar, and it looks like next Saturday is clear. I would like to start early so that all the children will have plenty of play time, and I will have plenty of time before I have to go to the club. You can stay with our guests. You don't have to leave the party."

"Liv, you know that's not going to happen. For me, there is no party without *you*. Our friends can stay as long as they want to, but you're *not* getting rid of *me*! If they want to hang out 'til we get back, they're welcome."

"Whatever you say. You're the boss!"

"In that case, as the 'boss,' I instruct you to hire Athene or one of that others to substitute for you. I don't want our guests to be deprived of our presence."

"It's done, Boss," Liv gladly submitted.

Fun Time at the Big House

Morgan spent Friday away from his office to prepare for their outdoor barbeque, swim, game, card, whatever party on Saturday. He took pride in preparing the variety of foods that would be available to fit all appetites—the carnivore, the pescatarian, the vegan/vegetarian, the finicky, the sugar-tooth, the glutton, the dieter, the allergic—all palates.

The tradition started out early in their marriage with their close friends and family (Walter and Lydia; Kevin and Eleanor; Arlan and Dionne; Howard and Kaye; Elizabeth and Allan; Holly and William; and Frank, Travis and Kyle and their guests). By now the number of adults had grown to about 60, mostly couples and extended family, with about 80 or so children of diverse ages. Morgan loved people, especially children, and he loved to entertain. For the average man, this would have been an impossible, daunting feat; but Morgan was completely in his element.

In addition to the regular play apparatus, Morgan made sure the play yard was safely equipped to provide the children of the various ages with objects and activities that were appropriate. He even arranged for a magic show, clowns, face-painters, and pony rides. There was sure to be something for everyone.

Their guests began arriving about 11 a.m. Most had been through the drill many times before and knew the routine. They knew where everything would be and just came in and did what they wanted to do. The children joined the Calais three in the play yard and began swinging, sliding, climbing, or whatever they wanted. The children who wanted to swim could do so when the lifeguards came on duty at 12:30.

By noon everything was in full swing. Music was playing, cards were being dealt, dominoes were being slapped, chessmen were being studied, hoops were being thrown, and, of course, food was being consumed. Liv was playing her role making sure everyone was having a good time and had whatever they wanted. She was waiting for a good opportunity to speak with Kyle. She spotted him talking with Morgan and another young man at one of the covered tables.

She caught Morgan's eye and signaled for him to leave as she walked toward them. Morgan promptly excused himself.

"Hi, Kyle," she said as the two men stood.

"Hi, Liv, it's good to see you." Kyle gave her a kiss on the cheek. "Do you remember my cousin, Victor? He was at your wedding. I know it has been a long while."

"I honestly can't say that I remember you specifically or that I would have recognized you on the street, Victor. I met so many people for the first time that eventful day, but I remember Kyle had a cousin at the wedding. I *can* say unequivocally *now* that I shall never *forget* you. You have my undying, heartfelt gratitude for what you have done for my family. May I give you a hug?"

Without waiting for a response, Liv embraced the blushing hero. The two men remained standing as Liv made no move to sit at the table.

"Kyle, I owe you an enormous debt of gratitude also for your part in protecting our family."

"'Our family' as in 'my family,' too?"

"Yes, Brother Kyle," she said, smiling. But, even more than that, I really, *really* owe you the biggest apology possible for how I behaved toward you. I feel ashamed of myself after all you were trying to do, after all you *did*."

"Sis, you don't owe me anything. You are a wonderful mother whose sons were missing, and you were understandably worried about their safety. No one can fault you for that. *I* certainly don't.

"Do you remember the toast I made at you guys' wedding reception?"

"You mean that long-winded dissertation you gave?" she asked as a jest.

"I guess it *was* that, wasn't it. But it was sincere! Anyway, I said something to the effect that you know when someone loves you because they will let you know when you are out of line. I knew you loved me. You could say that same principle applies in *this* situation. When you love someone, you continue to love them, even if they are angry or frustrated and speak their minds to you. You understand, you don't take it personally, and you continue to love them. *I* do. Sis, you don't need to even *think* about it. I would not have expected you to react any other way."

"So are we straight now, Kyle? Do you accept my apology?"

"Almost. It will be official when I receive a hug from my little sis."

"Thank you, Kyle," she said as they shared a fond embrace. "Now, come and let me kick your butt in a round of tennis! You can come, too, Victor, if you want to witness your cousin's painful humiliation on the court!"

(An old friend is forgiven) Morgan was checking the meat on the grill when his cell phone rang. He looked at the caller ID and saw that it was Travis calling.

"Hi, Trav! You're late. The party is in full swing. Where are you?"

"Hey, My Man. I'm really closer than you know. I wanted to talk to you first."

"What's up? Is Kyonne with you?"

"Of course! You know she wouldn't let me come without her. She loves you guys, especially the kids!"

"You know how the kids love their Uncle Travis and Auntie Ky! What's on your mind?"

"I brought someone else along, too, and I just wanted to make sure it would be okay with you. It's been over eight years, and he didn't want to impose if he would not be welcome."

"What are you talking about, Travis? I can't think of too many people that I wouldn't welcome to our home. Who is it?"

Travis hesitated a bit before he responded, "It's *Charles*, Morgan."

"Charles that we used to hang with years ago?"

"Yes, *that* Charles. He reached out to me several years ago, and we sort of kept in touch. Morgan, he really misses everyone. He even reached out to Kyle, whenever he could get in touch with him, and Kyle and I are both okay with him. We all know that things will never go back to the way they were. We are all older now. We all have different lives with no time for hanging out like we used to do when we were young and wild."

"Speak for yourself, Travis. You know I was never wild and rambunctious like *you* guys!"

"Okay, I'll give you that. You *were* the one who kept us all out of trouble.

"Charles hasn't had the nerve to contact you. He really regrets what happened and has been too ashamed to face you. He wants an opportunity to speak privately with you and to apologize to you. Knowing you as I do, I didn't think you would mind, and I encouraged him to come with me today. You don't mind, do you?"

"Mind? Of course not. I have never been one to hold a grudge, with a very few exceptions. In hindsight, though, I could have handled things a little differently with Charles. What happened was more of a knee-jerk reaction on my part. How close are you?"

"We're in-your-driveway close!"

"Well, what are you waiting for? Come on up!"

Morgan left tending of the barbeque to his brother-in-law and went to the front door to meet the three. "Come in! Come in!" he said, greeting Kyonne with a kiss on the cheek and Travis with a fist bump. "You guys know the drill. Go on out and make yourselves at home." The couple headed toward the patio, leaving Morgan and Charles in the entryway.

"Charles, welcome to my home," Morgan said, initiating a fist bump. "Why don't we go to the den where we can talk."

Charles was understandably subdued as he followed Morgan into the den. "This place hasn't changed much I see," he said, nervously trying to make small talk. "It's almost exactly as I remember it. We really had some good times here, the four of us."

"Yes, we did, Charles. A lot has changed in these past years. We've all gone our separate ways, though we do keep in touch. Every few months or so my wife and I throw these little get-togethers for our families and friends. Travis tells me that you want to talk. The floor is yours, my friend."

Charles was still reticent, not forthcoming. He knew this was his one shot, and he needed to take it. He began, "Morgan, I have thought about contacting you so many times to apologize for my actions. I can't tell you how much I have come to regret losing our friendship. You, Travis, and Kyle had been the only true friends I had ever had. We had so many good times together.

"You all knew that I was gay. I never tried to hide it, I *couldn't* hide it. It's who I was, who I *am*. It didn't make a difference to any of you. We were all just regular friends, doing guy stuff—playing basketball and tennis, watching sports, lifting weights in your gym, sailing, whatever we wanted to do. I crossed the line with Travis and Kyle, at different times. They put me in my place, and we were able to go back to the way things were.

"I don't know what got into me that night at that supper club. I almost couldn't believe it when I learned that you had married the proprietor, the one that Kyle and Travis had their tongues hanging out over. But *you*, Morgan, *you* showed no interest in her at *all*. When you didn't go with them up to talk to her and just stayed at the table with me . . . I guess I just misread the signs. I had *never* seen you with a girl, and in my mind, I just put things together in my head and came up with the wrong conclusion.

"I guess I thought you were just not ready to come out. I thought I could persuade you, help you along. When you kept telling me to back off, I just thought you were trying to keep up your front. I kept thinking what a handsome couple we would make.

"I realize it would be the same whether it was a man or a woman saying 'no' or 'back off.' 'No' means 'no,' and it should be honored, regardless. I went too far, and I paid the price. You really put a hurt on me that night."

"Charles, I'm sorry it came to that. I am sorry I felt I *had* to resort to physical violence. My patience failed me that night. I could have handled it much better. I am always preaching to my kids and all the students in our schools about using their words instead of their fists. I accept your apology, Charles, and I want to apologize to you as well. I let my anger get the best of me. I could have just gotten up and walked away since I had allowed myself to become so angry. I hope you had no permanent ramifications."

"I had no permanent *physical* ramifications, but worse than the physical pain was the loss of the comradery, the friendships, all of what the four of us had. I know things will never be the same, but I am grateful that you are allowing me back into your circle. Thank you, Morgan."

"No problem, Charles. Come on out and join the party!"

CHAPTER 31

LIFE TAKES ITS COURSE

It was *almost* business as usual as everything and everyone settled down. The only thing that kept it from being *completely* business as usual was the specter of the pending prosecution of Tyrone "Casanova" Adams and Frederick Underwood. As they soon learned, Tyrone Adams never regained consciousness. He remained in an irreversible coma and succumbed after about five months.

Being a man of compassion, Morgan took steps on behalf of Marty, including securing legal representation from among the Network, to ensure that he was placed in an appropriate facility where he would not be exposed to a general prison population. This he did out of appreciation for the significant role Marty played in protecting their sons while in the custody of the kidnappers. Fred Underwood entered a guilty plea and received the maximum sentence for his role.

Life Takes its Course

Things had been going quite well for the Calais Education and Community Centers, Inc. Families were increasing, school and college campuses were continuing to open across the country, lives were being changed, successes were being touted, the Network was increasing by leaps and bounds, and happiness abounded. Inevitably, life had to take its course.

Liv and Morgan were asleep when the telephone rang. They were both awaken, and Morgan answered, "Hello? . . ." After a very short pause, he continued, "Okay. Try to be calm. We'll be right there!"

Watching his expression, Liv knew something was very wrong. "What is it, Morgan?"

"Get your robe and put on your shoes," he said as he reached for his robe and shoes.

A sense of foreboding overtook Liv as she jumped out of bed and donned her robe. Because they were not putting on their clothes, only robes and shoes, she could only guess that they wouldn't be going far. That meant to her that something was wrong at her grandparents' home. She was afraid to ask.

Her heart began to pound as she followed Morgan down the stairs, out the door and through the path to her grandparents' home. As they left, they heard the siren of an ambulance sounding louder and louder. The paramedics had already entered when the two reached the door. The paramedics were heading toward the master bedroom, led by Dionne. Morgan and Liv were soon on their heels.

When they reached the bedroom, Dionne fell into Morgan's arms as the paramedics were trying to resuscitate Arlan.

"Dionne, come into the den and sit down while the paramedics are busy." Morgan urged. She couldn't will her legs to move. Morgan gently picked her up and sat her on the couch.

"He's dead! My Arlan is dead, I know! What am I going to do? What am I going to *do*? How can I go on?"

Liv sat down next to her grandmother and put her arms around her, trying to comfort her as Morgan returned to the master bedroom to check on Arlan.

"MiMi, try to relax. Whatever happens, it will be okay. *You* will be okay. Do you know what happened?" Liv asked, trying to put her own feelings aside for the sake of her grandmother.

"I know he's gone," she said more calmly. "He woke me up. He said he wanted to say 'goodbye.' He told me that he loved me, and that he wanted to thank me for all of the happy years that we had together. He said he could not have asked for a better wife. He said I should be strong, that when it was my time, he would be waiting for me. He kissed me. He said I shouldn't cry, but I can't help it. I'm missing him already."

"I know, MiMi, but you will be all right." Liv knew then that her grandfather would not be revived. She knew a few things about death, thinking back to the day Theo had died. "Did you call Mom?" Liv asked.

"No, I dialed 911, and then I called you. You were closer. Will you call your mother and Walter for me?"

"Yes, MiMi, I will."

The paramedics placed Arlan on the gurney and wheeled him out to the ambulance. Morgan followed them. "Will you be following us, Sir?" the paramedic asked Morgan.

"No, I won't. I know you can't affirm or deny, but I can see that he is already gone. He is okay. My place is with the rest of my family."

"You will probably receive a call from the hospital."

"Thank you."

Morgan returned to join Liv in the den. Liv knew looking at him that her grandfather had transitioned. He was later pronounced dead at the hospital.

"Does Mom know?" Morgan asked Liv.

"No. I was about to call her. Will you do it for me please, Morgan?"

"Yes, Sweetheart." Morgan left the room and returned after he had made the call. "Mom and Dad are on their way."

Liv was feeling the loss of her grandfather, but she was mindful of her grandmother and put up a strong front. "MiMi, can I get you anything? I know how much you like your herb tea. I'll go and bring you some." Liv went to bring hot water, mugs, and the tea bags, and the three sat quietly sipping the tea while they waited for Lydia and Walter to arrive. Morgan put Liv's recording of "Remember Me for Love" on, and Liv had to fight back her tears as they waited in silence.

Morgan opened the door when Walter and Lydia arrived. He greeted them solemnly and embraced Lydia. "Your mother and Liv are in the den." Liv stood to embrace her mother and to make room for her to sit next to Dionne. She hugged her father and went to get more hot water, tea and mugs.

"Morgan, I called Kevin and Eleanor. They will be here soon. I told them to bring the kids to your house. I don't know how they, or you and Liv, will want to tell the kids. You know how much they loved their PawPaw!"

"Yes, I do. That's good, Dad. I will go and wait for them there. I need to get dressed and check on the kids, anyway." Walter nodded and went to comfort his wife and mother-in-law.

Morgan had dressed when Kevin and Eleanor arrived shortly with their two sleepy children. They had dressed, but the kids were still in PJs. Morgan had Lydia taken to Alex's room and placed in the bed with Alex, who was still sleeping soundly. He took Kevin, Jr. and put him in the bed with Randy in the room both boys shared. All were sleeping peacefully.

As they were about to take the short trek through the garden, Morgan's cell rang. It was Walter. "Morgan, are Kevin and Eleanor there yet?"

"Yes, we are getting ready to head to you now."

"Why don't you just hang tight. We are coming to you. Dionne is having a problem being in the house here without Arlan. Lydia and Liv both think it's a good idea for us all to come to your place. Besides, I don't think the kids should be left alone in case they wake up and you and Liv are gone. Lydia is gathering a few things, and we'll be on our way."

"No problem, Pops."

Addressing his in-laws, Morgan said, "You guys might as well make yourselves comfortable. Everyone is coming here. Just relax. I am going to start preparations for breakfast. Can I get you anything first?"

"No, thanks, Morgan. I just want to try to get it together before Mom gets here. I don't want either of them to see me upset.

"Coffee is fine for me, Morgan," Eleanor stated. She knew not to ask if he needed any assistance with breakfast.

"Coffee coming right up. I'll just make a whole pot. I'm sure others may want some, too. I know *I'll* certainly need some."

Shortly the entourage arrived. Dionne had dressed, and Walter was carrying an overnight bag while Lydia carried an accordion folder. They all gathered around the formal dining room table while Liv went to get dressed.

Dionne was considerably more composed than when Morgan had left. He was happy to see her in that state of comfort. When Liv came to join them, Dionne began to address her family.

"My Family, that I am so blessed to have, we are one member short on this plane of life. No one can feel the loss to the extent that I do at this moment. There is no need for any of you to worry about me. Arlan prepared me for this event, and I think I have what people refer to as 'closure.'

"I don't call it that, for 'closure' to me signifies the end. We have only said 'goodbye' until I leave this plane to join him, which I know I will. We all will when our times come. That is for *God* to determine, as we know.

"We have not all been going to church on Sundays, praying, and fellowshipping, as just another thing to do. We know the purpose, the object. We all have faith and the covering of God. I accept His will. I *know* I will be all right. We *all* will be all right. God is *still* good! He has returned Arlan to Himself in His wisdom.

"But, we are all human beings with emotions that become raw sometimes, especially at times such as this. That's all right, too. Arlan is gone from my sight, but I see him with my heart. We *all* can do that. So, let's all just continue to do what we know to do, love each other, support each other, worship God, and live the best life we can until He calls us!

"Be mindful of the children. Help them to understand and not be unduly sad that their 'PawPaw' is not here with us in the flesh.

Remind them how much he loved them and is still watching over them from above!

"Well, I guess I've said enough. I love you all dearly!"

"We all love you dearly, too, Mom," Lydia said with a tear in her voice. "Everyone, Mom is coming to live with Walter and me. This is something that we have talked about in the past. My father made provisions, advance planning, and prepaid for both of their final expenses. He has left specific instructions that we will be following. He purchased two plots at Forest Lawn and wants a grave-side service with just the immediate family and very close friends.

"We will have a memorial service and a repast so that all of his friends and the church family can have a part in his home going celebration. He wanted a real celebration; and, Liv, he wants you to give a concert as part of that celebration. He wants you to dedicate that song you sing, 'Remember me for Love," to all his family, especially the little ones."

Liv inhaled sharply. Morgan took her hand and squeezed it, remembering how affected she had been with Theo's passing when she sang the song she had written for him at his request, "The Silence is Too Loud," that night at her Club a few days following his service. Liv squeezed Morgan's hand in response, signifying that she was all right. Liv had poured all of the love she had into the time she spent with her grandparents to make up for all of the years she had missed, not even knowing they existed until just before her marriage.

The tears that slipped over the rims of her eyes were not the result of sadness. She was remembering the surprise, joy and happiness she had experienced when Morgan had presented her grandparents along with her mother to her as his wedding gift to her. She squeezed his hand again and winked at him.

Arlan's wishes were carried out completely, according to his dictates. Dionne moved in with Lydia and Walter. All of her great-grandchildren were frequent overnight guests, taking advantage of being with their Gran-Gran and their MiMi at the same time!

CHAPTER 32

A NEW RESIDENT

A few months had passed since Arlan's home going. All of the grandchildren seemed to love spending so much time at their grandparent's home. It seemed that they loved swimming in Lydia and Walter's pool more than their own. Lydia and Dionne never seemed to get tired of having them around for a day, or a weekend, or however long, as often as possible.

It also freed up more time for their parents. No one was complaining. They still enjoyed their family Sunday dinners. Lydia and Dionne didn't mind chauffeuring the kids to the movies, on outings, and wherever they needed or wanted to go. It was a convenience for Morgan and Liv as they were engaged so frequently in traveling to different events in connection with their corporate business and their individual endeavors—Morgan with his speaking engagements, and Liv with her recording, acting and rehearsals, and her clubs. Nevertheless, they never failed to schedule quality time with their children.

Despite their busy schedules, they also always found time for their family, friends, and each other. It had been a while since they had hosted a yard party, and they were careful to manage their engagements to keep an upcoming weekend free.

The selected date had arrived, and their friends and family congregated again for a day of good times and fellowship. The usual bunch was there as well as several first-timers. The circle was continuously broadening, especially since Lydia's biological extended family had gradually been included.

Kyle's cousin, Vic, had become a regular guest. On this particular day, he and Kyle both came with dates. For Kyle, it was Aly, whom he had known for a long time and knew he would marry someday. Victor brought Ohlisa, the girl he had fallen in love with and was now free to think about "jumping the broom."

Vic had confided in his cousin that they were engaged but had not yet set a date. He was not as secure financially as he felt he needed to be. He had started his own business as a groundskeeper and landscaper. With his criminal record, he did not have as many options as he needed for gainful employment. He had always loved gardening and had a knack for landscaping. He felt he would eventually be able to generate sufficient income and would not have to be consumed with convincing would-be employers to take a chance with him as an employee.

He had invested in enough equipment and supplies and had a few clients and felt certain that as his work became known, he would secure more clients through word of mouth, eventually being able to buy a home and support a family adequately.

Kyle had suggested that he talk to Morgan and Liv about possibly getting work helping to maintain the grounds at local CECCA campuses. That would keep him busy and provide substantial revenue. He may have to wait a while before being in a position to purchase a home, but they would be able to make it pretty comfortably until then.

After feasting, the adults were mostly relaxing and lounging around, engaging in stimulating conversation, playing dominos, bid whist, or some other game. The kids were still occupying themselves in play, not quite settling down while they still had energy to burn. Kyle and Vic took this quiet time to speak privately with Morgan and Liv about Vic's situation. The two were taking a breather from all of the activity and were sitting alone surveying their guests.

"You guys need anything?" Morgan asked as the two approached.

"Not really, Bro. We just saw the two of you sitting over here all by your lonesomes and just wanted to disturb your peace."

"Well, why don't you guys take a chair and disturb our peace," Liv invited. They each took a seat.

"The party is great, as usual! Everyone is having a blast!" Kyle beamed.

Intuitive Liv addressed Vic. "You look like a guy with a happy secret, Vic. What's up with that?"

Suddenly at a loss for words, Vic replied, "Kyle told me about your sixth sense, Liv. It's obviously for real!"

"So what is the big secret, Vic?" Morgan inquired.

"I have asked Ohlisa to marry me, and she agreed. Can you believe that?"

"What is so hard to believe about that?" Liv asked. "You are a good catch, Victor. You will be a great couple. When is the big day?"

Knowing Vic's situation and his reluctance to ask for help, Kyle answered for him. "They haven't set a date yet, Liv. Vic feels he is not financially secure enough to be able to provide adequately for a family night now. He wants everything to be ideal first. I told him it doesn't work that way. It's just like waiting until you are ready to have a baby. You're never *ready*. It just comes, anyway! Like I told him, it didn't really matter if they are truly in love and if it is meant to be. I know they are."

"Vic, you know we, I should say, our entire family owes you a debt of gratitude. If there is *anything* we can do to help you, all you have to do is name it," Morgan said.

"Morgan, you guys don't owe me anything. I am not looking for a handout. That's not the kind of man I am."

"Morgan, it was my idea to talk to you and Liv. Vic is in business for himself. What he wants is work, an opportunity to grow his business. I thought, perhaps, he could do some work for you, for your schools," Kyle added.

"What kind of work are you looking for? What is your business, Vic?"

"Morgan, I have started doing landscaping and gardening. I have purchased the basic tools I need, and I have a few clients. I know that as my work becomes more widely known, I will be able to achieve what I want.

"I have always admired *your* landscaping. It's really fabulous. It looks like something *I* would have done myself! That is the caliber of work I do. I am confident in my ability. That is the kind of work I *love* to do. It's like an artist with a blank canvas. The possibilities of what that canvas can become is what inspires me. For me, a plot of land is a canvas; and I can see unlimited possibilities from the beginning!"

Morgan and Liv were both impressed with his confidence, ambition, and especially the passion he revealed as he spoke about his business. Liv was reminded of Morgan when he first told her of his vision for a place for his special friends. Even though Vic insisted they didn't owe him anything, they *wanted* to help him. They appreciated the fact that he wasn't asking for a handout. Regardless, they wanted to help him, but in a way that he would feel good about himself.

Morgan asked, "Vic, what do you think you would need to be in a position to get married immediately."

"There are only two things I would want to have, but they are lofty things—a secure, substantial income, and a suitable, affordable residence, or at least the ability to obtain one."

"Would you be willing to accept help from us?"

"Like I said, Morgan, I don't want a handout."

"I'm not talking about a handout. We appreciate the fact that you are *not* asking for a handout. As far as *we* are concerned, you could name your price, and we would gladly pay it. What I'm talking about is work so that you can pay your *own* way."

"In that case, of course! I would be a fool not to! What are you suggesting?"

"I am offering you an opportunity to work in your chosen field. We have two new sites under construction right now and three existing sites in San Diego and San Bernardino Counties. I can offer you a contract to get in on the development of the plans for the landscaping of the two sites in the works, and the opportunity to oversee and even participate in the upkeep of our local campuses. You can have as much work as you would like while still maintaining and expanding your current business and clientele."

Liv was thinking along the same lines and further. She didn't want to be the one to suggest it outright, but she did send a cue to Morgan. They had discussed what to do with the house that Liv's grandparents had occupied until Arlan's passing, but they had made no particular plans. It continued to remain vacant.

"Morgan, perhaps we can make some referrals for housing. You have people you can contact on Vic's behalf," she ventured.

Morgan looked at her, realizing what she was suggesting. He hadn't thought of it, but it seemed like a good idea to him. "As a matter of fact," Morgan said, I know a place that is available right now that you can consider, Vic. It's right here in the neighborhood."

"Oh, there is no way I could swing anything in this neighborhood, but it's a nice thought."

"Don't be so doubtful, Vic. Call me at my office Monday. We can make an appointment for you to come in and discuss this whole situation with the Director of our Real Estate Branch. You can get all of the specifications and submit a proposal for a contract. Our personnel can give you all the help you need in formulating a reasonable proposal that we can shoot to the officers and the Advisory Committee for approval.

"When you estimate what your proposed income will be, added to your current income, you can assess realistically when you will be able to get the house you want, where you want it. In the meantime, you and your bride can utilize the mother-in-law unit on the other side of the garden for a reasonable, affordable fee. Who knows, we might even be able to work out a deal where the rent can be subsidized by maintaining all of the grounds here."

"Are you talking about that big house over there, Morgan?" Vic asked in disbelief, pointing to the house where Liv's grandparents had lived until her grandfather's death.

"Why not, Vic?" Liv smiled at him. "It's vacant. We can save money on maintaining the grounds here, although Morgan will insist on taking care of his own gardens. That would be a win-win situation! All you will have to do is set the date—and invite us to the wedding, of course!"

Victor was overcome with gratitude. He could never have dreamed of such an ideal situation. "Morgan. Liv. I don't know what to say! This is *too* good to be true. You would really do this for me?"

"Victor, you have already earned whatever we can offer you. All you have to say is, 'I accept.' All we have to say is, 'Welcome to the neighborhood!'"

CHAPTER 33

READY TO BEGIN A NEW ERA

(2/21/2023) Reflecting on their first ten years of married life—their children, their family and friends, and the significant events that had taken place—as they had been doing over the past week, Morgan and Liv were more than ready to return home. They missed their children especially, as well as their family and friends. They had an incredible week together, but they had an incredible and satisfying life even at home, minus those few major events that had caused them problems.

They were scheduled to leave on an early flight the next morning, and everything was packed and ready to go. They had returned from their long, leisurely walk on the beach, had eaten a light meal, and had spent a relaxing hour in the tub. Now they were preparing to retire for the night.

"Liv, my wonderful wife and love of ten short years, are you happy?" Morgan asked as he took willing Liv into his arms and caressed her.

Liv looked at him and smiled, allowing the love she felt for him to emanate from her eyes to his. "I can truly say that I couldn't be happier. These ten years have brought so much joy, so much meaning, so much happiness! I have great hope—in fact, I *know* that our next ten years will be even better!"

"And I know that you're right! But now, let us prepare for bed. I want us to take full advantage of our last night in this beautiful paradise."

The pair knelt by the bed for their evening prayer, as was their custom. They began as always by acknowledging God as their Heavenly Father through their Lord and Savior, Jesus Christ. They gave bountiful praise and thanks for all of the blessings He had bestowed upon them as well as His many gifts. They had always considered themselves gifts to each other from God.

They asked for forgiveness of any sins they may have committed via commission or omission, and they asked for his continued covering of them and their loved ones as they continued their journey together through life on this earth. Above all, they acknowledged His sovereignty and sought his continuing guidance, asking only that His will be done in their lives and for their willingness to accept His will.

After their audible prayers, they remained for a moment on their knees in silent reflection and prayer.

They rose and engaged in a loving embrace. Morgan kissed her ear and whispered, "I love you, Mrs. Calais," and then kissed her passionately on the lips as they held each other closer.

"I love you more, Mr. Calais," Liv whispered back as they began to disrobe each other. "I desire to spend this, our last night here, in your arms as your Shulamite woman, O King!"

"Your desire is my desire. Your king will gladly make gentle, wild, and passionate love to his Shulamite woman!"

"But first, Morgan, can we talk about something?"

"What do you want to talk about, Love? Everything is fine, isn't it?"

"Yes, Morgan, it is. But how well do you remember our *first* first night?"

"As well as if it were *last* night, Babe."

"You asked me if I were curious about your relationships with your past girlfriends, remember?"

"I remember, but I don't think I called them 'girlfriends.' I remember your response vividly, however."

"Yes, so do I, and I still feel the same way I did then. Only, now, I know I can handle anything you might want to tell me about the subject, and why you didn't just come right out with it."

"Oh, Liv, Sweetheart! That's a long story. Are you sure you want to hear it right now?"

"Were there *that* many, Morgan? Maybe I *don't* need to hear it."

"I said the *story* was long, not that there was a long *list*!"

"Well, tell me the *story*!"

"Okay. It all started when I was 14 . . ."

"Fourteen?!"

"When I was *fourteen*, my father felt it was time for us to have '*that talk*!' He asked me if I were a *virgin* because if I wasn't, he said it was too late. All *I* could do was *blush*. I told him that I was curious, but that was as far as it ever went. I was heavily into sports and guy stuff. The conversation went something like this:

"Son, my father had this talk with me when I was about your age. I know he meant well, but I didn't believe him, although I knew what he was trying to do. He didn't want me to become sexually active until I was married. He was telling me what *his* father told *him*—that if he didn't wait, he would contract a serious disease, and his man member would wither, rot, and drop off! I know you are smart enough to know better, so I'm just going to tell you the way it is, the way I want it to be for you.

"You know how much I love your mother and you. Your mother is the only woman I have even been intimate with. We were each other's first love, and we were married before we first came together. I credit that fact for the long and happy, healthy relationship we enjoy to this day. This is what I want for you.

"There is something about sexualizing a relationship before marriage that has negative repercussions. It keeps people from seeing things as they really are. They make bad decisions and make serious mistakes, mostly in not being able to see, or in explaining away the red flags that are certainly present, and jumping into marriages that should never have taken place. They don't get to really *know* the other person until it's too late. They are often riddled with regrets.

"Son, you have two heads—a big head that is connected to your neck and contains a brain, and a little head below with *no* brain, only selfish desires. If you were flying in an airplane, which head would you want in the pilot's seat?"

"Of course, I would want the brain head to be in control of the plane! Wouldn't anyone with common sense want that, Dad?"

"Ideally, but there are plenty of examples where that is not usually the case as many men don't want or stop to consider the long-term consequences of their short-term quest to satisfy the dictates of their little heads. It's not just men. Women who are willing partners often, and for very different reasons, are guilty of not thinking of the long-term consequences as well. They see and hear what they *want* to, making themselves easy prey for the smooth talk and the sugar-coated bull unscrupulous men want to feed them.

"Son, you know your mother and I don't give much credence to your Grandmother Birdie's words many times. You know how she is always telling you about the woman who is destined to be your soulmate whom you will meet one day, fall madly in love with, and how blessed you will be, how blessed you *are*. On the off chance that what she says is true, I want you and this mystery woman to have the perfect relationship. So, before you decide to follow your little head instead of your big head when you think you have found the one for you and are thinking about being with her, will you promise me one thing?"

"I guess so, Dad, if I can. What is it?"

"Before you do *anything*, take her to meet Birdie and get her approval. Will you do that, Son?"

"Dad, we're talking about something that's a long way off. I'm not even *thinking* about girls like that right now. But if you think I will be able to have a good marriage like you and Mom if I do, then, yes, I promise."

"Thank you, Son. I just want you to know that keeping that promise may be hard to do many times. Though that little, one-dimensional head is inferior, it *can* be a powerful force and *very* persuasive. *You* have to keep him in tow. Make sure *he* knows that you are in control of *him*, not the other way around.

"Okay, Dad. Is that all?"

"Just one more thing." He removed a box from the bag he had with him and handed it to me. "Your mom and I got this for you."

When Morgan offered nothing further, Liv stated, "I have just two questions. What was in the box, and did you keep your promise?"

"In answer to your first question, it was the large, red-letter King James version of the Holy Bible that had been bookmarked to The Song of Solomon. My name was engraved on the cover. I always kept it by my bed."

"Now it's by *our* bed. And, Morgan, I know the answer to my second question. You don't have to answer it. After being married to you all this time, I *know* you. I know you *always* keep your promises," she said smiling at him and then kissing him fervently.

The pair enjoyed a magical night of love that rivaled their original wedding night. They finally fell into a peaceful sleep wrapped in each other's arms until the morning found them, ready to begin another decade of marital bliss.

An Ending.

INDEX OF SONG REFERENCES

OH, NO YOU DON'T!

(Eleanor H. Jones, Composer, Lyricist—a work in progress)

REMEMBER ME FOR LOVE

(Howlett Smith, Composer, Lyricist)

SILENCE IS TOO LOUD, THE

(Eleanor H. Jones, Composer, Lyricist)

WHEN I CAN TRUST MY HEART TO YOU

(Eleanor H. Jones, Composer, Lyricist)

www.ingramcontent.com/pod-product-compliance
Lightning Source LLC
Chambersburg PA
CBHW010406310726
48979CB00012B/2146/J

* 9 7 8 1 9 5 0 9 3 6 4 0 3 *